The beguiling creature performed
a polite curtsy, her eyes downcast.
Was she remembering the single
extraordinary kiss they had stolen
in a garden seven years ago?

He took her hand and bowed. "Charmed again,
Mrs. Huffington. How long have you been in town?"

"Not long, sir," she said as she looked up from their joined
hands. "I've only just returned from Kent."

He took a moment to absorb her remarkably green eyes.
Not emerald. Not greenish-gray or sea-green. Hers were
more...olive. And every bit as captivating as they'd been
years ago. His memory had not failed him. Nor had hers—
indicated by the subtle blush on her cheeks. Yes, she was
remembering that single astonishing kiss, too. Ah, but
she was no longer girlishly coy. No, this Georgiana was a
woman of considerable experience. One he would have no
qualms about seducing.

* * *

A Daring Liaison
Harlequin® Historical #349—February 2013

Author Note

Writing about the Regency world of the Wednesday League has always been fascinating for me. The things I've learned through my research have both surprised and dismayed me. The juxtaposition of the glittering society of the *ton* with the "seedy underbelly" of the rookeries and Whitechapel offer endless opportunities to my fertile imagination—which tends to run wild even in the best of circumstances. Adding to that mix, I've always been obsessed with the similarities between justice and revenge. When does one become the other? Or does it? I think I will always want to explore that question in my fiction.

Charles Hunter's story gave me ample opportunity to do this. Readers who have met Charles in earlier books may not recognize him as the single-minded, determined man in this book. As he searches for revenge he is faced with a different but equally important lesson—sometimes the heart sees more clearly than the eyes, and forgiveness can be more healing than revenge. But Charles must learn that lesson quickly if he is to save the woman he loves.

I enjoy hearing from readers, so please feel free to visit me at www.gailranstrom.com or email me at gail@gailranstrom.com.

And now, without further ado, here is Charlie's story.

A Daring
Liaison

GAIL RANSTROM

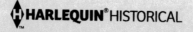

HARLEQUIN® HISTORICAL

Recycling programs
for this product may
not exist in your area.

ISBN-13: 978-0-373-30658-9

A DARING LIAISON

Printed in U.S.A.

Available from Harlequin® Historical and
GAIL RANSTROM

GAIL RANSTROM

was born and raised in Missoula, Montana, and grew up spending the long winters lost in the pages of books that took her to exotic locales and interesting times. That love of the "inner voyage" eventually led to her writing. She has three children, Natalie, Jay and Katie, who are her proudest accomplishments. Part of a truly bicoastal family, she resides in Southern California with her two terriers, Piper and Ally, and has family spread from Alaska to Florida.

Chapter One

London, April 1822

Charles Hunter always sat with his back to the wall to avoid unpleasant surprises—a tactic he had learned from his superior at the Home Office, Lord Wycliffe—and the Black Dog Tavern was not a place where one would want to be surprised. Charles watched Wycliffe come toward him now, wondering why he had arranged this meeting outside the office. The grim look on his face was not reassuring.

Trouble, then. Serious trouble, and highly sensitive if they couldn't they talk about it at the Home Office. He took a deep drink from his mug and gestured to the waiting tankard, which Wycliffe lifted promptly.

"Hunter," he said as he sat.

Charles nodded. "What is this about?"

"It's on the hush, Hunter. I can't make you take the venture, but it would be good for your career if you did. Probably get you that assignment to the Foreign Office you asked about. That's why I thought I'd give you first chance at it."

The Foreign Office? That was a plump little carrot to

dangle in front of him. He'd wanted to get the hell out of England for months now. Maybe a transfer would clear his head. Ever since he'd been wounded last fall, he'd been restless, angry and a bit reckless. Standing by one's best friend as he was shot through the head could do that to a man, he'd been told.

"What's it about?"

Wycliffe sighed and looked down into his ale. "Long story. First, have you met the late Lady Caroline Betman's former ward, Georgiana Carson, currently known as Mrs. Gower Huffington?"

Charles covered his surprise and damned the quick twist of his gut at that name. Did he know her? Hell, he'd been about to propose to her when her guardian informed him that his feelings were not returned. But that was before she'd married for the first time. She'd been so fresh. So beautiful. *So duplicitous.*

"We've met," he admitted.

"What do you think of her?"

"I've always thought she is a stunner. Intelligent and self-possessed, though guarded and…"

Wycliffe nodded again, as if confirming Charles's opinion. "Inscrutable?"

Charles shrugged. He'd been about to say *deceitful,* but perhaps that had only been his experience. "Aloof, I'd say. And not given to emotion."

"Odd for a woman who's been married twice."

"And widowed twice, and hides in the countryside now, from what I hear."

"Then you didn't know?" Wycliffe narrowed his eyes as he sat back in his chair. "Mrs. Huffington has come back to town."

The connection was lost on him. What did Georgiana Huffington, née Carson, have to do with Wycliffe's assignment? He rubbed his shoulder, still aching from the ball he'd taken when his friend was killed last October. "Aye, she's come back to town and…?"

"Good Lord, Hunter! Where have you been? Allow me to catch you up." Wycliffe leaned forward again and lowered his voice as if he feared they might be overheard. "Rumor has it that she killed her husbands."

Charles stared into his ale, remembering his obsession with the woman seven years ago. He'd been taken with those olive-green eyes—and the promise of lush curves beneath her demure girlish gowns. She'd been shy, sweet and possessed of a gentle humor he found endearing but there had always been a hint of darkness and mystery about her. "She doesn't look like the type."

"You, better than most, know that appearances can be deceiving. Why, you've witnessed things that would shock the ton into speechlessness—with the possible exception of me."

Aye, the deceit and duplicity he'd seen beneath innocuous appearances no longer surprised him. He was a jaded man.

"But I am glad you find her appealing. That will make your job easier."

A job involving Mrs. Huffington? Never. Charles laughed and shook his head. "I am on holiday. Personal matters to settle."

"Come, now, Hunter. I know you are not spending your leave playing with the demimonde and dancing with new country lasses fresh into town for the season. Not while Dick Gibbons is still at large."

Gibbons. That misbegotten, vile, flea-infested bag of manure. *Gibbons* was the personal matter he intended to settle before taking another assignment. He'd wager all he owned that Gibbons was the man who'd killed his friend and put a bullet in his shoulder. "I have business of my own to attend, Wycliffe. I am not inclined to help you with any 'unofficial' problems at the moment."

Wycliffe sat back in his chair and tapped the table with one finger, a jaded expression on his face. "The truth is that you need to kill Gibbons before he kills you, eh? I've seen all kinds, Hunter, but the Gibbons clan is beyond my comprehension. I cannot think what could account for their felonious nature."

"It's in their blood," Charles murmured. "It's who they are and what they were born to be."

"I've known good men with no better beginnings. You do not really believe in 'bad blood,' do you?"

"Aye, I do. And I believe if it's birthed a Gibbons, you'd do the world a favor to exterminate it before it can spread."

Wycliffe gave a short laugh. "And nature and upbringing have no bearing? Are inconsequential?"

Charles shrugged. "I'd say they count for very little."

An arched eyebrow was Wycliffe's reaction. "I can see this is not the night for a philosophical discussion."

It certainly wasn't. Charles brought the conversation back to the point. "So if you think the Huffington woman is guilty of something, put someone else on her trail."

"That's precisely why I need your help. It isn't official, you see. Not yet. It is…delicate, and requires someone who is socially adept, accepted at all levels of society and who has a light touch."

"If it is not official, why are we poking our noses in what doesn't concern us?"

"Requests from some rather prominent people. Her former husbands' families are suspicious of the nature of the deaths. Too coincidental, they say. Too convenient. For her.

"She has profited nicely from both deaths. And her

last husband, Gower Huffington, was quite wealthy. No immediate family, but he has a distant nephew who was expecting to inherit. He thinks Mrs. Huffington cozened his uncle into changing his will and thus cheated him of his due."

Disgruntled relatives looking for an inheritance were not reason enough to drag his attention from Dick Gibbons. He shook his head again. "Not interested."

"You haven't heard the rest." Wycliffe finished his ale and pushed his chair back. "About her and Adam Booth."

A cold feeling settled in the pit of Charles's stomach at the mention of his friend. "What about Booth?" Adam had taken a bullet that had been meant for Charles, and Charles had been carried away with a bullet in his left shoulder. Dick Gibbons had been gunning for Charles, not Adam. His friend had just gotten in the way. And what did any of that have to do with Mrs. Huffington?

"He'd been courting Mrs. Huffington. 'Tis rumored they'd signed marriage contracts the day he was killed."

Charles remembered Booth's interest in the widow, but he hadn't realized how serious it was or he'd have warned his friend against her. He took a long, slow drink, digesting this information.

Wycliffe pressed his advantage. "Furthermore, Mrs. Huffington's former guardian, Lady Caroline Betman, died rather suddenly. Her death is being seen as yet another convenience for Mrs. Huffington. Each death was ruled accidental, save Lady Caroline's, which was thought to be natural. That is why the investigation must be kept unofficial. There is no new information that would warrant reopening the inquiries. Gathering that information would be your task."

Charles was forced to admit that Mrs. Huffington looked guilty of *something*. And he'd known unlikelier killers. "I only knew her briefly seven years ago, and have no way of knowing what she may or may not be inclined to do. In fact, I can think of no reason to take this assignment. I need to find Gibbons before he finds me."

"That's what I've been trying to tell you. Maybe it isn't Gibbons you are looking for."

For a moment—just a moment—Charles thought Wycliffe was suggesting… "Mrs. Huffington?"

Wycliffe spread his arms wide. "Why not? If she is guilty of killing her husbands, then why not Adam Booth? Even *his* father has paid a visit to the secretary. You always said it was not like Gibbons to miss, nor was a pistol his first choice of weapons. What if it wasn't Gibbons holding the gun that night after all?"

That supposition gave Charles a moment's pause until logic took over. "What could her motive be? She wasn't married to Booth, so she did not stand to inherit. Would she not have waited until the nuptials?"

"Lady Caroline had negotiated a nominal settlement should Booth not wed her, no matter the reason. Afraid he'd back out, no doubt."

Bloody hell! Was everything he'd believed wrong?

"Two husbands? And both of them dead?" Lady Sarah Travis asked without preamble, her violet eyes wide with astonishment.

Georgiana Huffington was well aware that the Wednesday League book club had convened an emergency meeting on her account. The ladies were quietly dedicated to helping women who, for one reason or another, found themselves in a pickle.

She gave a decisive nod, feeling the color rise to her cheeks. It was always the same—this reaction. Perhaps it was because she was only three-and-twenty. Or perhaps they were wondering how she could possibly have had such colossal ill fortune. They might as well know the worst immediately. "And one fiancé," she admitted with a breathless sigh.

Grace Hawthorne leaned forward and placed her teacup on a low table. "My dear! That is...too heartbreaking."

Lady Annica Auberville and Lady Charity MacGregor, the other two women present, nodded their agreement.

"Is this why Gina has brought you to us?" Lady Sarah prodded with a sideways glance at her sister-in-law, Eugenia Hunter.

"She said you might be able to help me."

Lady Annica placed her teacup beside Mrs. Hawthorne's and studied Georgiana intensely. "I confess I do not know how."

Dizzy with the implications of what she was about to say, she took a deep breath before she could say the words aloud. "I have begun to wonder if their deaths were altogether natural."

She expected protests, or at least some sort of reassuring denial. But the ladies merely studied her as if she had said something perfectly reasonable. For a long moment, the only sound in Lady Sarah's elegant sitting room was the rhythmic tick-tock of an ornate tall case clock in one corner.

Finally, Lady Sarah nodded. "Please rest assured that anything revealed in this group is utterly confidential. And we shall expect the same of you."

She heaved a sigh of relief and nodded her agreement rather vigorously. What she was about to say was bad enough, but to risk it being repeated was untenable.

The women smiled and Lady Sarah inclined her head. "Could you give us a brief summary, Mrs. Huffington? A sick feeling settled in the pit of Georgiana's stomach. "I was first married at seventeen, barely three months after entering society. His name was Arthur Allenby. The night of our vows he tumbled down the stairs, having had a bit too much celebration."

"Consummated?" Lady Annica asked in a very frank manner.

Dear sweet Allenby. He'd been so eager for the marriage bed, and then... "No. He fell before, well, you know. Mr. Allenby's family returned my dowry, added considerable compensation and sent me back to my aunt Caroline's at once. I was a reminder of the tragedy, they said. Then, after my mourning and an extra year, came Gower Huffington. We wed two years ago. In December. We traveled to his country estate for our honeymoon." This time there had been a consummation. He'd been quite eager and quick—over before she'd been able to ease the pain. And once again, for good measure Gower had said. She had dared hope she would come to tolerate it in time. "A day or two after we arrived, he went for a walk and did not return. By the time the woodsman found him the next day, he was quite dead. His heart gave out, the coroner said."

She glanced at Lady Annica and answered before it was asked. "Consummated, no issue. Mr. Huffington's lands were not entailed, nor his fortune. He had no other close heirs and left me quite comfortable."

"And...and you wonder if these unfortunate incidents were entirely natural?" Lady Sarah repeated.

"It seems rather odd to me that neither of my marriages have lasted longer than a day or two. It could be a tragic coincidence." Georgiana hesitated. The final story was shorter, and even more tragic. "But last fall, before Aunt Caroline and I left town so quickly, I was betrothed to another man. He was killed barely a day after signing our contracts and before any announcements had been made."

Even Gina's eyebrows went up at this. "Who was it, Georgiana?"

"Mr. Booth. Mr. Adam Booth."

"I was at the Argyle Rooms that night! I recall the incident—in the street outside Argyle House."

Georgiana nodded. She still did not know the particulars of that event, except that she had been assured it had nothing to do with her. But still…

"Too much for mere coincidence," Lady Annica mused. "Do you have any particular reason, aside from the untimely nature of the deaths, for suspecting foul play, Mrs. Huffington?"

"I have been over it in my mind endlessly. I did not know of anyone who wished them ill, nor can I think of anyone who would wish *me* ill. There is simply neither rhyme nor reason to it all, and that, I think, is the reason it took me so long to see the unlikelihood of mere coincidence."

Grace Hawthorne put her teacup aside. "Has there been a threat to you personally, Mrs. Huffington? A note or a warning? A near call, an unaccountable accident, odd occurrence?"

"Nothing. I vow, each time it came without warning. One moment, all was well, and the next…"

"Disaster," Gina finished for her.

"The most troubling was my betrothal to Mr. Booth. Our engagement had not even been announced, and he was dead. We—Aunt Caroline and I—were assured that the matter was quite unrelated to our betrothal, but…"

"But?"

"The facts speak for themselves. And, to be blunt, I would almost rather think there is something or someone else behind these things than to think of myself as being cursed. I've heard it whispered in the ton that only a madman would propose to me now. And I've heard there are some who are speculating that I hastened my husbands' ends."

"Do you want to be married again?" Lady Sarah asked with a note of wonder in her voice.

Georgiana shuddered. "I've had quite enough marriage and mourning, thank you." Not again. Never again. Marriage and men were not for her.

Lady Sarah sat a little straighter. "Then the worst that could happen is that we are unable to get to the bottom of this and that the rumors persist. But if you do not wish to marry again, those consequences are not so very dire."

"No," Lady Annica corrected. "The worst that could happen is that we stir the pot and it somehow comes to a boil and implicates Mrs. Huffington and she is arrested."

Arrested? If she was found guilty, she would hang. Dare she risk that?

"Is there anything—anything at all—that you have not told us, Mrs. Huffington?"

Georgiana shifted in her chair. Should she mention the little items recently gone missing? The occasional uneasy feeling that she was being watched or followed? Or that something was not quite…right? No. She needed these women to help her, not think she was confused or mad. Clara, her maid, had said it was merely her imagination, brought on by the circumstances of her husbands' deaths. Even Aunt Caroline had told her she was seeing things that were not there.

"I can think of nothing important. Truly. Nothing."

"Were you terribly in love, my dear?" Lady Charity asked.

"Love? I… Lady Caroline assured me that love follows marriage. She approved of my husbands and was as distressed as I over their deaths—perhaps more so. She desperately wanted to see me settled."

Gina filled the gap for her. "Lady Caroline expired just before Christmas."

"Then you are quite alone in the world, are you not?" Mrs. Hawthorne asked. "Such tragedy in your short life."

Georgiana waved one hand in dismissal of the unwanted sympathy. "I only want to clear my name and reputation. And if my husbands were murdered, I want to find out who is behind it and obtain justice for them. That is the least I can do."

Lady Annica clapped her hands. "Justice. The very thing we stand for, Mrs. Huffington—Georgiana, if I may? We are all on first names here."

"We must ask you to think carefully about our next question, Georgiana," Lady Sarah warned. "How closely do you want to be involved in the investigation?"

"Very closely, indeed," she vowed. If someone was singling out the men she married, she wanted to know why.

"Excellent. I shall make all the arrangements and send you notice of where and when we shall meet next. Leave your schedule open, dear. We shall likely begin tomorrow."

His hand raised, Charles was about to knock on his sister's door when it opened and nearly caused him to stumble. Thank God he'd arrived in time.

"Charles! Heavens, you nearly frightened us to death."

He looked over his sister's shoulder to see her usual collection of friends—Lady Annica, Grace Hawthorne, Lady Charity MacGregor, Eugenia and, yes, the infamous Widow of Kent. His first love, his deepest cut and now his quarry.

Sarah followed the direction of his attention and smiled. "Charles, have you met Mrs. Huffington?"

"I believe I had that pleasure some years ago," he said, removing his hat. "Refresh my memory?" He was rewarded by Mrs. Huffington's little flinch at the slight.

Sarah stood aside to allow Mrs. Huffington to come forward. "Georgiana, may I present my woefully wicked brother, Mr. Charles Hunter? Charles, may I present Mrs. Georgiana Huffington?"

The beguiling creature performed a polite curtsy, her eyes downcast. Was she remembering the single extraordinary kiss they had stolen in a garden seven years ago? He took her hand and bowed. "Charmed again, Mrs. Huffington. How long have you been in town?"

"Not long, sir," she said as she looked up from their joined hands. "I've only just returned from Kent."

He took a moment to absorb her remarkably green eyes. Not emerald. Not greenish-gray or sea-green. Hers were more…olive. And every bit as captivating as they'd been years ago. His memory had not failed him. Nor had hers, indicated by the subtle blush on her cheeks. Yes, she was remembering that single astonishing kiss, too. Ah, but she was no longer girlishly coy. No, this Georgiana was now a woman of considerable experience. One he would have no qualms about seducing.

"Is Kent your home?" he asked to break the silence.

"It was until my marriage…s. And is again now."

Quite interesting, the way she included her deceased husbands in one group. He wondered, perversely, if he should offer condolences or congratulations.

Before he could say anything, she tucked a stray wisp of dark blond hair back into her bonnet and continued a little breathlessly. "I have come to town to meet with my aunt's factor and solicitor to settle matters regarding her estate."

He noted a quick flash of pain in her eyes, just as quickly hidden—genuine grief for her aunt, then, but only scraps for her husbands. And Adam Booth? What had she felt for him? "I am sorry for your loss…es, Mrs. Huffington."

A sudden spark in her eyes told him she'd caught his deliberate mocking.

He became aware of the other ladies watching them with interest, and that he was still holding Mrs. Huffington's warm, delicate hand. He released it and gave her his best devil-may-care grin as he bowed and stood aside to let them pass. A fair beginning. Having been reintroduced by his sister, Mrs. Huffington was unlikely to suspect the real reason he was about to show a singular interest in her again.

But he'd been surprised by the sudden flash of anger that surfaced at his memory of that kiss—a kiss so remarkable he'd been about to propose. A kiss he still remembered seven years later. A kiss, as it turned out, that had been nothing but deceitful.

Chapter Two

Georgiana looked down at the darkened city street outside her window. There were a few trees in the small square across the way, two or three benches and a grassy patch for children to play. A little piece of the country in London. The thought made her a bit melancholy. She'd lived most her life in Kent, shut away with her guardian. Lady Caroline's tragic disfigurement had isolated her from the world but for her brief and successful husband-hunting forays for Georgiana. But she could not regret those quiet, idyllic days. In fact, she yearned for them. A life in the countryside free of the controversy and scandal of her circumstances seemed the most desirable of all goals. The moment she could conclude her business, she'd hasten back to Kent and retire there.

London was too unsettling. Too demanding. Too dangerous.

She leaned against the window casement and pulled the lace curtain aside to watch the flicker of the lamppost below and try to organize her mind for the days ahead. But all that came to her was Charles Hunter. Her first love. Her greatest shame.

She'd met him years ago, in her come-out season, and

she'd thought him terribly handsome and quite amusing. She'd made the mistake of allowing him to kiss her in a garden one summer night, and that had been her undoing. That kiss had been deeply stirring and had led to more than she intended.

Upon their reintroduction this afternoon, she'd confirmed he was quite the best-looking man she'd ever met. But now there was nothing of his youthful openness left. He was still tall and dark, like his brothers, and he had the same startling violet eyes as his sister, but he seemed more guarded, more…dangerous. What had happened to him during the intervening years?

Back then, he'd been her favorite, and she'd thought she was his. But after that kiss he'd turned moody and began to avoid her. She wondered if she'd done something wrong, commited some gaucherie, or somehow offended him. When she'd complained, Aunt Caroline informed her that some men were fickle, and lost interest when a woman came too easily. Charles Hunter, she was told, was a rake—the sort who liked the chase more than the capture. Had the kiss been his capture? Humiliated, she'd begun to avoid him, too.

Now? Well, he was Lady Sarah's brother, and she would likely be encountering him on occasion. But she was seven years older and wiser. She could hold her own with a man like Mr. Hunter. His subtle challenge and the ever-so-slight insult this afternoon aside, she could be as polite as he. Yes, warm and polite on the surface, cool and distant beneath—that was the way to deal with a man of his mettle. Surely ignoring his little barbs would be easy for her now that she had some measure of sophistication and experience.

The mantel clock struck the hour of eleven just as a knock sounded on her door. Sanders, her footman, entered carrying a small silver tray bearing two letters. "Mr. Hathaway said these came for you a bit ago, madam. I think one is from that solicitor fellow."

Her solicitor? Oh, pray he had found time for her in his schedule. "Why did he not bring it to me when it arrived?"

"Mr. Hathaway was on his way out to fetch blacking for the stove and andirons, madam. He left them in the foyer and Clara told me to bring them up." Sanders placed the little tray on her night table.

Blacking? Where would her butler find blacking so late at night? Georgiana sighed as she realized her household had become used to functioning by itself during her mourning. It might take her a while to get matters back in hand.

Sanders added wood to the fireplace and turned to Georgiana. "Will that be all for tonight, madam?"

"Yes, thank you. Please send Clara up."

He gave a crisp bow before leaving her alone in her room. She looked around and sighed. In London three days, and they'd just managed to settle in. She hadn't thought to send servants ahead to prepare for her arrival. Aunt Caroline had always tended to such matters. The house had needed airing, the linens washing, the furniture dusting and the floors polishing. But now she was ready for her stay, no matter how long. The only room they hadn't opened was Aunt Caroline's. She was not quite ready for that yet.

How odd, she thought as she turned to the four-poster bed and removed her apron. She and Aunt Caroline had talked endlessly about everything in the world, but they'd never talked about this—about the small details of her aunt's final wishes.

The threat of tears burned the backs of her eyes and she blinked rapidly to hold them at bay—she had promised herself that she was done with them. She'd cried oceans of tears in the past seven years, but her deepest sorrow was for Aunt Caroline.

She removed her lace cap, tossed it on her dressing table and pulled the pins from her tidy bun. The weight of her hair tumbled down her back and she ran her fingers through it to remove any remaining hairpins as her maid bustled in.

"Ready for bed, madam?"

"Yes, Clara. I think we are all exhausted. Please tell everyone to sleep late."

The plump woman smiled. "Aye, madam. Won't have to tell them twice, I vow."

Georgiana laughed. Sleeping late was a treat Aunt Caroline had always offered after an unusually long day of work. "If you will just help me with my stays, I shall do the rest myself." She undid her tapes, lifted her work dress over her head and turned her back to the maid.

Clara went to work loosening the laces of her corset until it fell away, leaving Georgiana only in her chemise. "Aye, madam. I think we're all settled in, like. Everyone is excited to be back in town. Why, even Mr. Hathaway has a spring in his step."

Her staid butler? Imagining Hathaway excited about anything was nearly impossible.

"Cook and me think he has a sweetheart." Clara giggled. "He was sad to leave last fall and he perked up the minute we got here."

And now he was going out at night to buy blacking. Georgiana smiled. She wondered if she'd have to hire a new upstairs maid soon. She hoped Hathaway's sweetheart was not a cook, because Mrs. Brady was truly gifted in the kitchen.

Clara picked up the brush but Georgiana took it from

her and sat at the dressing table. "Go on to bed, Clara. I'll finish up. And mind you, lie abed in the morning."

Clara bobbed a curtsy and practically ran for the door before Georgiana could retract the offer. She began to pull her brush through her hair and then set it aside to open her little jewelry case.

Silly to look again, she knew. It hadn't been there yesterday and wouldn't have magically appeared today. But she'd have sworn she'd left the little opal ring here last fall. Aunt Caroline had given it to her on her sixteenth birthday and it was precious to her. Even more precious now that Auntie was gone.

She closed her jewelry case with a sigh and turned to the letters on her tray. She broke the unfamiliar seal on the first one—not from her solicitor but from Grace Hawthorne. She and her husband, a diplomat, were hosting a reception for the American ambassador tomorrow evening and requested her attendance—a very proper and sedate way to reenter society after her most recent mourning. She would send her acceptance in the morning.

The next letter was, indeed, from her solicitor. He would see her Friday morning and hinted that he had news for her. Whatever it was, she could not be surprised. She and her aunt had shared every detail of their lives. Well, every detail but for those in her will.

Georgiana went to her escritoire and opened her appointment book. She scratched the Hawthorne reception tomorrow night and her appointment with the solicitor the day after into the book, then blew the candles out, dimming the bedroom to the indistinct glow of the fireplace.

After she shed her chemise and donned her nightgown, she went back to her window to open it to the soft breeze. A movement in the shadows across the street set her heart to racing. The overwhelming sensation of being watched sent a shiver though her and she rubbed her arms to banish the sudden gooseflesh that rose there. Someone walking over her grave, her aunt used to say. The edge of the curtain drifted back into place as she backed away from the window. Had it been her imagination or a foreshadowing of things to come?

Charles shifted in the darkness. He hadn't meant to let the sight of Mrs. Huffington in the window draw him closer to the light, but he'd forgotten himself in his study of her. She was so bloody beautiful that he could well understand men getting lost in those soulful green eyes and proposing in the face of almost certain death.

But was she a victim or a villainess? That was the question Wycliffe wanted answered. And *he* needed to know if she'd been the cause of Adam Booth's death and his wound. He rubbed his shoulder absently, the muscles still stiff from the injury.

Georgiana Huffington's entire future depended upon what he uncovered. And, as heart-stopping as she was, he could not afford to allow his baser instincts to interfere. He'd never compromised an assignment before, and he wouldn't start now. Seduce her, perhaps, but be drawn in by her supposed innocence? Never. He knew better.

Ah, but anticipation of tomorrow night at the Hawthorne reception made him smile to himself. Mrs. Huffington's dismay should be quite amusing when she realized he would not be so easy to avoid as he'd been years ago.

A cold shiver worked its way up his spine. Someone walking over his grave? He glanced around and strained to hear any sound, no matter how faint. Damn Gibbons and his cutthroats. Charles hadn't been able to relax for months, but this was different. His every instinct warned him danger was in the wind. Breathlessly, he waited. Moments passed before he breathed again. A falling leaf? A stray cat?

Only stillness. And oppressive atmosphere.

He turned away, grateful that Thackery's was nearby. He'd find his friends and indulge in a bit of gaming. Perhaps a bit of female companionship.

Charles paid his respects to Adam Hawthorne and his honored guest, the American Ambassador Richard Rush, and moved away. The press of guests at his back waiting for introductions relieved him of the responsibility of making polite conversation.

He was pleased to find there was an orchestra. Dances, he had found, were quite convenient to get a lady alone for a private word. All he needed was the lady. He waited in the foyer to watch the wide entry door. Sooner or later, Mrs. Georgiana Huffington would come through it, and the game would begin.

Charles's anticipation rose with each passing moment. The memory of her standing in the window in a nearly transparent nightgown, her hair falling around her in a golden aura, was enough to keep him standing there for hours. How would that glorious mass feel slipping between his fingers? What lay beneath that alluring nightgown he'd glimpsed? Did she still kiss like a wild angel?

He straightened as his sister and Mrs. Huffington came through the door, followed by his brother-in-law, Lord Ethan Travis. He hovered until they had been presented to the ambassador and then followed them into the music room.

Mrs. Huffington was elegant in a soft gray satin that draped to reveal her excellent figure. Rather than drab, as it might have been on any other woman, the sheen of soft gray became her, nicely setting off her delicate coloring and hair. Was the gown a remnant from her previous half mourning? Her hair had been contained in a graceful coronet from which a few curls were left to dangle and caress her long, graceful neck.

For one prurient moment he found himself wondering if the hollow of her throat was still soft and sweet, if he would be able to feel her heartbeat there, quickening against his lips. Did her passions run hotter now that she was an experienced woman? How fierce would she be in making love?

Sarah noticed his approach and smiled a welcome. "Ah, I thought you'd be here, Charles. With your imminent appointment to the Foreign Office, you could scarce afford to miss this event. The American ambassador—perhaps you will be sent to America."

His imminent appointment? Now, why hadn't he heard this? Another of Wycliffe's ploys to convince him to investigate the Widow of Kent? He forced a smile and bowed. "Dear sister. Mrs. Huffington." He greeted the ladies. "I trust you are well?"

Sarah turned to Mrs. Huffington, deferring to her for an answer.

"Very well, thank you," she said. Her full lips curved in a smile both wise and innocent.

Charles knew when a woman was attracted to him, and knew by her smile that she recognized the attraction was still mutual. The question was what she would do with that knowledge. Time to test the waters.

"Have you taken care of your business in town, Mrs. Huffington?"

"I've done no more than make appointments, sir. I think all of London must be waiting on someone or other."

He laughed at her assessment. "Then you will be with us for a while yet?"

"So it would seem."

"And I am doing my best to keep her diverted," Sarah said. "I am taking her to my modiste tomorrow."

Ethan slipped his hand into Sarah's, an endearing gesture that belied their four years of marriage. "Her favorite establishment," he explained. "Though I always suspect there is some manner of mischief afoot there."

Sarah nudged him. "Tease! The only mischief is to your accounts. Marie is simply the best dressmaker ever. One has not truly arrived in London until one has had a gown fashioned by Madame Marie. Her judgment is unerring."

Ethan read Charles's expression, smiled and edged a knowing glance toward Mrs. Huffington. "Have you seen the Hawthorne gardens, Mrs. Huffington? The topiary is extraordinary."

"I've not had that pleasure, Lord Ethan."

Taking the cue, Charles offered his arm. "Allow me to show you the grounds, Mrs. Huffington."

She hesitated, then blinked and took his arm, her hand trembling just a little, and he surmised she had been about to refuse. Did she realize he was on to her "poor widow" act? That his interest in her now was due to his suspicion of her? Or was she remembering their last encounter in a garden?

"Bring Georgiana back before long, Charlie. I really must introduce her around," Sarah called after them.

He gave his sister a sardonic wink. Sarah had admonished him more than once for his rakish ways, but he was not about to lie just to set her mind at ease. Instead, he led Mrs. Huffington through the ballroom and out to the terrace.

"I fear I've appropriated you with falsehoods, Mrs. Huffington," he admitted.

"You have no knowledge of topiaries?"

He smiled down at her, a bit diverted by the subtle scent of her perfume—a note of flowers blended with ambergris—similar to the scent his former mistress had used. But on Mrs. Huffington it was quite heady. Lush and seductive. "None," he admitted. "Absolutely none."

"Then we shall have to bumble along on our own, shan't we?"

Quite adventurous of her. He'd just given her the perfect excuse to return to the house, and she hadn't taken it—not that he'd have let her escape. Perhaps she had her own reasons for wanting to speak to him alone.

They strolled deeper into the twilight, guided by the lantern-lit paths. She did not prattle on like most women in like situations. To the contrary, after her initial reluctance, she seemed composed and calm, and he supposed that was due to the familiarity of such a walk. Had her husbands strolled with her through gardens before going down on bended knee?

They reached a path of hedges trimmed in various forms. He paused at one with a sharp spire. "Here we have the ever-popular boxwoodicus pointum."

She laughed, a sound that sent a shiver up his spine. "I shall commit that to my memory, Mr. Hunter."

He led her a bit farther from the house, curious how far he might take her. Far enough for privacy? "How have you come to know my sister?"

"I am not long in her acquaintance," she admitted. "Miss Eugenia O'Rourke—oh, sorry, Mrs. Hunter since her marriage to your brother, but she was an O'Rourke when I met her—introduced us."

"And how do you know Gina?"

"Last fall when Aunt Caroline and I came to town, we met in mutual company. I was previously acquainted with the Misses Thayer, who made the introductions."

"Hortense and Harriett? Aye, the twins know everyone between the two of them. Did you all go about together?"

"Occasionally." She paused and looked up at him as if she would say more, then glanced down again and the moment passed. "Not long after our arrival, Aunt Caroline and I returned to Kent. There was…trouble. And Aunt Caroline felt we should go home."

Trouble? Was that how she thought of her most recent conquest's death? Aye, he'd wager that would send her back to the countryside to hide. He stopped and took her hand, mildly surprised by its softness and warmth. "May I offer my condolences on your aunt's death? I am told time will ease the loss."

Tears welled up in her eyes and she brushed them back with her free hand before they could fall. "It was quite unexpected. I do not believe she was much in pain."

As they continued to stroll in silence, still holding hands, Charles was surprised that she hadn't sought to break the contact. All the better for him, since accustoming her to his touch was a part of his plan. Her little half smile was back and he breathed a little easier. He'd learned that the more a woman smiled, the less suspicious she was.

After a moment or two, she spoke again. "Did I hear your sister say that you are bound for the Foreign Office?"

"It has been mentioned to me as a possible option, but I have not made a decision. I have unfinished business where I am."

"And where is that, Mr. Hunter?"

"London," he told her without a twinge of conscience. Though it was no secret that he was with the Home Office, he perpetuated the myth that he was a minor clerk to

Lord Wycliffe at Wycliffe's suggestion. Only his brothers knew the extent of his activities.

"The Foreign Office sounds wonderfully exotic. I think I would love to travel, though I have not done enough of it to know."

Charles shrugged. "My family has always believed in service to one's country. All of us have traveled extensively, and allow me to assure you, Mrs. Huffington, that there is no place on earth like England."

"Still, I have nothing left to hold me here, and it might be nice to see something of the world. That is the one benefit that Aunt Caroline's infirmity denied me."

He looked down at the top of her head, bowed to the pebbled path. Her scent, the soft warmth of her hand as it rested in his, the curve of her throat that begged his kisses, and the fullness of her lips just waiting for his. His eyes slipped lower to the provocative swell of her breasts above the modest neckline of her gown. Though they were mostly hidden from view, his imagination fueled an immediate and strong response in his body. One that he hoped Mrs. Huffington was yet innocent enough to miss.

He shook his head to clear it. Was this part of her allure—this mixture of worldliness and innocence? The undeniable appeal that had lured two men, perhaps three, to their deaths?

"Is something amiss, Mr. Hunter?" she asked.

The lowered intimacy of her voice caused him to stop and face her again. There was an unquestionable risk in growing closer to the woman, but he was a man who'd always liked the thrill of danger. "Mrs. Huffington, I hope you will not think me presumptuous, but how long do you plan to be in town?"

"No longer than it will take me to settle matters regarding Aunt Caroline's estate. I find London society a bit…ruthless."

He, too, lowered his voice. If the chit was flirting, he'd give her more than she'd bargained for. "If you are referring to the gossip shared over teacups, I cannot deny it. But I hope you will be staying longer."

Georgiana's heart tripped. He leaned closer. Too close. "Are you flirting, Mr. Hunter?"

He gave her the boyish smile that used to turn her insides to mush. "Neither of us is innocent of the world and its…pleasures."

She held her breath as he lifted her hand and bent his head to brush his lips across her knuckles. A dark lock of hair fell across his forehead, and instant warmth seeped through her. She knew quite well that Aunt Caroline had been right about him. He teased, he flirted and once he'd stolen a kiss, he was on to the next woman. Who would know that better than she? Charles Hunter was an irresistible rake who had broken half the hearts in the ton. But not hers for a second time. She was immune.

After two marriages and a rather serious courtship, she had experience of a man's passion. But Charles Hunter's slow, easy grace was nothing like poor Arthur's, who'd done no more than kiss her before his tumble down the stairs. Nor was his seduction akin to Gower's quick, hard passion, come and gone in a blink. Yet not so sweet as Adam Booth's humble kiss.

No, Mr. Hunter was in no hurry, and that unsettled her. He was a challenge to everything she'd come to believe—that love and passion were not for her, and marriage would be a disservice to any man for whom she bore any fondness at all. But it might almost be worth a kiss or two, since she no longer bore any fondness for him. Just curiosity. Could he still render her senseless with his kiss? Cause her heartbeat to race? Kindle a burning in her soul?

She looked up into those deep unfathomable eyes and he seemed to read her mind. He lowered his head toward hers, parting his lips just slightly. She wanted to cry. To run. But she wanted to kiss him even more. Aunt Caroline's voice echoed in her mind. *Once a man like Charles Hunter has what he wants, he will go on to the next conquest.*

Slowly, reluctantly, she withdrew her hand. "You are most gallant, sir, but I think we've…studied the topiary rather longer than we intended."

He offered his arm, which she took. A frisson of misgiving warned her that there was more to Charles Hunter than Aunt Caroline had suspected. The night had deepened and the shadows encouraged her to say things she might not have dared in daylight. "Why did you really ask me into the garden, Mr. Hunter?"

He seemed surprised by her frankness. "I should think that would be apparent, Mrs. Huffington. As you have become my sister's friend, we shall be often in the same company. 'Twill be more pleasant if I can count you a friend, too."

Friend? Their brief moment of familiarity had passed, and the time had come to be polite again. "I believe we have established that much, sir."

He guffawed. "I like the way you speak your mind, Mrs. Huffington. Quite refreshing. Is there anything coy about you?"

"Heavens! I hope not. If you hadn't noticed, I'm a bit past the blushing maiden stage of my life. And, alas, there is no one left to remind me of my manners."

He arched one dark eyebrow. "Do not look to me for reminders, Mrs. Huffington. Had I my way, you'd be joining the gentlemen for cigars and brandy. I am far more likely to encourage your frankness than complain of it."

They entered the terrace doors to the strains of a waltz already in progress. Mr. Hunter swept her into his arms without a "by your leave" and led her into the whirl of soberly dressed gentlemen and gaily gowned women.

"Why, yes, Mr. Hunter. I'd love to dance," she said with mild reproach.

"The first of many to come."

Oh, she doubted that. Too much Charles Hunter would have her undone and forgetting both her scruples and Aunt Caroline's warnings. A moment later the dance ended and Mr. Hunter took her arm to lead her back to his sister.

Their way was blocked by two couples who had stopped to chat.

"…just as brazen as you please," one woman was saying. "And now it seems she has dug her talons into Charles Hunter, dragging him into the gardens like a common trollop…."

Georgiana's cheeks burned.

"I would think she'd have the decency to remain in the countryside," the other woman agreed. "Everyone knows what she is."

"And what is that, Francine?" one of the men asked, his gaze flicking over the woman's head to meet Georgiana's eyes.

"Why, a schemer at best. A murderess at worst," the woman answered. "And if I were to choose between the two—"

The scorching heat was replaced by a sudden icy coldness in the pit of her stomach. She could not mistake the mocking glance of the man who'd asked the question. She looked up at Mr. Hunter, and the expression on his face was terrifying—dark and furious. She started to turn, thinking he would quickly lead her around the group.

His grip tightened on her arm. "Hello, DeRoss. Everly. *Ladies*," he said with an inflection that cast doubt on the name.

Georgiana was torn between amusement and humiliation.

"Hunter." DeRoss, the man who'd asked the question, looked pointedly at Georgiana, pressing the introduction.

Mr. Hunter gave a slight smile, but there was something predatory about it. She suspected there was worse to come and lifted her chin with every bit of pride she could muster.

"Have you met my sister's dear friend, Georgiana Huffington?" he asked as he placed his hand over hers where it rested on his arm. The move was proprietary and flattering. And false.

Mr. DeRoss and Mr. Everly both gave the barest of bows and Mr. DeRoss spoke for them both. "Charmed, Mrs. Huffington."

She curtsied as slightly as they'd bowed. "Gentlemen," she murmured.

But Mr. Hunter was not inclined to stop there. "Miss Wilton-Smythe and Miss Grayson, allow me to present Mrs. Huffington."

Georgiana nodded and the women did likewise.

"I importuned Mrs. Huffington to allow me to show her the topiary. Quite artistic, were they not, my dear?"

My dear? He really was going a bit far. "Quite, sir. Exceeded only by your knowledge of the subject."

He laughed. "You are most welcome to whatever random knowledge I possess." Turning to the others, he said, "Must be getting Mrs. Huffington back to my sister. She will be waiting."

"Lady Sarah?" one of the women asked.

"I only have the one sister," he said. He turned Georgiana in Sarah's direction and led her away. "I've found it's always best to face bullies down," he said. "Let them know you're equal to them and that they cannot force you into a corner."

"But what was the point of mentioning your sister?"

"She has a reputation in the ton, Mrs. Huffington. Whoever Sarah approves publicly will be accepted without question."

"Ah, so then…"

"Those women will say nothing further against you."

Lady Sarah aside, she did not think any of them would want to cross Charles Hunter again. "But they will not like it," she said. "And they will be waiting for me to do something wrong."

He looked down at her, one eyebrow cocked and a challenge in his words. "Then your task is simple, Mrs. Huffington. Do nothing wrong."

She shivered as he released her hand. What a pretty pass things had come to when even her professed friends did not think she would be able to keep out of trouble! Worse—that she, herself, doubted it, too.

Chapter Three

Georgiana took long strides, still fuming as she swept out of her bank, her bulging reticule stuffed with two thousand pounds in banknotes tucked tightly under her arm. How could things have gotten so out of hand in just a few months? While she had been languishing in Kent mourning Lady Caroline's death, every distant relative of Lady Caroline and Gower Huffington had been conspiring against her!

"Madam, could you slow down a bit?" Clara asked, trotting along behind her. "'Twill make no difference if we're a few minutes late at that fancy French dress shop."

Georgiana slowed her pace to accommodate her maid's shorter legs. "Sorry," she murmured.

Now able to catch her breath, Clara began prattling on about the doings of the household, leaving Georgiana's mind to return to the problem at hand—how would she find the resources to look into her husbands' deaths and fight for her rights at the same time?

The worst of it was that Walter and Robert Foxworthy, Aunt Caroline's second cousins on her mother's side, had filed for conservatorship over her. Conservatorship? According to her solicitor, Mr. Goodman, they were suing for the right to control her inheritance and her into the bargain! *Untenable!* How *dare* they?

They had never bothered to visit even once in the past twenty years or more. Why, she wouldn't know them if she bumped into them on the street. Furthermore, warning her that the matter could take years to settle, Mr. Goodman had advised her to withdraw a considerable sum of money from the bank before her funds were frozen.

If that were not enough, he informed her that she was being sued by a Mr. York, Gower's cousin twice removed. She hadn't even been aware that Gower had a nephew, let alone that he claimed to be the sole heir to Gower's fortune. Indeed, Mr. York was claiming she had used duress to make Gower change his will in her favor! Why, nothing could be further from the truth. He'd changed his will in her favor even before they'd said their vows.

She had hoped her business in town would be settled today, and instead she had this new set of problems and another chore. Mr. Goodman had given her a packet that contained a copy of Aunt Caroline's will for her information and a few letters to her old friends. All were now safely tucked in her reticule along with that absurd amount of cash.

Common sense told her she should go back to Kent and await the outcome of the Foxworthy petition and the York suit, but how could she do that? She had to defend herself against these scurrilous charges. Her life and future were hanging in the balance! Any plans of hastening back to the countryside to avoid Mr. Hunter's attentions were now out of the question. He'd advised her to stay out of trouble and now, through no fault of her own, trouble had found *her*.

The ladies had arrived at La Meilleure Robe. Georgiana left Clara in the waiting room and joined them in the back fitting room. They brushed her apology for being late aside with kind reassurances.

"These little lulls give us a chance to actually discuss the books our husbands think we are reading," Sarah said.

"What book do they think you are reading?"

"*The Pirate,* by the Wizard of the North," Lady Annica said.

"It would be a good idea for you to read the book, too, dear," Grace Hawthorne said. "In the event someone should ask. I have an extra copy if you'd like."

Georgiana nodded. "Thank you, Mrs. Hawthorne."

"Grace," the woman corrected. "I shall have a footman deliver it to your home."

A handsome woman with the bearing of a queen entered through a side door and clapped her hands. "Ah! We are in pursuit, eh? Well, come. 'Oo is my client?"

Sarah nudged Georgiana toward the dressmaker's platform. "Madame Marie, this is Mrs. Georgiana Huffington."

The dressmaker circled Georgiana, her gaze sweeping up and down, assessing her figure. "Ah, yes. I know just the style for you, petite. And the correct color for you is violet. Any violet, but especially deep violet. Please say you never wear yellow."

"Never again." Georgiana vowed to go home and cull anything yellow from her wardrobe as she undressed to her corset and chemise.

Marie nodded and began taking Georgiana's measurements with knotted string behind a short dressing screen. Barely a moment later, a pleasant-looking man entered the room and was introduced as Madame Marie's husband, Mr. Francis Renquist. Gina explained that he had been a Bow Street Runner and was the group's chief investigator. He'd been briefly informed of her dilemma.

He nodded acknowledgment to Georgiana and then chivalrously avoided looking at her. "I have a few questions before I can begin, Mrs. Huffington."

"Ask anything, sir."

He took a small pad of paper and a lead pencil from his waistcoat pocket and prepared to take notes. "Do you know of anyone, no matter how far-fetched, who might have any reason to kill your husbands?"

"None," she answered quietly as Madame Marie continued to knot her string. "That is why these events are so bewildering."

"Do you have any former suitors who might bear a grudge?"

"No. Between marriages and mourning, I have not been much in society."

"Could it be possible that either of your husbands had enemies? Former lovers, mistresses, or rivals?"

"I...I do not believe so, sir, but I was not married to them long enough to become familiar with their personal affairs."

"Had any of them been affianced before you?"

"I do not think so."

"And you, Mrs. Huffington? Are there any men you jilted or who paid you court and who could be angry? Narrowing the field, so to speak, to have a second chance at you?"

Charles Hunter swept briefly though her mind, but *he* had snubbed *her,* not the other way around. She arched her eyebrow at the man. "I think I'd recall such a thing."

He allowed a small smile to quirk the corners of his mouth. "Aye, you probably would. Well, then, shall we look at the money? Who, apart from you, stood to profit from your husbands' deaths?"

"No one, I thought. My first husband made settlements

for that possibility in the marriage contract, but I did not inherit the bulk of his wealth. Certainly not enough to murder for. And Mr. Huffington did not have any close relatives, though he did have a cousin twice removed who has made claims against his estate. He says that he was Mr. Huffington's heir, but he did not come for the funeral or send condolences. Neither has he called in the year and a half since. Mr. Huffington's friends, though, were all quite considerate." A few had even offered to "ease her loneliness," but none had paid her serious suit.

"Aside from that, I have just learned that my aunt's second cousins have filed for conservatorship over me on the grounds that I am unstable due to the deaths of my husbands. I think they are simply making a grab for Aunt Caroline's estate."

Mr. Renquist frowned and his pencil flew across his paper as he made notes. Several of the ladies raised their eyebrows at her announcement and she knew they were wondering how she would handle such an occurance.

Madame Marie took a few more measurements and stood back with her hands on her hips.

"A lovely figure, Mrs. 'Uffington. I believe we shall try the new lower waistline. *Bien entendu!* I will begin at once," she said, bustling from the dressing room.

Georgiana turned to Lady Sarah. "Do I not have to choose a style from her books?"

Lady Sarah merely smiled. "Trust her, Georgiana. She will delight you."

Finished with his notes, Mr. Renquist took a deep breath and continued. "That brings us to you, Mrs. Huffington. Is there anyone in your past who might have a reason to kill your husbands?"

She was prepared for that question since she'd asked it of herself many times. It was that very question that had sent her straight to Gina and the Wednesday League book club. "I have no relatives, which is the reason Aunt Caroline raised me. Though I called her 'aunt' we were not blood kin. She had no brothers or sisters, just her second cousins. The entailed lands reverted to the crown upon her father's death, and the rest were solely hers. I shall learn her wishes for the final disposition of her estate once I have read her will. But she led me to believe that no one else had a right to make a claim on her estate."

Mr. Renquist looked pained. Clearly, he would rather have someone to point a finger at than have her as the only logical killer. "I am bound to say, Mrs. Huffington, that it looks bad for you. Still, if there is something afoot, we shall uncover it. Are you willing to do your part?"

"Whatever you think reasonable."

"Go about in society. Make note if anything odd occurs, or if anyone suspicious lurks near you. Should there be something out of the ordinary, or anything too similar to the circumstances leading to your previous marriages, come to me at once."

She nodded. A quick glance at the other ladies reassured her that this was not an unusual request.

Mr. Renquist continued, "I will meet you here at your fittings. If you wish to see me sooner, send word to Marie and she will arrange it." He gave a short bow and was gone.

Bemused, Georgiana stared at the closed door as she edged from behind the screen. *I am bound to say, Mrs. Huffington, that it looks bad for you.*

As Lord Wycliffe and Charles entered their box at the Theatre Royal, Wycliffe inclined his head to the ladies in the box across from them and Charles lifted one sardonic eyebrow. Perhaps it was the threads of distinguished gray at Wycliffe's temples, or the fact that he was unmarried, considered good looking, and possessed of a title and position—whatever it was, Wycliffe did not lack for female attention and did not hesitate to reciprocate.

As if reading Charles's mind, Wycliffe turned to him and smiled. "I say, Hunter! I always get more attention from the ladies when I'm in your company."

"'Tis true," Sir Harry Richardson said with a wide grin and a slap on Charles's back. "Why, even the demireps love our Charlie."

"Ah, there's our pigeon," Wycliffe said, inclining his head toward a box to their left.

Charles followed his line of vision and saw Hortense and Harriett Thayer, along with Mrs. Huffington, entertaining a number of men in their box. His brother James was there, too, accompanied by his bride, Gina—the perfect excuse to pay his respects.

"Do you really think that divine creature is capable of cold-blooded murder?" Richardson asked Wycliffe.

"Capable? Yes. From what I've heard, she is more than capable of anything she should choose to do. Morally inclined? That is another question entirely, and the one we must answer to the Secretary's satisfaction."

Charles cocked an eyebrow. "Is that possible?"

Wycliffe laughed. "Peel is a reasonable man, for all his innovative ideas about reform and establishing a metropolitan police force."

He gave a sigh, knowing now that they'd be answering to the Home Secretary himself for all that the investigation was "unofficial." Suddenly the case had taken on a more ominous tone. More urgent.

"What do your instincts tell you about the woman?" Richardson asked.

"I hardly know. We have not talked at length, but she

is a congenial sort. Quite pleasant to look at, and she possesses an infectious laugh. She expressed an interest in travel."

"She is not—"

"No, she has no immediate plans to leave the country. She mentioned that she has business to attend, then will consider it. We have another fortnight to find our answers, at a minimum."

Wycliffe frowned. "Who is her solicitor?"

Charles had had enough time in the past two days to discover a good many facts about the infamous widow. "Goodman is her solicitor."

"If we need to delay her in London, I will persuade him to hold up Mrs. Huffington's business matters."

Wycliffe could be very persuasive and Charles hoped that wouldn't be necessary. His superior could have a very heavy hand on occasion.

Richardson nudged him with another glance at the ladies as the orchestra signaled an intermission. "Are you going to introduce us?"

Still watching Mrs. Huffington, Charles considered the question. She was airy tonight, dressed in a heavenly froth of willow green with a fluid overdress of translucent cream. Even from this distance, he could see the graceful column of her throat, the lush curve of her breasts and the sensual way her lips curved into a smile when she saw him across the distance.

To his dismay, he suddenly realized that he wanted her. Despite her rejection. Despite the intervening years and marriages. Despite that she could be a cold-blooded killer and may have contracted the murder of his best friend and his wounding, he still wanted her.

That thought disturbed him. She was an assignment. No more. She was a potentially murderous female who'd gotten away with two crimes, perhaps four if her aunt's death had not been natural and Booth had been one of her casualties. She was intelligent, clever and forthright—a lethal combination in a woman. And because of those things, she could easily have stymied the authorities. However he dealt with her, he would have to keep on his guard.

He noted the eager light in Richardson's eyes and the interested spark in Wycliffe's expression and sighed. "Come on, then."

Within moments, the introductions were performed and several conversations were struck up, leaving Charles free to watch. Hortense and Harriett quickly snagged Harry Richardson's attention, and after a few quiet words with Mrs. Huffington, Wycliffe turned to greet Jamie and Gina. Seizing the opening Wycliffe had given him, Charles nodded to the widow as she raised her fan and snapped it open.

"You look flushed, Mrs. Huffington. Are you feeling well?"

"Very well, thank you, Mr. Hunter. Just a bit warm."

"I believe there is time for a breath of fresh air, if you'd like."

"Thank you. That should be just the tonic I need." She retrieved a cream cashmere shawl from the back of her chair and took his arm.

Charles was pleased to find that none of the others followed them. A few moments alone with Mrs. Huffington would seal their friendship and relax her suspicions. He couldn't help noticing the heads that turned to watch them descend the double staircase to the rotunda and exit the building. Tongues would wag, he was certain, but gossip would work to his advantage, discouraging other potential suitors by signaling his own interest.

Once they were on the street, he draped the shawl over her shoulders against the cool night air and turned her toward the square. Covent Garden, alive with excitement until the wee hours, always had something interesting to offer.

"I never grow bored in London," Mrs. Huffington said as if reading his mind.

"And yet you've spent most your life shut away in the countryside."

She laughed and looked up at him, stopping his breath with her beauty. "Aunt Caroline was not comfortable in London after her accident. I might have made another decision."

Ah, yes. Her disfigurement. "When did that occur?"

She shrugged and her shawl slipped down one creamy white shoulder. "Aunt Caroline said it happened the year before I was born. She did not like to speak of it, so I did not ask more. And as much as she dreaded London, the dear woman made certain I had my come-out. She so badly wanted to see me happily married that she brought me to town to husband-hunt."

A task she had excelled at, evidently. "How gratifying you had no problem finding one. Or two. Still, 'tis a pity she did not live to see you happily married."

"She did. Twice, remember? It was only after my last fiancé's tragic death that she lost heart for my future."

He looked down at her to see if she was serious. They had touched on this subject before, but she had never admitted to having a fiancé. Perhaps he was making progress in gaining her trust. He decided not to pursue that particular subject just now since Booth's death only angered him. "Did she believe you were happily married?"

"Though I scarcely knew the men, I was quick to assure her that I was more than content with the matches."

"And were you in actuality?"

"I had no particular objection to them, and Aunt Caroline was so eager for my happiness that I could not disappoint her."

"Is that why you married so quickly each time?"

"I married because she urged me to. I'd have been perfectly happy to wait for…"

"Wait for what, Mrs. Huffington?"

She sighed and shook her head. "For her death, sir. I would rather have stayed with her and eased her old age, just as she eased my childhood."

"Is that why you returned to Kent after each of your husbands' deaths?"

"Yes, and there was nowhere else to go. I could have stayed at Mr. Huffington's estate, but I was quite alone and did not know anyone in Yorkshire. Aunt Caroline sent for me, and I was happy to go."

"I must say that I find your equanimity refreshing," he said. "Most women go on about marrying for love, and yet you managed to find contentment, brief though it was, with two men. And a fiancé?"

She laughed at his assessment. "I was not married long enough to be disappointed, Mr. Hunter. As for love…" She shrugged. "Perhaps that requires a certain fierceness of character that I do not possess. In regard to my…equanimity, I have a practical nature. And practicality tells me that marriages are seldom made for love. They are made for gain, position, consolidation, convenience or simply to produce an heir."

"So you've never loved deeply?"

"Certainly I have. Lady Caroline. My darling spaniel. The memory of my mother and father."

"But not a man?"

"Once I thought…" There was a long pause before she stopped and looked up at him. "No. Not a man."

The moment stretched out as Charles wondered what it would be like to be loved by such a woman. If she loved, would she love fiercely?

"Flowers fer the missus?"

He turned to find a young girl staring up at him. She had a small wooden box filled with posies slung around her neck and was holding one made of violets and lily of the valley. Innocent, yet provocative, like Mrs. Huffington. He took a sixpence from his waistcoat pocket and flipped it to the child. She snatched it out of midair and gave him the posy before dashing off down a side street, not even offering change.

Basking in her brilliant smile and with a small bow, he presented the flowers to Mrs. Huffington.

She accepted them and lifted them to sample their fragrance. "Thank you, Mr. Hunter. You are the first to ever give me flowers."

A muzzle flashed. Instinctively, he pulled Mrs. Huffington into his arms before he dove for the ground. The deafening report of a pistol shattered the night as the bullet whistled past his left ear, and fury filled him.

Bloody hell! The flower girl had been sent to distract him.

Chapter Four

A shrill scream split the air in the echo of the gunshot even as the sound of running feet increased. Help arriving? Or pedestrians escaping the chaos?

Georgiana felt the reassuring weight of Charles Hunter across her, and the rise and fall of his chest against hers, and sighed with relief. He was breathing. He was alive. Thank God.

He lifted himself slightly, as if he was unwilling to expose her if the danger was still present. His glance bored into her, as if searching for signs of injury or hysteria. "Are you…"

"I am well, Mr. Hunter," she answered, trying to give the impression of aplomb even as she cleared her throat to steady her voice. "And you?"

He grinned and she realized he had anticipated hysteria. He eased himself to the side. "Well enough, Mrs. Huffington."

"What—"

"Hunter! Good God, man! What happened?"

Mr. Hunter sat up and helped her into a sitting position as Lord Wycliffe and Sir Harry arrived at their side. "'Twould seem buying a lady flowers has become a capital offense."

Lord Wycliffe's narrowed gaze swept the surrounding square and paused at each deepened shadow. At a subtle gesture, Sir Harry spun about and headed in the direction from which the shot had come. "No warning?"

Mr. Hunter uttered a curse under his breath as he stood and lifted her to her feet. "A flower girl stopped us as we strolled. The moment she had her coin, she dashed for the alley. A second later—the shot. I'd wager she'd been hired to stop us long enough for the shooter to take aim, and then run away."

Oh, dear Lord! Another man she'd been with had nearly been killed! She was *cursed!*

"You think the flower girl was involved?" Lord Wycliffe asked.

Mr. Hunter glanced quickly in Georgiana's direction and she made a pretense of brushing the dust from her gown and examining herself for damage, though her trembling hands were apt to betray her. Apparently assured of her well-being, he turned back to Lord Wycliffe.

"Aye," he said in a hushed voice. "Paid to distract us. As for knowing why, that's anyone's guess."

But Georgiana had a guess. Whoever had killed her husbands, and perhaps Mr. Booth, had now turned his attention to her. Or Charles Hunter. Her heart pounded against her ribs at the thought of Charles lying in the street with a bullet in his chest. She turned slightly to pretend attention to her costume, trying to cover her fear and wondering what else they might say if they thought she wasn't listening.

"Gibbons?" Lord Wycliffe asked.

There was a pause and then Mr. Hunter's voice answered in a hushed tone. "Unlikely that Gibbons would have missed once we were still for longer than a moment, and I doubt he'd part with a ha'penny to hire a flower girl."

Who was this Gibbons person, and why would he want to kill her?

From the corner of her eye, Georgiana noted that Lord Wycliffe slid a glance in her direction. "Do you think…"

"Possible," Mr. Hunter answered.

She shivered with that implication. She knew what they suspected. That someone had tried to kill *her*. Was that better or worse than someone trying to kill the men with her? Icy cold crept through her as she surveyed the crowd, looking in one direction and then the other. Was a killer still watching? She caught sight of the edge of a cape rounding the corner of the Theatre Royal. She shivered. She really must get a grip on her imagination!

She met Charles's gaze, painfully aware that attention was directed at her and they were likely wondering if she really was such a dreadful person that someone wanted her dead. She banished the terrifying notion and gave them an uncertain smile. "At least no one was injured. Thank heavens for that."

"Are you not frightened?" Charles asked.

Terrified! But she had no intention of discussing it. "S-surely the whole thing was some sort of accident, was it not?"

Lord Wycliffe seized on her excuse. "Pistols misfire all the time, Mrs. Huffington. Very sensible of you to understand that."

The thought flashed through her mind that his lordship was a dreadful liar for a man in his position. "Nevertheless, I should like to return to the theater, if you do not mind. I would think the intermission is well over and my friends will be looking for me."

Mr. Hunter and Lord Wycliffe flanked her as they turned toward the theater. She glanced over her shoulder one last time, her skin prickling with the feeling that someone was watching. She was sure of it. As sure as she'd been the other night at her window.

"How perfectly dreadful!" Hortense exclaimed. "Why, you could have been killed."

Harriett's eyes narrowed and an angry furrow creased her brow. "Really! Men ought to be more careful. I do prefer swords to pistols for that very reason. You wouldn't have an accident like that with a sword, now, would you?"

"You have a point, Miss Harriett," Lord Wycliffe replied with a wry grin.

The orchestra struck a chord to signal the end of the intermission, and Harriett lowered her voice. "Furthermore, men who discharge their pistols in public ought to be horsewhipped."

Hortense nodded her agreement. "At the very least."

Georgiana noted the twinkle in Lord Wycliffe's eyes. She was relieved that neither of her friends seemed to be taking the incident as a personal attack. One could argue that one shot was much like another, but she was not reassured. That shot had seemed deeply personal.

"Mrs. Huffington, are you quite all right?" Mr. Hunter asked yet again, noticing her distraction.

"Quite," she said as everyone turned to her. She gave them a cheering smile and shrugged. "Nevertheless, I should like to go home."

"Why, of course, you poor dear," Harriett said. "You've had a frightful experience. We should have thought of that, but you seem so composed."

"I am just exhausted. But please do not shorten your own evening. I shall hire a hackney."

"You'll do nothing of the sort," Mr. Hunter said, shooting a meaningful look at Lord Wycliffe.

Ah, so contrary to their assertions, he and Lord

Wycliffe actually did suspect there was something sinister in the wind.

Mr. Hunter took her arm and led her from the theater as the performance resumed. On the street, he signaled a hackney, handed her up and followed her in. The jarvey cracked his whip and the carriage lurched forward, propelling Mr. Hunter into the seat beside her instead of across from her.

"Beg pardon," he murmured as he settled next to her.

She gave him a sideways glance and arranged her skirts to keep them from wrinkling, then folded her hands in her lap, trying to give the appearance of sublime unconcern. She did not want him to know how acutely aware of him she was—of his warmth, his size, his sensual mouth or the devastating effect he was having on her senses.

"I have a vague recollection of glimpsing you last fall, Mrs. Huffington. Were you in London as late as September?"

So it was to be inconsequential conversation, was it? And a tacit agreement to ignore their earlier acquaintance? But she couldn't ignore the fact that he smelled utterly masculine—like good shaving soap and starched linen.

She gave herself a mental shake and turned her thoughts to the conversation. "Yes. In fact, I believe I saw you at the Argyle Rooms the night my...Mr. Booth was shot."

"Did anyone ever mention to you that someone else had been shot that night, too?"

"I believe so. One of his friends, I was told, but the injury was not life threatening." She looked at him and surprised an almost incredulous look on his face. But she had told him about Mr. Booth before, hadn't she? Why should he be surprised?

A muscle jumped along his jaw and he took a deep breath. "You were saying, Mrs. Huffington?"

"Oh, yes. That we left for home a day or two after that. There seemed no point in staying and Aunt Caroline was never very comfortable in London."

"I understand. London, for all its glamor, can be an unsettling place."

She smiled. "I would never call it peaceful."

He shifted to face her, and a small smile quirked the corners of his mouth. "Somewhat of an understatement, that."

She looked into his deep violet eyes and wondered where her wits had gone. Two husbands and a fiancé, and it had taken Charles Hunter and a vow of celibacy to make her heart beat faster—the very definition of irony. He had, in fact, been the only man who ever had ever made her heartbeat race. The only man who had ever made her lose her wits with a single kiss.

Her little voice, the one that whispered good sense when her heartbeat tripped along a wayward path, told her to demur. Told her, in fact, to run home as fast as she could. Charles Hunter could have her rushing headlong into a relationship she'd sworn never to have again.

"But I must say, Mrs. Huffington, that you have a very cool head. Not many women could be shot at and then dust themselves off and get on with their lives."

"If there was another choice, sir, I missed it."

Charles laughed at her attempt at irony, then grew sober. Perhaps it was just as well that she didn't know he was the other man shot last fall. That knowledge could put her on her guard and he wanted her as unguarded as possible. He reached out to tuck an escaped lock of hair behind her ear. The strands felt like silk against his fingers. "I gather you've learned to cope with shocks."

A shadow passed over her face, and her dark lashes lowered to shield her eyes at his reference to her husbands' deaths. Was she hiding something? Preparing to lie? "When you are at fate's mercy, Mr. Hunter, there is little else you can do."

"Fate?" he echoed. "Is that how you define your ill fortune with husbands?"

Her gaze, half angry, half bewildered, snapped upward to meet his. "Or that I am cursed. What else can it be?"

"Coincidence?" he ventured.

She relaxed and shrugged. Had she thought he was making an accusation when he'd only meant to open the discussion? Mention the elephant in the room that everyone seemed intent on ignoring?

"'Tis just that I hardly know what to say. How can I explain such odd occurrences? And how shall I explain my late fiancé? Mr. Booth had just signed the contracts before he was killed. Am I supposed to believe that, too, was coincidence?"

Charles gritted his teeth. Booth. His head spun with Wycliffe's unsubtle suggestion that the shooter hadn't been Dick Gibbons. Had, in fact, been Georgiana Huffington. He fought the impulse to ask her where *she'd* been when those shots had been fired.

Long adept at covering his emotions with innocuous expressions and meaningless banter, Charles did nothing to betray his anger and suspicion. If Mrs. Huffington had been responsible, in part or whole, for Adam Booth's death, what had she hoped to gain? Without the nuptials, she was not entitled to anything more than the small settlement her aunt had negotiated. Could she have done it to preserve her freedom rather than for gain? Did she not like her aunt's choices? Or was she a secret man-hater who disposed of any who threatened her freedom? If so, he sure as hell knew how to find *that* out.

"Rational explanations or evidence aside, Mrs. Huffington, what do you think is behind it?"

Her bewilderment looked genuine enough. "Fate is as good an explanation as any I've pondered. Unless…"

"Pray, enlighten me."

"If…if it is not a curse or coincidence, then it has to be deliberate. And if it is deliberate, then it must be personal. And if it is personal, then someone, for some unknown reason, wanted Mr. Allenby and Mr. Huffington dead— perhaps even Mr. Booth. And if that is true, then I am the common thread between them. But if that is so, then why hasn't an attempt been made on *my* life?"

"Aside from tonight, you mean?"

She turned her lovely face up to his, and her expression was one of bewilderment. "To make me suffer? Or to hang for the crimes? Or could that person simply be taunting me until he is ready to kill me, too?"

Ah, she was good. He almost believed her. "Why? Who would despise you so much?"

"I cannot think of anyone I've wronged deeply enough to warrant such hatred." Something of her desperation reached him. If she was telling the truth, she would be frantic, indeed. Her eyes were luminous in the dark coach. "That is why I must get to the bottom of this before something else calamitous can happen."

Better and better. She was falling like a ripe plum into his open palm. "I collect it wouldn't be much of a life if you feared any man you showed an interest in could die, and that you must always watch over your shoulder."

She cocked her head to one side and her lips quirked

in a sardonic smile. "Was that supposed to be comforting, Mr. Hunter?"

"Were you looking for comfort or honesty, Mrs. Huffington?"

"Honesty," she conceded.

"I am prepared to help you, if you desire it."

"Help me what?"

"Find out if there is anything sinister behind your ill fortune and the odd things that have been happening to you. That gunshot tonight, for instance." Could have been Dick Gibbons targeting him, but she did not need to know that. "Apart from that, I think you will be needing a male escort. Delightful though they are, I doubt the Misses Thayer can offer you much protection."

Her deep shudder told him that she'd feared the same thing. Mrs. Huffington was not just in fear for the lives of men who knew her, but in fear for her own life—unless this was an act to disarm him.

"I am nobody," she murmured. "I cannot in my wildest imaginings think why someone would want Mr. Allenby or Mr. Huffington dead. Or Mr. Booth, for that matter. Nor is there anyone who might wish me dead. It has to be something else. And that is why..." She blinked and pressed her lips together as if she'd said too much.

"Why it is a mystery you are compelled to solve?" he finished for her. "Again, one with which I am prepared to help you."

"I scarcely know what to say, Mr. Hunter. I appreciate the sentiment, but you would be putting yourself in danger." She sighed and only the steady clip-clop of the horses' hooves broke the heavy silence.

Charles took her hand, so delicate and small in his that he almost regretted what he was about to do. She was playing into his scheme, offering an opportunity only an idiot or a man with scruples would waste—and Charles was neither. No, he was a man about to test whether she was a man-hater or not. With his other hand, he lifted her chin to look up at him. Slowly, relentlessly, he lowered his lips to hers.

They were soft, plush, voluptuous and they trembled just a fraction. A studied response? Or genuine? He didn't care which. He lost himself in the taste of honey, her heated moan and her almost unwilling response. He sensed that she wanted to deny him, but was unable. Could there be any sweeter revenge for her previous rejection than that?

And that was his last rational thought as he answered in kind, releasing her hand to draw her closer. His reaction was purely visceral—as primal and basic as that long ago night when he'd fancied himself in love. Time had done nothing to dull that edge. He wanted to lose himself in her, bury himself in her softness, feel her heat surround him, lay her bare to his study, watch her face as she found release in his arms. He was older now, more experienced than he'd been back then, but knowing what lay ahead only deepened his hunger and quickened his urgency.

Seven years had changed Georgiana considerably. She was no longer a maiden. She was a woman of experience, schooled to passion. No demurring now. No fear. No crimson blushes. She arched to him, her breasts crushing against his chest. He felt a shiver of passion shoot through her and nearly choked on his body's response—a desire so strong he was hard-pressed to contain it. And, sooner than he'd thought, he had the answer to his question. No, Georgiana Huffington was no man-hater, and yes, she would love fiercely. Or, at least, *make* love fiercely.

And who had the upper hand now?

"Charles…" she murmured when he softened his kiss.

The single word was more declaration than denial. She wanted him. *Him.* Whom she'd had so little regard for that she'd had her aunt reject him. Well, she could have him. Far be it from him to leave a lady wanting or waiting.

Her shawl slipped down her arms, baring her slender neck. The warmth of her skin and the subtle scent she wore rose to him, wrapping him in a seductive cloud. He answered in the only way he could.

He relinquished her lips to nip at one earlobe, tugging gently until, with a faint moan, her head dropped back to expose her throat. He accepted that invitation and traced a path of kisses to the hollow where her heart beat closest to the surface. Lingering there, he triumphed in her gasp and the quickened beat against his lips.

Georgiana Huffington was his for the taking, and he was mystified by how deeply he wanted her, too. Could it be possible to love and hate at the same time? To want to give both pleasure and pain?

She tangled her fingers through his hair and held him close, lifting her throat to his lips with a longing sigh. He left that sweet spot, moving downward, scraping her delicate skin with the coarse stubble emerging from his morning shave. She shivered and wiggled closer.

He wove his fingers through her hair to hold her immobile while he continued his exploration. He moved his other hand to push the willow-green bodice lower. Even through the gloom of the coach, he could see the delicate pink contrast of her breast appear above the trim, and his sudden need to sample it was greater than he'd thought possible.

He captured the little crown between his teeth and drew it deeper into his mouth. The peak, already firm, tightened into a bead against his tongue, teasing, tickling. He rolled it against the roof of his mouth and she made a soft keening sound. As she'd done all those years ago, before she'd stopped him with a desperate cry.

But there was no plea for mercy this time. No demurring. Her hand, still tangled in his hair, pressed him even closer—so deeply that he feared he'd hurt her. He swept his hand downward to lift her hem and skim his palm up the inside of her thigh. Past stocking, past garter, past a soft chemise, until he found the soft heat of her sex.

She shivered and twitched as if she would draw away or stop him. But he nuzzled her breast again, drawing her ever deeper into his mouth, and she hesitated. That split second was all he needed.

He stroked lightly and she was almost wanton in the way she arched to his teasing touch. He circled her opening with one fingertip, gathering the dew of her passion, and then slipped it upward to find the source of her need. At his first touch to the little nub, she moaned and pressed against his palm. Oh, she was ripe and ready, but he was in no position to join her—damn the luck. Their coach had just passed the park across from her home.

Ah, but he could bind her to him with a lesser satisfaction and leave her still craving more. The next time they met she'd be ready and eager for anything he'd be willing to give. She'd think him smitten and never suspect that he had other motives.

With a few deep strokes, she was finished, gasping and trembling in his arms. She seemed so surprised, so genuinely disconcerted, that he almost believed she had not experienced that particular pleasure before. He eased his hand away and smoothed her skirts as the coach drew up outside her town house. He tugged her bodice up to cover that wanton nipple and lifted her shawl to cover her shoulders. No trace remained of their indiscretion.

"'Ere we are, gov'nor," the driver said as he threw the door open and lowered the step.

Charles exited first and flipped the driver his coin before he lifted Mrs. Huffington down. He steadied her as the coach pulled away, leaving them in the dim glow of a streetlamp. Even in the darkness, he could see the deepness of her blush. A bit late for that, was it not?

"I...I..." she stuttered. She held his arm as she steadied herself.

He grinned. He liked having the upper hand and vowed not to give it up again. "An auspicious beginning to our new arrangement, is it not?"

"I...that...shouldn't have happened."

"Tush! 'Twas little more than a kiss. And we've done that before, so nothing new at all."

"Did...did we kiss back then? I'd forgotten."

Her words were so patently a lie that he laughed. On the strength of that long-ago kiss, and before her aunt had invited him to tea to "talk," he'd been eager to ask for her hand. This "kiss" had been even more powerful, but he was older and wiser now, and he'd known how to use it to his advantage. No longer a callow lad apt to challenge her, he merely smiled, evoking another telltale blush.

She turned toward her door and took an unsteady step. He gripped her arm again and walked up the steps with her. It was not his intention that she take a tumble because he'd weakened her knees. No, her next tumble, though she didn't know it yet, would be directly into his bed.

With one hand on the door latch, she turned to him. "Mr. Hunter, I scarcely know what to say."

"Good night will do." He arranged the shawl around her shoulders and grinned. "Or, 'Until tomorrow, Mr. Hunter.'"

A spark in her eyes told him that her wits had returned. "I think it should be 'Never again, Mr. Hunter.'"

He laughed outright as he gave her a low bow and entered the street.

Around the corner and down a narrow lane, Charlie found himself deep in thought. Though he'd been loath to admit it, that "kiss" had taken a toll on him, too. One that left him barely able to stand straight.

In the coach, though, the years had slipped away the moment their lips had met and he'd been vulnerable again, young and eager to please. Everything he'd done since then, good and bad, everything he'd become, was because of that kiss. Because of Georgiana.

He hated that feeling. Hated that she could still do that to him—make him remember their long conversations and how she'd said she wanted the same things from life that he did—loving each other, learning, a family, travel, extending themselves in service to those less fortunate, growing old together. He felt he'd found the one woman in all the world who could fill his every need, and he had vowed to fill hers.

But now he knew the spell she could cast over him. Knew how deeply he wanted to possess her. And how deeply she wanted him, too. But that was physical. He could still give her that much. So he would take her. Enjoy her. But never fall prey to her wiles again.

Yes, he'd been deliberate. He'd meant to disarm her and draw her closer to him. He'd meant, in fact, to take her completely and lull her into believing he was smitten with her. But…his conscience had pricked him as deeply as a sword point. If she was innocent of the charges, he'd have a damn lot of explaining to do. But if she was guilty…oh, hell! If she was guilty, he'd want her still. As frequently as he could manage before she climbed the gallows.

He was so lost in his thoughts that he almost missed the movement in the shadows. How had he missed that he was being followed? He barely had time to prepare when, with a suddenness that kicked his heartbeat to a higher level, he was attacked.

A knife slashed across his midsection and he spun away to avoid it. When the knife became caught in his jacket, he used the momentum to gain control. Fear, followed quickly by anger, infused him, making him reckless.

His attacker made a fist of both his hands and brought them down on Charles's shoulder, trying to drive him to the ground. His arm went numb and he dodged away, leaving nothing but air to brace the man. He went down on his knees, catching himself by throwing his arms out to break his fall.

Charles took the knife by the hilt and freed it from his jacket as he gripped a handful of the man's hair and jerked backward. He held the knife to his throat, ignoring the throbbing in his shoulder and arm.

"Gor!" the man wheezed as he looked into Charles's face.

Not Gibbons! Damn it all! "Who are you?" he snarled.

"Don't matter," the man gasped.

"What the hell do you want?"

"Uh…yer watch and coin."

A lie if ever he'd heard one. He pressed the edge of the knife against the man's Adam's apple until a fine line of red appeared and a single drop trickled down the man's neck. "Don't lie to me if you want to live."

The man whimpered. "Easy, gov'ner."

"Who sent you?"

"Nobody. Just bum luck…"

He emitted a muffled shriek when Charles increased the pressure on the blade. "Give me the name."

"He'll kill me!"

"And I'll kill you if you don't."

"Gibbons! Dick Gibbons!"

Charles slipped the knife downward, wiped the blade on the man's jacket and released his filthy hair. Just like Gibbons to hire a street ruffian. "Go back to him and tell him to do his own dirty work. Tell him I'm waiting for him."

The man scrambled away, half crawling and half tripping over his own feet in his haste.

Charles tossed the knife into the shrubbery and peered into the midnight mist. Anyone else? No, too quiet now. He rubbed his shoulder and continued, keeping watch this time. Two attempts in one night. The bastard was stepping up his game. He'd better find Gibbons before Gibbons found him.

Chapter Five

Georgiana slammed her bedroom door and leaned back against it as if she could hold her shame at bay. She'd sent Clara to her bed with a sweep of her hand. No more conversation tonight!

How could she have confided all her deepest fears? How could she have allowed him such liberties? How could she have cast caution and the lessons of the past to the wind?

Because it felt so good. So right.

She threw her reticule across the room and dropped her shawl where she stood. He'd bewitched her! That could be the only explanation. She'd never allowed liberties like that before, except with Gower—and that had been required because they'd been married. In bed. And he hadn't made her feel the things that Charles Hunter had. Things that left her breathless and trembling. Craving more. She'd never suspected—never dreamed—there could be such delight. She collapsed on her bed, her knees unable to support her through the vivid memory of the unexpected passion he'd awakened in her.

Oh! And it was *Charles Hunter* who had taught her that. He must be laughing up his sleeve right this very minute. Or telling his friends how easily seduced she'd been. For the second time! Or plotting how he might avoid her in the future, now that he'd made a fool of her again.

Never again.

She stumbled to her dressing table and pulled the pins from her mussed hair, dropping them in a gilt pin dish. She needed to compose herself or she'd never sleep tonight. Not that she'd slept well at all since arriving in London.

She suspected she was losing her mind. Aside from the shocking incident with Mr. Hunter, there were other signs of madness. She hadn't told him everything. In fact, she hadn't told Mr. Renquist everything, either. They'd think she'd gone quite balmy. Perhaps they'd even think she was unhinged enough to have killed her husbands herself. She couldn't risk that. She'd almost rather believe she *was* cursed than that those little things meant she'd gone insane.

There were dozens of them—those little things— her forgetfulness, the missing items she'd sworn she left here last fall, the things she'd brought with her from Kent that she could not find now, the vague uneasinesses, the prickle of hair on the back of her neck warning that she was being watched or followed.

She might have suspected one of the new servants, but the missing items were inconsequential, really, and of little value beyond sentiment. A tortoiseshell comb, a ribbon, a brass locket she'd gotten at a country fair. Oddly, when she'd made a fuss over a small golden ring with a tiny garnet that had gone missing, the household had been in an uproar until one of the servants found it in the garden. Georgiana couldn't imagine how it had gotten there since she had no recollection of being in the garden.

Clara said she was too high strung, that her nerves were

spent and her imagination had run away with her. Furthermore, Clara informed her, grief could make a person think and do very odd things.

Like allow Charles Hunter to...

No! She would not spend another moment thinking about that! Or about him. If she had any sense at all, she'd leave London immediately. But since she could not, she would face Mr. Hunter down. Offer him impudence for impudence.

She opened the drawer of her dressing table and removed the bottle of laudanum Aunt Caroline had kept on hand to help her sleep. She hadn't used it before, but tonight, at least, it would help her forget the news from her solicitor and her wanton behavior with Mr. Hunter. She removed the cork and took a sip, ignoring the instructions to measure the dose carefully. She couldn't possibly be any more reckless than she'd already been.

Marcus Wycliffe heaved a world-weary sigh as he and Sir Harry Richardson sat at the small table on either side of Charles. "We searched every hole and shadow near Covent Garden. No trace. And, of course, no one saw anything. All we can say for certain is that Mrs. Huffington did not fire the shot."

"Aye?" Charles took a deep drink from his tankard. "Well, that does not eliminate the possibility that she had help."

Wycliffe winced. "Are you backing out?"

Charles had had time to consider that option in the hour he'd been waiting for Wycliffe and Richardson to arrive. Anger and desire mingled into a heady brew every time he thought of Georgiana Huffington. Sense told him to walk away. Something dangerous and darker urged him to continue. His darker urges were always stronger. "I've already made a beginning. Mrs. Huffington is unaware of the Home Office's interest in her. Our meeting went well."

Wycliffe quirked an eyebrow at Charles. Even through the dim tavern light, the man could be intimidating. "Went well? How well?"

Charles had no intention of telling his superior that he'd left the woman in question still trembling from his touch. She might be his assignment, but he was still discreet enough to know that some things were none of the Home Office's business.

Richardson, however, sat back in his chair and regarded Charles with a sly grin. "Details, man. We want the details."

"Our conversation was quite enlightening. She is shrewd enough to know how she appears to the ton. She realizes that people are talking, and she has thought ahead to the necessity of finding a palatable answer to the mystery. She has even voiced a concern that she might be next—which is something I do not think we can rule out entirely after the shooting tonight."

Wycliffe placed his tankard on the table in front of him. "Did anything she said, no matter how subtle, lead you to believe she might be the culprit?"

"She'd be too clever for that and seems to be willing to explore even far-fetched explanations."

"As a diversion?" Richardson suggested.

Charles had considered this possibility. Mrs. Huffington was certainly intelligent enough to attempt that sort of diversion, but he doubted she was desperate enough for that yet. For a split second, he'd thought perhaps she had set that street ruffian on him, but no. The man had confessed it was Gibbons. He shook his head. "I wouldn't rule out the possibility, but I do not think she considers me threat enough yet to attempt the deception."

"It's that congenial demeanor you put forward. No one

ever suspects you're up to anything deeper than your next pleasure."

Charles smiled at Richardson's conclusion. "It has served me well thus far. Mrs. Huffington suspects me of nothing but passing interest. If she were guilty and suspected my intentions, she would be unlikely to risk piquing my attention. In fact, I begin to suspect you only cast suspicion on Mrs. Huffington to persuade me to take this infernal case, Wycliffe."

Wycliffe gave him a canny grin and signaled the bar for another ale. "So *do* you suspect something?"

"I don't believe in coincidence. Someone or something is behind these deaths and attacks. And I was nearly killed on my way here tonight. All these events appear to have a common thread, and that appears to be Mrs. Huffington."

"Christ! Two attacks in one night? Someone really wants you dead. Do you think she could have hired someone? Paid someone to shoot and miss, just to misdirect suspicion? Then kill you on your way here?"

Charles thought about how close that shot had come, how open she had seemed in the coach, how truly bewildered by events. "The man tonight said Gibbons sent him. As for the incident in Covent Garden, I think we must consider the possibility that Mrs. Huffington could have been the target."

"Who—"

Charles shrugged. "Her husbands' families? Someone from her past? I need to know more before I can hazard a guess. I am gaining her confidence. And, should I make the proposal I am thinking of, I imagine there is a fair chance she will take it."

"What sort of proposal?" Wycliffe asked. He lifted his fresh tankard and watched Charles over the rim.

"Why, marriage, of course."

Richardson leaned forward, his bright blue eyes widening. "Are you mad?"

He laughed. "Aye, I suspect I am."

Wycliffe snorted. "I've heard she has said she will never marry again."

"That suits me well. I don't mean to actually go through with the nuptials. Just propose. Lead the ton and the public at large to believe it is true."

"To provoke an 'accident'?"

"Exactly."

"Will she go along with your plan?"

"I have ample reason to believe she will. She says she wants to get to the bottom of this, so it would be difficult for her to refuse my help."

"And what if no one attacks?"

"They will. Or she will. The temptation will be too great for the killer to resist. Booth was engaged to her for mere hours before he lay dead in the street."

"Damn it all, Charlie, I do not like this," Richardson muttered in a low tone. "You'd be a target."

"Have you forgotten Gibbons? I am already a target."

Wycliffe sat back in his chair. "When do you plan to make this proposition to Mrs. Huffington?"

"Tomorrow." Charles glanced to the establishment's dingy window, where a faint trace of dawn lurked. "Tonight, actually. We are both invited to Thayer's musicale, and I shall contrive to escort her home. Once we are alone, I am certain I can persuade her."

Richardson chuckled but wisely said nothing.

Wycliffe sighed. "I do not know if you are brave or foolhardy, Hunter. Guard yourself well."

Charles milled with the rest of the attendees at the Thayer musicale, holding a glass of wine in one hand and a small plate of pastries that had been forced upon him by his hostess in the other. He had arrived late and hadn't been able to spot Mrs. Huffington. The soft glow of candlelit chandeliers cast moving shadows and made it difficult to recognize anyone until he was nearly upon them. But now that the performance was over, he wandered toward the dais to position himself to view the room.

The soft chords of the pianoforte carried to him as he approached. *Ah, and here she was.* He deposited his plate on a passing footman's tray and paused to watch the scene. Harriett and Mrs. Huffington sat together on the bench, Mrs. Huffington with her hands poised upon the keyboard. Harriett was giving her some sort of instruction and both were laughing.

For a moment, Charles could almost believe both women had nothing more than the next fete to worry about. Mrs. Huffington's skin glowed as warmly as the candlelight. Her gown, sumptuous lavender-blue satin, was cut to emphasize her striking figure, and the lush swell of her breasts straining at the organdy edging of her bodice was almost more than he could bear. His mind filled with the memory of their coach ride last night—how the tight little buds teased his tongue, how she had sighed and tangled those same fingers she now placed upon the keys through his hair and held him closer.

He swallowed a gulp of wine, praying that would douse his rising hunger and other parts of his body that were also rising. Alas…

"Mr. Hunter!"

Drat. Harriett had spotted him. She smiled and waved. "Mr. Hunter! How nice to see you."

He stepped forward and gave her his best casual smile. "And you, Miss Thayer. A thoroughly delightful presentation, by the way. Though it does not seem possible, I vow that you and your sister improve each time I hear you play." He glanced at Mrs. Huffington and nodded. "Mrs. Huffington. I trust you are well this evening."

Only the slightest stain of pink rose to her cheeks. "Quite, sir."

"I was just demonstrating to Mrs. Huffington the technique for sharing a keyboard in a duet. Though she plays quite well, she is rather clumsy when trying to share the keyboard."

Mrs. Huffington laughed. "Had I anyone to play with when I was learning, I am certain I'd be better."

Oh, that simple phrase brought to mind all manner of possibilities. Indeed, he'd have been more than happy to play with her, to teach her, well, perhaps not the pianoforte…. He finished his wine before he could say something unforgivably crude.

Harriett glanced between him and Mrs. Huffington and stood with a meaningful smile. "I believe I have neglected my duties long enough. Now that you have someone to keep you company, Mrs. Huffington, I will excuse myself."

Mrs. Huffington's mouth opened as if she would object, but Charles offered his hand to help Harriett down from the platform. That done, he turned back to the object of his search and held his hand out for similar duty. "How was your day, Mrs. Huffington?"

She rose from the bench and smoothed her gown before taking his hand, almost reluctantly. "Well enough, sir."

Ah, she was in a bit of a pique about last night. Well, tonight would go no better for her. "Did you come alone tonight, Mrs. Huffington?"

"I live less than a quarter of a mile away, Mr. Hunter."

He cringed. "Never say you walked."

"Very well. I won't."

He stopped to face her. "Have you no sense at all? Someone may have tried to kill you last night, and you go out in public without a care to your safety?"

To his amazement, she laughed. "For a moment I thought you were going to lecture me on the unsuitability of a woman arriving on foot or alone. And I was going to remind you that the only real danger to me occurred in a coach last night."

He could only look at her wide, innocent eyes and marvel at her impudence. Women did not mention such things—they ignored them.

She blinked, a tiny smile hovering at the corners of her luscious mouth. "Why, Mr. Hunter, whatever is wrong?"

"I—" He began to stroll again, trying desperately not to like her. He could not afford to lose his objectivity. "I had some matters I needed to talk to you about, Mrs. Huffington. Matters I think could be of advantage to us both."

"Then by all means, sir. Speak."

"Private matters."

She sighed. "Hmm. Private matters. You do realize the brief coach ride to my home will not allow for…private matters, do you not?"

He glanced down at her, strolling by his side, not sparing him so much as a glance. So that was her game. Turn the tables on him by laying their intimacy bare? Was that her way of rebuking him? Well, she could think again. He'd trafficked with far too many courtesans to be embarrassed by sexual nuance. "You seem different tonight, Mrs. Huffington."

"Do I? Perhaps it is because I am feeling a bit more… familiar with you."

"I am pleased to hear that, *my dear.*" He paused to note her reaction to the endearment and was not disappointed. A slight frown knit lines between her eyebrows. If she was going to toy with him, she had better be prepared for the consequences.

"Are you not frightened for your life, sir? Almost certain death awaits the objects of my affection."

"I enjoy a bit of danger. Adds spice to the game, eh?"

It was her turn to stop and glance toward the door and long for escape. "Then it is difficult to say which of us is the greater fool."

"Quite a pair, are we not? And that brings me to my proposition."

"Proposition? Oh, I think not, sir."

"My coach is waiting outside, Mrs. Huffington. Shall we discuss it on the way home?"

Chapter Six

Georgiana found herself whisked out the door and deposited in Charles Hunter's carriage before she could even take leave of her hostess. Where had she gone wrong? A dose of his own medicine had not cured Mr. Hunter of his relentless baiting. Instead it had seemed to double his determination.

Occasionally, when he looked at her. she thought he might like her just a little. But more often his words had an edge to them that put her on her guard and made her feel as if he did not like her at all. But if that was so, why did he pursue her so persistently? Whatever was going on in his mind made Georgiana uneasy and she suspected Charles Hunter knew that. And encouraged it.

She could think of only one way to end it. "Mr. Hunter, what is it that you want from me?"

He looked surprised as the carriage started off with a jolt. "I am not certain what you mean, Mrs. Huffington."

"I think you do. A moment ago you were calling me 'my dear' and now you are all formality again. What is it you want?"

"My proposition, you mean?"

"Precisely."

"I propose to escort you to and from all public functions. We mix in the same circles, are invited to the same affairs and know the same people. It should be an easy task, and I flatter myself in thinking I could keep you safe."

"From what?"

"Accidental discharges of pistols, among other things. You mentioned last night that you think there might be more than mere chance behind your many misfortunes. That you feel compelled to find what might lie at the bottom of it. The answer to your questions, as it were. I stand ready to help you with all of that, and more if necessary. And the first step is to be your escort."

Could he be serious? He'd mentioned it last night, but she thought he'd been joking, or trying to cozen her before trying to seduce her. She shook her head. "No, Mr. Hunter, but thank you for your concern."

"I promise not to interfere with your current husband hunt, as you so aptly described it."

There it was again. That harsh edge that told her he was not at all fond of her. "I did not say I was on a husband hunt, Mr. Hunter. To the contrary. I shall never wed again."

"I am relieved to hear it. But things could change if the right man comes along. In that case, I would gladly step out of the way."

"And if someone should *put* you out of the way before that happens? You are not forgetting what happens to men who become involved with me, are you?"

He laughed and a shiver went up her spine.

The carriage pulled up at her town house and Mr. Hunter opened the door before his driver could dismount the box. He hopped down and reached in to lift her out.

She braced her hands on his shoulders as he swung her down and closed the carriage door.

"Home, Peter. Do not wait for me," he called before escorting her up the stairs and holding his hand out. "Your key, Mrs. Huffington?"

She gave him what she hoped would be a quelling glance as she rapped on her door. A moment later her butler, Hathaway, opened the door. When he saw who was on the step, he opened the door wider and stepped aside.

"Madam," he said in a disapproving voice.

"Hathaway, this is Mr. Hunter. He has seen me home."

Her guest moved past her into the foyer and glanced around before gesturing at a door on the right. "Library?"

"Yes."

"I'll take that nightcap now."

"What—"

But he was already heading for the library. She handed her shawl and reticule to Hathaway, feeling an absurd need to explain. "Mr. Hunter believes I need an escort for my safety."

Hathaway's expression did not change, but the corner of one eyebrow twitched. "Will you be needing me, madam?"

"Ah, no. I don't—"

The butler bowed sharply from his waist and disappeared. Georgiana knew she would not see him again tonight. According to Clara, Hathaway disappeared most nights after everyone was settled in and did not return until the wee hours of morning. To see his ladylove, she'd said with a smirk. Georgiana could only hope he was less stern with his "ladylove" than he was with his employer.

She sighed and followed Mr. Hunter into the library. He'd already found the brandy decanter and was pouring a measure into a crystal glass. "Would you like me to have a word with Hathaway?" he asked.

"A word? Why?"

"Someone should remind him who is paying him."

Precisely. And it was long overdue. Since her guardian's death, in fact. Still, "I suspect he does not like working for me. He barely tolerated Lady Caroline. But he was hired by Lord Betman just before his death and has been with the family since. I cannot recall a time he was not a part of life at Betman Hall."

He carried his glass to the fireplace and left it on the mantel while he bent to stir the coals to life. "Then let him resign his position and find work more to his liking. I would consider hiring someone who is loyal to *you*, Mrs. Huffington."

"Hathaway is loyal. He is just cross because he had to wait for me to come home before he could call on his lady friend."

Mr. Hunter's lips quirked as if he was fighting a smile. "That is his job. It is what you pay him for."

"Thank you, but no. I will handle Hathaway."

He looked at her as if he doubted she was equal to the task, and she bristled. "Somehow we have managed without you, Mr. Hunter. And where would you be the next time Hathaway needs a reminder?"

He straightened and rested his elbow on the mantel. His grin was a bit unnerving and she could only imagine what he was thinking. Indeed, she now regretted asking the question.

"As...as for your proposal, I cannot think of any advantage to that. Only some rather serious consequences. To you, and to me." *Oh! Why did he not say something? What was he thinking?* His silence coupled with that little smile was nerve-racking.

The library door opened and Clara bustled in. "Mr. Hathaway sent me, madam. Said you might be needing me?"

Mr. Hunter's eyebrows shot up at that statement. No doubt he was wondering what Hathaway thought they were up to. Dismissing the maid would only cause household gossip. "Clara, this is Mr. Hunter. He was good enough to escort me home."

Clara dropped a proper curtsy and smiled, obviously smitten with Mr. Hunter's dark good looks. "I told her not to walk, I did."

He came forward and gave the maid a polite inclination of his head, a nicety most servants were not afforded. "So you are the one responsible for Mrs. Huffington's impeccable appearance?"

Clara giggled—actually giggled. "Aye, sir. But it's no problem. Mrs. Huffington could make sackcloth and ashes look stylish."

"And a good thing that black actually becomes her, eh?"

Clara nearly choked on her laughter. "Oh, sir! You're a wicked one, you are."

A wicked one? But Clara's flirtatious smile belied her words. Then she covered her mouth with both hands, apparently realizing she had overstepped her place.

"I've been called worse, Clara," Mr. Hunter interceded.

Indeed, Georgiana could think of a few names herself.

"But, as you can see, we are just having a nightcap and Mrs. Huffington will be up shortly."

"Aye, sir," she said, turning on her heel and heading back out the door.

Mr. Hunter took her hand and led her to a chair, indicating that she should sit. Like her servants, she did as he wished, then cursed herself for complying so readily. What was it about this man that was so compelling?

"I have been thinking, Mrs. Huffington, that we should dispense with the ploy of my being your escort."

She took a deep breath and nodded, fighting both relief and disappointment. "I am pleased you see the sense in that, Mr. Hunter. It would be quite awkward—"

"Awkward? Yes, I suppose so. Your 'escort' sounds as if we are having an affair. In fact, I propose we make it an engagement."

Engagement? Had he lost his mind? "But…I… Are you mad?"

"Probably. My friends and family will certainly think so. But I cannot think of a more efficient way to prove or disprove your theory of a curse."

"I think it far more likely that the events were coincidence, or that someone holds a grudge against me or my husbands. And I cannot think why any of this is your concern. Unless… Has your sister asked you to assist me?"

"Sarah? No. The truth is, I find you—"

"Oh! Do not think you can flatter me, sir. I am acutely aware of how you think of me. It is in your eyes and manner. I have not forgotten our earlier acquaintance, and the way you—" She broke off when she saw the flint-hard look enter his eyes.

"Then shall we say that I cannot resist a mystery? You do not have to like me, Mrs. Huffington, nor must I like you. The fact is that you require some assistance with your current situation, and I am prepared to lend it. Although I will grant you that is a daring liason, my reasons are my own. And, you must admit, we have a certain fascination for each other. A certain…*je ne sais quoi.*"

There it was—last night in his coach. The physical manifestation of their mutual attraction. Physical. Nothing more. "That will not occur again, sir. So if you are lingering in the hopes of finding me unguarded again, disabuse yourself of the notion."

He laughed as he took her hand to lift her to her feet. He did not step back to accommodate her and she found herself barely an inch from his chest. She looked up, almost afraid of what she'd find in his eyes.

Heat. Smoldering heat. It rushed through her veins, prickled her skin and left her breathless. *Fascination.* Yes, that was the word for it.

"Come, now, Mrs. Huffington. Since you dislike me so, it should not inconvenience you in the least should something untoward happen to me."

He lowered his head, his lips moving against hers as he whispered, "With very little effort, we shall be able to give a convincing performance. Whatever is between us, Mrs. Huffington, will pass for affection with just a bit of help from us."

"I...I..."

"You're welcome." He stepped back and headed for the door. "Rest tomorrow, Mrs. Huffington. Monday we shall announce our engagement."

Comfortably settled in his favorite chair before the fireplace in the library, Charles read the *Times* and sipped coffee. Sunday newspapers were filled with all manner of useful information. Auctions, shipping news, birth, death and marriage notices, engagement announcements, the scandals of the day and other news of society were standard fare. Though he had little use for the gossip, he found it convenient to catch up on what was happening in his own circle.

One news article, however, caught his attention. A man had been found murdered in Whitechapel early yester-

day morning, his throat slit ear to ear. The report was of
a robbery, but from the description, Charles knew it was
the man who'd attacked him after he'd taken Georgiana
home from the theater. This, then, was the price of fail-
ure. Gibbons had stolen back the money he'd paid and
killed the man so he couldn't talk. Charles would have to
be even more careful now.

Crosley knocked softly, knowing Charles preferred to
read uninterrupted. "Sir, you have callers. Shall I ask them
to come back at a more convenient time?"

Callers? On a Sunday afternoon? He glanced at his
valet over his shoulder. "Who is it?" He prayed it wasn't
Georgiana Huffington demanding that he cease and de-
sist. He'd expected something of the sort ever since he'd
left her last night.

"Lord Wycliffe and Sir Henry Richardson, sir."

Although Charles had sent for them, he hadn't expected
them so early in the afternoon. "Show them in, Crosley,
and put on another pot of coffee."

Reluctantly, he folded his paper, put it aside and pulled
two more chairs in front of the fire. The day had turned
gloomy with spring rains turning the streets into a maze
of puddles and mud. His friends would appreciate a warm
fire and a hot drink.

"Bless you," Wycliffe said as he entered the room.
Richardson was fast on his heels and rubbing his hands
together in an effort to warm them. Crosley had taken
their coats and they looked as if they were prepared to
stay awhile.

Richardson glanced around the room, his gaze stopping on Charles's cup.

"Crosley is bringing coffee," he said and gestured to
the chairs.

Wycliffe settled in with a sigh. "Have you any news?"

Richardson grinned. "She gave you a set-down, did she not?"

"I did not give her a chance. We will announce our engagement tomorrow night."

"As the proverb says, *Keep your friends close—and your enemies closer,* eh?" Richardson raised his eyebrows.

Wycliffe folded his arms over his chest. "Does *she* know she is becoming engaged?"

"It was mentioned. She may have other ideas, but they will come to naught. She needs help, and she knows it. She is not foolish enough to refuse."

"I am beginning to think I have done Mrs. Huffington a disservice in appointing you to this investigation."

"I think you've made the very best choice possible," Charles countered. "Why do you suddenly think I am not the man for the job?"

"You are starting from a presumption of guilt rather than innocence. Everything you uncover, everything you learn, is tainted by that perspective."

"Are you afraid I will build a false case against her?" He couldn't deny that, in the beginning, the thought had occurred to him. But he wanted to see the true killer of Adam Booth punished.

"I sense something deeper between you. Do you have a...history?"

"We flirted during her come-out year, then moved on. As you know, she was quickly engaged to Arthur Allenby."

Wycliffe became contemplative. "You did not renew your flirtation after Allenby's death?"

Annoyance tweaked Charles when he realized that Wycliffe had a bit more than a suspicion that he and Mrs. Huffington were something more than acquaintances. He was spared the necessity of a reply by the arrival of

Crosley with a tray bearing cups and a coffee service. The awkward silence continued as Crosley served them and then departed, closing the library door behind him.

Richardson broke the silence as he settled back in his chair and sighed contentedly. "There is a subtle note of anger when you speak of Mrs. Huffington, Hunter. I propose you let me take over and you can chase clues."

"Not a chance," Charles growled. The very thought of Richardson cozying up to the woman in question caused a burning in his stomach.

Wycliffe reached inside his jacket and pulled out a packet. "We will stay the course. The last thing we need at this point is for Mrs. Huffington to hasten back to Kent before we can find an answer." He handed the packet to Charles. "Here is Lady Caroline's profile. It goes back to her presentation at seventeen."

Charles took the packet and set it aside. "And Georgiana Huffington?"

"What we know of her is in that file—everything from the time she became Lady Caroline's ward. She was barely three years of age then. I doubt there is anything worth knowing further back."

"Give me a day to look this over." Charles gestured at the packet. "These events, the deaths, may have nothing to do with Lady Caroline. We cannot ignore the possibility that the answer lies with someone in Mrs. Huffington's past. I met her the year she came out. Something caused her to change that year. Perhaps there is a clue in that."

Richardson finished his coffee and placed the cup and saucer on the tray. "She has no past beyond Lady Caroline. No family at all. Georgiana was the daughter of Lady Caroline's friend. The woman's husband, an officer in the Royal Navy, was lost when his ship went down off the coast of France, and she died within months."

Charles said nothing, but reserved judgment. All he knew for certain at this point was that things—and people—were rarely what they seemed. And that babies did not just appear out of thin air. No, if he wanted answers, he would have to get them from Mrs. Huffington. As soon as possible.

"One more thing, Hunter. Have you met Lord Carlington?" Wycliffe asked and waited for Charles's nod before continuing. "Gossip has it that he and Lady Caroline were sweet on each other her first season. In fact, it was rumored that an engagement was in the offing. Then Lady Caroline's accident sent her back to Kent to recover. As you know, she did not return until she brought Georgiana for her introduction to society."

"You think he might know something?"

"He may be the only one still living who could fill in the holes of Lady Caroline's story and know what happened that season. If she had secrets, she might have confided in him."

Charles nodded. He'd call on Lord Carlington tomorrow. He glanced at the packet on the table beside him. There had to be something in there—some clue that would explain the odd occurrences.

"Meanwhile, Hunter, you should know I still have runners looking for Dick Gibbons. He will eventually surface, and when he does—"

When he does? "You will send for me. I mean to have the pleasure of dealing with that scum myself."

Chapter Seven

Georgiana read her aunt's will for the third time. She had expected most of what she'd found there—generous bequests to family retainers, instructions for the disbursement of a few personal items to an old friend, a sealed packet to be hand delivered to Lord Carlington and one for herself. The rest and remainder of her worldly goods were to go to Georgiana. Funds, investments, real property and personal effects, including the Betman jewels and Betman Hall, were all to be hers. Generous, certainly. Undeserved, perhaps. But hers, nonetheless. And no mention of the Foxworthys.

She had long been aware that Caroline's fondness for her was born more from obligation than any true affection. Still, the fact remained that she'd been closer to the woman than anyone else from the moment she'd been taken to Betman Hall. Their relationship hadn't been everything Georgiana had longed for, neither had it provided her with a sense of belonging, but it had been enough for a little girl who'd been left in a foundling home for three years before anyone had come for her. Enough for a penniless orphan who'd been destined for a life of servitude and poverty.

The chime of the tall case clock in one corner of the study pulled her from her musings and she set the personal packet aside with the others and took a sip of her tea, pondering the meaning of it all. Aunt Caroline had never mentioned friends aside from the two to whom she'd left bequests, and those friendships had been maintained through correspondence since her disfigurement. No friends had come to call, nor had she called on them when in town. But one acquaintance, Mrs. Thayer, had agreed to be Georgiana's sponsor for her introduction to society, as Lady Caroline would not make an appearance herself.

Lord Carlington's connection to her aunt was a complete mystery. Lady Caroline had been as close to a recluse as anyone Georgiana had ever known. When they'd come to town, she'd worn a veil and dealt with invitations and other social obligations by mail. She'd even remained behind closed doors whenever anyone called on Georgiana. When had she known Lord Carlington?

Georgiana now wondered if she had been mistaken in the extent of Caroline's outside connections. After all, Caroline had never even mentioned the Foxworthy brothers, let alone made a provision for them. But Walter Foxworthy was suing to control it all, and Georgiana into the bargain. Heaven only knew what surprises might lie ahead for her in the next weeks.

Well, she'd put it off long enough. It was time to deal with Aunt Caroline's last requests. With no small measure of trepidation, she broke the seal on the thick packet with her name on it and dumped the contents onto her lap. No personal items, just three sealed letters with names and addresses on the outside. And a fourth for her.

She broke the seal on the letter with her name and unfolded the page.

My dear Georgiana,
I am sorry to lay this burden upon you, but there is
no one else I can trust—only you. I know you will
faithfully follow my instructions to the letter.

You must personally deliver the enclosed be-
quests, Georgie, lest they fall into the wrong hands.
And you must be present when they are opened, lest
there be questions. The reason for this will become
apparent presently.

Wrong hands? Whatever could she mean?

Save the delivery to Lord Carlington for last. He
will have many questions for you, but you will have
few answers. Tell him, please, that I never stopped
loving him.
There is so much I should have told you, so much
I would still like to tell you, but that would be a dis-
service to you. Please always know that you eased
my loneliness and delighted me with your compan-
ionship.
Now and ever, Caroline

Georgiana glanced at the following pages and sighed.
Just more lists and an occasional name. She had no heart
for reading more and folded the instructions. She did not
know what she'd expected, but surely more than this.
Some personal words, some endearment. As always, Caroline had evidenced a gentle kindness, but…but there
was something missing. No mention of love, or even of
fondness. She'd been an obligation, if not an imposition.
She'd known it, but she had wondered if, at the end, her
guardian would give her that crumb. *I love you, my dear.*
She fought tears as she slipped the stack of letters back

into the packet and wondered what it would feel like to be truly loved. For a brief moment in time, she'd thought Charles Hunter had felt strongly for her, but then Lady Caroline had advised her that his emotions were simply the excitement of the hunt. Oh, but they'd been so indescribably thrilling. She'd felt almost as if she were flying for those brief weeks all those years ago—loving, feeling loved. Almost feeling as if she belonged. But she'd never felt it again, nor would she feel it in the future. No more marriages for her. No more hopes of love and a family of her own.

She leaned back in her chair and closed her eyes, remembering what Charles Hunter had done to her in his coach. She wasn't foolish enough to think that was love. Sometimes she suspected he could barely tolerate her. But if anyone had been wronged back then, surely it had been her.

Was it a mistake to let him pretend they were engaged? Even prepared, he was risking his life. Why would he put himself in such a position? The chase? The passion? The conquest? His love of danger?

She stood and went to stir the coals in the fire as the afternoon drizzle continued outside the window. She supposed his reasons really didn't matter. She only needed to know what—or who—was behind her ill fortune. She wanted to obtain justice for her deceased husbands.

Charles handed his dripping hat and coat to Hathaway, ignoring the man's disdain. He fought the temptation to say something scathing since he did not want to overstep Mrs. Huffington's authority with her servants, but if she did not handle this man soon, he would.

"I shall inform Mrs. Huffington that you are here," Hathaway said, a slight curl to his lip.

Charles clenched his teeth and ground out, "Never mind, Hathaway. I shall announce myself."

"But, sir—"

He did not acknowledge the man's protest as he continued toward the library. That much of the house, at least, he was familiar with. She stood as he entered the room and the expression on her face surprised him. Fear? Surprise?

"Oh! Mr. Hunter. I did not hear the bell."

He went to the decanter on a side table and poured himself a glass of sherry as if he was completely comfortable here. In fact, when he glanced at the two chairs facing the fireplace with a small table between them, all he could think of was a day long ago, when he'd sat where Miss Huffington sat now, listening to Lady Caroline tell him in detail how unwelcome his attentions were to her ward. He swallowed the sherry and poured another before facing her, squelching the old anger at Miss Huffington's cowardice in not facing him herself.

"Hathaway let me in. I told him I'd announce myself."

"I see."

Disapproval from her, too? The sherry hit bottom and he smiled with the warmth and confidence it brought. "You had better get used to it, Miss Huffington. Once we announce our engagement tomorrow, people will expect me to become a frequent caller here."

"But my servants will talk."

"Servants always talk. There is nothing we can do about that but use it to our advantage." He poured another glass and took it to her before sitting in the vacant chair. "We shall let them believe our engagement is genuine. If we are to carry this off, no one must know the truth."

She nodded as she took the glass and sank back against the cushions of her own chair. "Very well. Is that the purpose of your visit here today? To accustom the servants to your presence?"

"No. I have been thinking about your concern that the answer to this mystery could lie in your past. I've come to ask you what you remember."

She looked down at the fire. "I do not recall a past, Mr. Hunter. My earliest memories are of seeing Aunt Caroline for the first time and being terrified. I was just a toddler, you see, and did not understand her disfigurement. I thought she was a monster, and when I was taken away with her, I...well, I cried."

He recalled seeing the vivid scars on Lady Caroline's face through the veil she wore, so he could imagine the effect it had had on a small child. He hadn't been terrified, but he'd been curious. "Did she ever speak of her injury?"

"Never. I asked once, when I was a bit older, but she struck me and told me to never mention it again. I did not." Her hand rose to her cheek as if she could still feel the sting.

"You frequently refer to her as your aunt, yet she was your guardian rather than a blood relation, was she not?"

She nodded. "Though she was the only mother I ever knew, she had no wish for me to take her name. She said I was born a Carson and should remain so until marriage. And I was a bit old to start calling her mama at that point. We were content with things the way they were."

He did not know whether to feel sorry for the lost child she had been, or to be envious of the peace and solitude of such a life. He had a picture in his mind of two women living quietly in the country, without expectations, without intrigue or drama. That is, until Lady Caroline decided it was time for her ward to marry.

"Do you recall them? Or anything about them?"

"My parents?" She took a sip of her sherry and looked

thoughtfully into the fire. "Just what Aunt Caroline told me. My father was a naval officer and my mother had come from a good family. Aunt Caroline met her through mutual friends and they struck up a friendship at once. When my mother married, Aunt Caroline stood up with them and even became my godmother when I was christened. My father died first, when his ship went down in a Channel storm, and my mother died several months later. I was given to a foundling home while the hospital searched for any remaining family. When there was none, they took Aunt Caroline's name from the parish baptismal register and notified her."

"And this took, what, two, three years?"

"Yes. Aunt Caroline told me I was no better than a savage when she rescued me. Truly, I have no clear memories of my own. I cannot imagine what my life would have been like had she not come for me."

"Where was that? Kent?"

"Cornwall. A village called Mousehole."

Mousehole. The far end of England. A village of pirates and wreckers. The nearest naval garrison to that godforsaken place was in Plymouth. If she'd been taken from Plymouth to Mousehole, then someone had wanted her lost forever. But who, damn it? And why?

He'd send Richardson to Kent tomorrow. If he learned nothing, he'd send him to Cornwall. If anyone could ferret out the truth, he could.

"And that is all you remember?"

She nodded and her smile was sad. "I do not even have a likeness of them, though Aunt Caroline told me I resemble my mother. If there were ever portraits, they were stolen by authorities or the foundling home. Aunt Caroline said they were all scoundrels, every one." She clasped her hands together and sat forward in her chair. "Do you really think this is important?"

"You are the common link between your husbands, Mrs. Huffington. If these incidents are not coincidental, then I've come to believe it is your past we must look into."

"I was a penniless orphan, Mr. Hunter. What could I have worth killing for?"

"You *were* a penniless orphan. From the moment Lady Caroline Betman made you her heir, you could have become the object of envy or resentment."

A frown knit faint lines between her eyebrows. "If that is so, then it is the Foxworthy brothers who bear scrutiny. They thought they were Aunt Caroline's heirs. They have brought suit to become my conservators. Well, the eldest brother has, Walter, I believe."

This was a surprise to Charles. He did not like surprises. "And who, perchance, are they?" He placed his glass on the side table before he could snap the fragile stem.

"Distant cousins of my aunt. I do not think she liked them, since she did not mention them in her will, nor did she ever invite them to visit. Truly, I would not know them if they knocked upon my door."

"And they would inherit the bulk of the Betman fortune should something happen to you?"

"I...I suppose. I do not know much of inheritance laws, but I am certain they would have some sort of claim. After all, they feel it is within their rights to claim conservatorship over the assets and me into the bargain. In fact, if I become engaged again so soon, it would lend credence to Mr. Foxworthy's contention that I am incapable of rational behavior."

Walter Foxworthy. He would know everything worth

knowing about the man by this time tomorrow. If anyone would make a claim on Georgiana Huffington, it would be him.

He stood. "I shall be by to pick you up at seven o'clock tomorrow evening. Lord Carlington is hosting a ball at the Argyle Rooms. I think a quiet announcement to family and friends of our pending nuptials would be an appropriate place to start. Unless—" he turned to her with a quirked eyebrow "—you'd rather have a formal announcement with all that implies."

Her eyes widened and something churned in his stomach. As she stood, a faint scent of lilac wafted up to him. Lord, she did not have to do much to bring him to a boil.

"Goodness, no! Even if it were real, making a formal announcement would be inappropriate. We must not make too much of this or it will be awkward to extricate ourselves when it is over."

He gave her a grim smile. "That will have little significance, Mrs. Huffington. I do not intend to marry, and you've declared you are done with matrimony. It will signify nothing if we are both branded as jilts."

"Very well. If you are not concerned over your reputation, why should I be?"

Ah, she was peeved. But why? His offhand approach to their plan? Or did she, indeed, mean to seek out a third husband, despite her protests? It was time to remind her who she was playing with. He stepped closer to her and tilted her chin up to him. "I think we should behave in a more familiar manner, Mrs. Huffington. How can we hope to convince society we are fond of each other if we snap and address each other with formality? Yes, I think I shall call you Georgiana on occasion, and you should refer to me as Charles. If we were really betrothed, such familiarity would be convincing, would it not?"

"I…I…"

"I think so, too," he said as he lowered his lips to hers. After a moment of shock, she relaxed and accepted his gesture. Her lips trembled just enough for him to know that she was not as calm as she seemed. No doubt she took comfort from the fact that they were in her home, and he would not dare take advantage of her here.

Poor deluded thing.

He slipped his arm around her and drew her close, relishing the feel of her soft breasts crushed to his chest and her little intake of breath when she felt the evidence of his arousal against her. The way she parted her lips—half innocent, half wanton—was incredibly erotic to him. An enigma he wanted to explore. Indeed, if it was not imperative that he hand on this information to Richardson at once, he would take this not-so-innocent kiss a great deal further.

Reluctantly, he released her. "I think I am going to enjoy this charade, Georgiana."

"Magnifique!" Madame Marie exclaimed as she inspected her handiwork. "Turn about, Mrs. 'Uffington. 'Ave you ever seen anything so lovely?"

Georgiana could barely look at her reflection in the mirror the next afternoon at La Meilleure Robe. Self-loathing rather than modesty was the cause. She could not wipe from her mind how she had allowed Charles Hunter to continue his attempts to seduce her when she knew full well that he only wanted the challenge, and did not bear any particular fondness for her.

"Come, little Georgiana. Do not sulk. When the seams are all sewn, you will like it better. No?"

"Oh! I was thinking of something else, Madame. Of course I like the gown." She finally gave herself a critical glance in the tall cheval looking glass. The gown was really quite remarkable. The color was as stunning as Madame had promised, and the style was...well, unlike any other she owned.

Aunt Caroline had picked all her gowns from a fashion book and had employed the village dressmaker to execute them. Gina had told her once that she'd thought Georgiana dowdy when they'd first met. But no one would think her dowdy in Madame Marie's gown. The cut emphasized the curve of her breasts and the slender figure beneath. So this was what Madame had meant by using the new lower waist. The woman was a genius.

Georgiana smoothed the drape of the soft violet silk over her hips and sighed. "I've never had a gown more beautiful, Madame. I think I should have one in every color."

The modiste chortled. "Not every color, I think, *chèri*. But a few more of this cut would discourage your competition. No?"

Her competition? For what?

"I shall change the colors and trim. Per'aps add a flounce at the 'em on one, or embroider the 'em on another. They will never realize it is the same as this one. Oh, I should like to shut their mouths."

Georgiana noted the frown on Madame Marie's face and realized the woman was talking about something specific. "What have they been saying, Madame?"

"Oh, I did not mean... Well, per'aps you should know. Two exceedingly plain women were in for fittings yesterday. One said that Mrs. 'Uffington is a brazen 'ussy. That no man will propose to you, no matter 'ow you bait the 'ook. The other said you are like Circe, casting a spell over unwary men."

Georgiana felt the heat rising in her cheeks. "I am not

casting a spell or a hook, Madame. I am in town on business."

The woman dimpled. "Of course you are, *chèri*. They are simply jealous, yes?"

"Yes. I mean...no!"

Madame laughed a full-bodied enjoyment of Georgiana's confusion. "Ignore them, *chèri*. Enduring such talk is the fate of every great beauty. And when this gown is finished, you will 'ave the envy of everyone who sees you."

Georgiana was about to protest when there was a soft knock at the side door to the fitting room.

"Come, François. She is decent."

Mr. Renquist peeked around the door before entering. He went to a far corner and leaned one shoulder against the wall, but not before Georgiana noted a look of appreciation pass over his usually inscrutable face.

"Not much to tell, yet, Mrs. Huffington. Just a few items of interest."

She nodded, waiting for what he'd been able to discover.

"Cautious questioning has led me to believe that the incident outside the Theatre Royal the other night was no accident. Mr. Hunter has made an enemy. The gossip in the rookeries has it that *he* was the target of that attack."

Georgiana did not know whether to be relieved or worried. If she was not the object of the attack, was someone targeting Charles because of his appearance with her? "Do you know who was behind it or why, sir?"

"I cannot confirm anything, Mrs. Huffington. A theory has been mentioned, but I have been unable to trace the rumor. I would not feel comfortable mentioning a name until I can confirm the information."

As much as she would like to press for an answer, she

had to respect his wishes. In truth, it made little difference which of them had been the object of the attack. The fact remained that Charles was facing danger in her presence. "What next, Mr. Renquist?"

The man straightened and put his little notebook back in his jacket. "I have gone over my notes from our last meeting, Mrs. Huffington, and I think I shall look into the Misters Foxworthy. Because of their ploy to become your conservators, they have a great deal to gain by keeping you unattached, and the most to lose from any possible remarriage."

That fact had occurred to Georgiana. Any insights she could gain would be an advantage in dealing with the brothers—Walter in particular. But what of the other claims against her? "Have you any news of Mr. York?"

Mr. Renquist shrugged. "I shall send someone to investigate just to be certain, but I do not consider him as a part of this whole mess, Mrs. Huffington. For one thing, he was related to your second husband and, therefore, could have had no interest in your first husband's death. And secondly, he has not expressed any particular concern over any remarriage. His suit is more of the common variety of a disgruntled relative who had lived in expectation of an inheritance. Perhaps he has borrowed against future funds and now finds himself in a very bad position with his creditors. Whatever the reason, I think we can dismiss him as a killer."

"Should I make him an offer, sir?"

"That is your decision. How much money would satisfy him, and how badly do you want him disengaged from your life?"

"Very badly," she confessed.

"On the other hand," Mr. Renquist continued, "if the rumors are wrong and the shot outside the Theatre Royal was actually meant for you, Mr. York would be the likely suspect. No attacks had been made on you until then—on the settlement of your second husband's estate. I would advise caution in any event."

Georgiana sighed. This was all such an impossible muddle.

Chapter Eight

Charles waited on the steps of the Argyle Rooms in Little Argyle Street for any sign of his coach. The evening had turned into a series of frustrations. He'd been delayed at the Home Office, then subjected to a lecture from his eldest brother, Lord Lockwood, on the dangers of becoming involved with Georgiana Huffington, and finally had been summoned to the Argyle Rooms for an early private conversation with Lord Wycliffe. He'd been remiss in not interviewing Lord Carlington after Wycliffe suggested he might want to look into that possible lead.

He watched his coach round a corner and slow as it pulled up to the broad steps and breathed a sigh of relief. He'd sent his driver to retrieve Mrs. Huffington rather than make her wait for his arrival and he'd been half afraid she'd refuse to come alone. Thank heavens she was a sensible woman.

Rather than wait for the footman, he stepped forward, flipped the step down, and opened the door.

"I was beginning to think I'd been kidnapped," she said as she took the hand he offered to help her down from the coach. "Your driver was quite mysterious."

She was especially lovely tonight in a deep blue frock

with an embroidered hem and neckline in a darker hue. She was sure to draw attention, and he wanted to make certain the whisper of their engagement was circulating before anyone else could make a claim on her. "I apologize, Mrs. Huffington…Georgiana. I was called here early for a meeting and I did not want to leave you waiting at home."

"Yes, but I wanted to talk to you before we made an appearance. You have not made the announcement to anyone, have you?"

"Second thoughts, my dear?"

"For your sake, sir. Not mine."

"Come, now. I thought we'd decided I would make an admirable target. Would I not?"

"No! Yes. But you would be killed, would you not?"

"We've been over this, Georgiana. I am willing to take the risk."

"I am not."

He lowered his voice suggestively. "Have you grown fond of me, Georgie?"

He noted the tightness in her jaw and knew she was holding back a scathing retort. He supposed it was a good thing that one of them had some measure of self-control. He took her arm and led her up the stairs to the grand foyer, then handed her mantle to a footman before leading her up the wide staircase to the private rooms.

"My family is here tonight. Shall we start with them?"

"Start? Oh, you mean…" She heaved a sigh of resignation. "Can we not tell *them* the truth, Mr. Hunter?"

He shook his head. "I think it best if you and I are the only ones who know. Conversations can be overheard, Georgiana. Should Sarah and Lockwood comment privately in a corner, someone nearby could learn the truth.

And you know how quickly scandal travels in the ton. Our game would be up before it began."

"Your family will not like it."

"Nonsense! Sarah will be delighted. She has made it her calling in life to see all her brothers married. She has begun to despair of me, so she will be relieved by our announcement."

Georgiana looked up and gave him a sad smile. "Not if she loves you and wants to see you live to a ripe old age."

He guffawed. "Well, if that is the case, she will keep it to herself."

She murmured something under her breath that he could not make out. Disagreement, he gathered.

At the top of the stairs, Charles turned her down a corridor to the series of rooms reserved for Carlington's ball. Rather than having a footman announce every new arrival, Lord Carlington, himself, headed a small reception line. Charles felt Georgiana stiffen at his side and wondered at her sudden hesitation. She was shy, but she was not ordinarily timid.

"Lord Carlington, may I present my...dear friend, Mrs. Georgiana Huffington?" He then turned to Georgiana and smiled reassurance. "Mrs. Huffington, please meet Owen Trent, Lord Carlington."

Georgiana performed a flawless curtsy—deep enough to be deferential, but not so deep as to be falsely flattering. Lady Caroline had trained her well.

Their host performed an equally flawless bow. "Mrs. Huffington. I am pleased to meet you, at last. Your reputation precedes you."

She blushed and Charles wondered if he should try to fill the suddenly awkward silence, but she recovered quickly. "And I have heard of you, Lord Carlington. I am delighted to put a face with the name at last."

Carlington gave her an odd look, half bewildered, half admiring. "We must find time to discuss mutual friends, Mrs. Huffington. If not this evening, then in the near future?"

"I shall look forward to it, Lord Carlington."

The press of the last arriving guests behind them forced them to move forward into a large ballroom lit with brilliant chandeliers and an orchestra at the far end. They paused at a table laden with filled wineglasses and canapés. He handed a glass to his companion.

"How do you know of Carlington, Georgiana?"

"I've only heard his name. I believe he knew Aunt Caroline when they were younger."

"Ah. Well, brace yourself. Here comes my sister and her husband. Have you met Ethan?"

"Lady Sarah introduced us when I went to her...reading group."

Charles thought back to that day less than a week ago and remembered the surprising nature of his reaction. Even though he'd engineered that meeting, he hadn't expected her to still cause such a strong reaction in him. Physical, he told himself. Purely physical.

"Here you are, Charlie," Sarah greeted him with a kiss on his cheek. She gave Georgiana a sweet smile. "And, Mrs. Huffington, how nice to see you again. Will you come to our book club meeting again day after tomorrow?"

"I should love to come, schedule permitting. How kind of you to ask, Lady Sarah."

"Are you very busy, then?"

Charles seized the opportunity. "She has affairs to put in order before the nuptials."

Ethan raised an eyebrow and Sarah's eyes widened. "Nuptials? Are you marrying again, Mrs. Huffington?"

Georgiana opened her mouth and Charles knew she was going to deny him. "I—"

"She has accepted my proposal. I've been hoping to catch her between husbands for quite some time now. I've been successful at last."

"This is so sudden." Sarah looked as if she were doing her best to cover her astonishment. He could not tell if there was a slight element of dismay in her eyes. "I...I did not know you were long acquainted."

"Not as sudden as it might seem. We met years ago, when Georgiana was first brought to town. Is that not right, my dear?"

She gave him a sideways glance before donning a smile and answering. "Yes. But Charles was not serious minded at the time."

He had not been serious? Was the treacherous little chit turning her motives around on him? That was a foul play and he'd pay her back in kind.

"That very much sounds like my brother," Sarah admitted. "But he has always said he will never marry. It seems Cupid has aimed his arrow true."

He clutched at his heart. "Aye, and 'tis a deep wound." He looked down into Georgiana's face, reading her near rebellion in her dilated pupils. "I pray no one will say anything to dissuade her."

Sarah looked as if saying nothing would be difficult for her. The silence became awkward and Ethan finally spoke.

"Then I wish you bliss, Charles. It has been a long time coming."

Charles expelled the breath he'd been holding. Despite his reassurances to Georgiana, he'd been worried there would be objections. There might still be, but at least his family would hold their tongues for the moment.

He glanced toward the door with an air of unconcern.

"Carlington is done receiving his guests. I'd like to have a word with him."

Ethan was quick to seize the opportunity to escape the tension, too. "I shall go with you, Charles. I've been meaning to talk to him."

"Take care of Georgiana while I'm gone, Sarah," he instructed. He did not want to give her a chance to back out.

As they moved to intercept Lord Carlington, Ethan lowered his voice and said. "Is it true, Charlie? Did you narrowly miss the opportunity to become Mrs. Huffington's first late husband?"

"Truer than I like to think."

"You do not intend to go through with it, do you?" Travis lowered his voice. "It's a ruse, is it not? You are trying to draw a killer out?"

"It is not a ruse, and Lockwood has already given me this lecture, Travis. Do not waste your breath."

"I am certain you've considered the consequences."

"I have."

"When do you intend to do this?"

When, indeed? "There are matters she needs to tend to before she is free to think of planning a wedding."

"Meantime you are a walking target, Charlie. If her curse does not kill you, Gibbons will. Have you lost your mind?"

Very likely. As they approached him, Carlington smiled a welcome. Thank heavens he could put an end to this conversation. He shot Travis a warning look as they joined Carlington.

Their host offered them a welcoming smile. "Travis. Hunter. Are you enjoying yourselves?"

"Very much so, Lord Carlington. Good of you to invite us."

"Ah, well. A ball is not complete without three or four

Hunters in attendance. And since I do not have a wife, having the event here relieves me of the responsibility of finding a hostess. Quite satisfactory, in all."

Carlington had had some great disappointment in love, according to the rumor mill. Charles was beginning to suspect just what that disappointment had been. He gave his brother-in-law another quelling look. Travis was discreet to a fault. If he caught on to Charles's ploy, he would not say anything.

"I am curious about what you meant when you said that Mrs. Huffington's reputation preceded her," he said.

Carlington looked chagrined. He raised his glass and took a drink before he spoke. "I have watched Mrs. Huffington from afar. I knew her guardian, you see. Lady Caroline Betman. Lovely woman. For her sake I've kept my eye on the girl since Lady Caroline brought her home. I had not met Mrs. Huffington's mother, but I knew a great many of Caro—Lady Caroline's friends. She certainly is a beauty."

"I think so," Charles admitted.

Travis put his glass down on a side table. "Charles has just announced to the family that he and Mrs. Huffington intend to marry."

Carlington's eyebrows shot up. "Indeed? Well, that is very interesting." The older man grinned. "I had not known that you have a death wish, Hunter."

Charles laughed. "Go on. Tweak me all you want. It won't change a thing."

"I am glad to see you have a sense of humor about this." Carlington laughed. "I hazard you are going to need it."

Charles grinned and steered the conversation back to his original purpose. "Then you knew Mrs. Huffington's guardian well?"

Carlington sighed. "It is a little-known fact that she

and I were on the verge of betrothal. Her father and mine were in accord that it was a good match. There seemed to be no impediment."

"What happened?" Travis asked, and Charles made a mental note to thank him.

"One night we were dancing and laughing, the next she was gone. The first thing I heard was that she'd had a tragic accident that had left her scarred. Her father swept her back to Kent and she declared she would not return to London. She begged I would not hate her for her change of mind. I couldn't hate her, of course. I only wish she'd allowed me to visit."

Charles recalled those shocking scars. He could well understand Lady Caroline's reticence. She could never have been the sort of wife a man in Lord Carlington's position needed—a public hostess, the mother to the Carlington heir, a force in London society. And her pride would have prevented her from allowing Carlington to see her in such a condition.

"But when you have a moment, Hunter, bring Mrs. Huffington to me for a visit. I would very much like to hear about Lady Caroline's life. I always imagined she'd found a way to fill it when she took in her goddaughter."

"I shall. I believe she would enjoy talking to someone who knew Lady Caroline."

So that was Lord Carlington. From across the room, Georgiana watched the handsome man with silvery-gray hair—the very same man to whom she would deliver a packet from her aunt. The man who had caused Aunt Caroline to sigh whenever his name was mentioned. The man who might hold the secret to what had happened to Aunt Caroline all those years ago.

"You seem distracted, Georgiana," Lady Sarah said.

"It is just that I almost feel as if I know Lord Carlington. I heard my aunt mention him on occasion and with a great deal of respect."

"He is a very good man from what I hear," she agreed. "Is he married?"

"I do not believe so. I've never met a Lady Carlington."

Had he remained single because of Aunt Caroline? It was quite unusual for a man in his position—a man who should be providing an heir for his title—not to marry. Or was he simply not inclined toward matrimony?

"Georgiana, may we speak frankly?"

She suspected what was coming. Questions about her relationship with Charles. "Of course."

Sarah took her hand and led her to a small settee on one side of the ballroom. "I want you to know that I…I have reservations about your engagement. Please understand that it has nothing to do with you. But, well, I suppose it does, in a way. Until we find out what is behind your ill fortune with husbands, do you really think it is… ah, prudent to be announcing yet another engagement?"

Georgiana sighed. "Not prudent in the least. And I have begged Charles to delay the announcement, but he is determined. He thinks it will be a help to me. He means to draw out the villain, if there is one. Believe me, I have warned him, begged him, threatened him. I have sworn that I will not marry him at all. But he intends to go through with this, no matter what my wishes are in the matter."

"You could simply refuse him. Tell him that you have no intention of marrying him. Ever."

She glanced around to be certain they were quite alone before speaking. "I have, in fact, thought of that. But it would make no difference at all. He was determined to help me even before he proposed that we…marry. For some unaccountable reason that eludes me entirely, he has taken on my cause."

Sarah blinked her wide, violet eyes. "Love, perhaps?"

Oh, how she wished she had not promised Charles she would not divulge their plan! "P-perhaps. All I know is that he will not be dissuaded. I have tried everything I can think of, to no avail. But…"

"But?" Sarah prompted.

"But, please, if you can, change his mind. Should something happen to him, it would be my fault. I could not live with that. "

Sarah sighed heavily and laid her hand over Georgiana's. "Charles is stubborn. If his mind is set on this course, then he will follow it. But, Georgiana, dear, I would be remiss if I did not remind you that he may have his own enemies. He does not speak of it in front of me, because he knows it would upset me, but last fall when he was shot outside the Argyle Rooms the assailant escaped. The villain is, by all accounts, a very dangerous man, and may still be stalking Charles."

Georgiana could scarcely comprehend the enormity of this information. *Charles* had been the other man shot when Adam was killed? Why hadn't he told her that? She pressed her fingertips to her temples, trying to remember what she'd overheard between Charles and Lord Wycliffe outside the theatre. Gibbons? Was that the name?

"Oh, dear. I've upset you," Sarah said.

Georgiana shook her head. "I simply cannot think straight. There are so many things filling my head that I cannot put them in order. Sarah, why did you not tell me your brother was the other man injured the night Mr. Booth was killed?"

"I thought you knew. Why, it was in all the newspapers a day or two after it happened. The two of them were dear friends."

By then, Georgiana and Aunt Caroline had been in a coach on the way back to Kent. She shook her head and forced a smile. "It is of little consequence, Sarah. Since Charles did not mention it to me, I imagine he does not wish to discuss the incident. And, truthfully, neither do I."

"Good, because here come the men. I shall see you Wednesday, if not before. We can discuss it then if you'd like."

They stood and Charles offered his hand. "I hear a waltz, Georgiana. Will you favor me?"

She placed her hand in his and allowed him to lead her onto the dance floor and into the dance. He spared an unconcerned glance at the sidelines. "The rumor is already under way, Georgiana. The speculation has begun."

She noted a few elderly matrons watching them and talking behind their fans. "How could people possibly know? We've been here less than half an hour and talked to only a handful of people."

"It takes less than that to start a rumor in the ton. I did not lower my voice when announcing our intentions to Lord Carlington, and that was enough."

"I thought they'd at least wait until we left."

Charles merely laughed. "Are we about to fuel the fire by making our first quarrel public?"

"The whole plan was ill-conceived and a dreadful mistake."

"Is that you speaking, Georgiana, or my sister?"

"Me! Oh, your sister is dismayed, but she covered her disapproval. She is quite concerned about you."

His face froze with a frown. "I warned you that might be the case."

"You'd have done better to warn me who *would* approve."

"Do not goad me."

"I am not goading. I am deadly serious. We must stop this silly rumor at once. I cannot think what convinced me to go along with it."

"Would you like me to remind you?"

"You took advantage of my desperation. I should never have allowed it."

"I feel compelled to ask you again, Georgiana. Have you grown fond of me? Are you worried for my well-being?"

She deliberately missed a step and allowed her heel to come down sharply on his instep. A wince and narrowed eyes were her reward.

"Is this how you've treated all your fiancés, Georgiana?"

"I treated them as they deserved."

"Ah, so a cross word was provocation enough to kill?"

Did he really think…? A twisting in her stomach warned her to say no more where they might be overheard. "I have a sudden headache. I would like to go home, please."

"We've scarce arrived."

"Now." She left him standing on the dance floor and headed down the corridor to the grand staircase.

Charles caught up with Georgiana as she entered the street looking for a hackney in the crush of evening traffic and late arrivals for Carlington's ball. Fortunately his coach was still at the corner. He draped Georgiana's mantle over her shoulders and took her elbow to guide her toward his vehicle. She looked up at him with such deadly cold that he feared she might pull away and denounce him.

He supposed he deserved that. He really had gone too far with that last accusation. Ah, but her denouncements and unwillingness to go through with their charade had reminded him of her jilt so many years ago. He was dismayed to find that it could still cut so deeply.

A prickling of his skin warned him to glance around. Something in the air was not quite right. Again, that uneasy feeling that something was about to happen. But there was nothing in the crowds surrounding them to cause a threat.

He scanned the sea of milling faces across the street and his gaze caught on one. Despite the beard he'd grown, Charles would know Dick Gibbons anywhere. The man grinned and drew one filthy finger across his neck in an unmistakable threat, then pointed it at him.

He released Georgiana's arm and stepped in front of her. He had not taken two steps before a passing coach cut him off. By the time it passed, Gibbons had disappeared. Or was he still hiding in the crowds? Should he give chase and abandon Georgiana to her own devices? Or get Georgiana home safely and pursue Gibbons another day?

He turned back to her, finding a perplexed look on her face as she, too, gazed across the street, then back at him. "Who was that?"

He returned and took her arm again. She relaxed ever so slightly and without hesitation allowed him to escort her to the coach and hand her up before calling their destination to his driver.

The coach pulled into the street at once, but immediately stalled in the traffic. "Do you know that man, Georgiana?" he asked without preamble.

To her credit, she did not ask which man. "I have seen him before, I think, though I cannot remember where."

"Outside the Theatre Royal?"

She frowned. "I…do not think so. Everything happened so fast that I only saw shadows and movements, but I have no recollection of faces."

Had she seen him when she had hired him to kill Booth?

"Who was it, and what did he want?"

"His name is Dick Gibbons, and he wants to kill me."

Her little gasp was convincing. "Why? What have you done to him?"

"He thinks I killed his brother."

"Did you?"

He shrugged. "I would have, given half a chance. I suppose I was the cause of his death, one way or another."

"That is a very mysterious answer, Charles."

"The truth is that I did not pull the trigger, but I caused it to be pulled."

The coach lurched, the driver having apparently found a hole in traffic. They moved ahead slowly but steadily. Georgiana gave him an exasperated look, as if she could not trust a thing he said.

"He killed Adam Booth and wounded me, Georgiana. The question remains, why?"

Her eyes widened. "Adam… But he must have had a reason."

"And I *will* uncover that reason. The person responsible will pay, and so will Dick Gibbons."

"But you said Mr. Gibbons is responsible."

"He is a thief and an assassin. He kills for money. I want him and the person who hired him. I thought I knew who that was."

Her eyes widened into two pools of unfathomable green. "He is an assassin?"

"Among other things. He is the vilest of the vile. He is the worst sort of scum London has to offer. Dick and Artie Gibbons would do anything for a tuppence. They robbed, raped, pillaged and murdered their way through London. They were known for their filth and utter lack of morals. Artie is dead, thank God, but Dick needs to be put down like the rabid dog he is."

He remembered his conversation with Wycliffe before this case began and repeated the words he'd spoken then. "If it's birthed a Gibbons, you'd do the world a favor to exterminate it before it can spread," he muttered under his breath.

She had gone quite pale and a deep shudder shook her body. To be fair, he could not picture Georgiana seeking out and meeting a man like Gibbons in a back alley to pay him money to kill someone. There had to be another explanation. He took a deep breath and got a grip on his anger.

"Then…then you think it was him—this Mr. Gibbons—outside the Theatre Royal? And that he wanted to kill you and not me? And that he never had anything to do with my situation?"

Never say never. "Unlikely, Georgiana."

The silence stretched out for a moment and he finally turned to her to find her fixing him with a cold stare.

"When were you going to tell me this, Mr. Hunter?"

"I did not think it was necessary for you to know. As I said, Gibbons evidently has nothing to do with your situation. We are still searching for that person."

"And when were you going to tell me that you had your own enemies? Enemies that have nothing to do with my 'situation'?"

"Never. Unless it affected the investigation into your problem."

She sat back against the leather squabs, staring straight ahead. Neither of them spoke again until the coach pulled up at Georgiana's town house. She reached outside the window and opened the door herself. "Thank you for the escort home, Mr. Hunter. No need to see me in."

But he was fast behind her. He had no intention of allowing her to back out of their arrangement. He waved his driver off and followed her up the steps to the door. Before she could turn the knob, the door opened and Hathaway's stern visage blocked the passage. Georgiana slipped past him, but Hathaway moved in front of Charles.

Oh, he was not in a mood for this! "Step aside, Hathaway," he warned.

"I believe Mrs. Huffington is retiring for the night, sir. Good evening."

He caught a glimpse of Georgiana disappearing into the library, and something snapped when Hathaway began to close the door in his face. He put one arm out to stop the door and the other out to seize Hathaway by his starched collar, twist and slam him against the doorjamb.

"You presume too much, Hathaway. I've had enough of your insolence to Mrs. Huffington and her guests. Do not forget who is in charge in this house, or you and I will have words. Do you understand?"

Hathaway's rheumy blue eyes widened and his mouth went slack. Lack of oxygen? The man could strangle for all he cared, but Hathaway nodded, a look of desperation on his face.

Slowly, Charles released him and pushed past him on his way to the library. "Do not wait up. I'll show myself out," he said over his shoulder.

Chapter Nine

Georgiana knew Charles had followed her into the house. She heard the sharp crack of the doorjamb when he confronted Hathaway and almost turned back. That was her fault. If she had dealt with Hathaway herself, this wouldn't be happening. Oddly, she cared more what Charles thought than she did if Hathaway quit and left her in the lurch.

Hathaway had been Caroline's servant and he'd always treated Georgiana like an outsider. She had hoped he would adjust in the months since Caroline's death, but instead he'd grown even more churlish. Doing without his constant insubordination and disrespect might even be a relief.

Still, Charles was presuming far too much where she was concerned. He really had no right to intercede with the servants or to invade her home without invitation. The man needed to be taken down a peg or two.

She went to the sideboard and poured herself a glass of sherry. She'd never needed its calming effects more. One gulp finished the glass and she poured another as the sherry's heat crept downward to warm her middle. One more and she'd be ready to deal with Charles Hunter.

Alas, there was no time for more. Charles, imposing and angry, came to stand beside her at the sideboard. He chose brandy, and not a small amount, either. More judicious than she, he only sipped.

"Show Hathaway the door, Georgiana. The man is out of control. He works for you. Not the other way 'round."

"He? He is out of control? You are in quite a foul mood tonight, are you not? From my arrival at the Argyle Rooms to your dressing down of Hathaway, you have been singularly unpleasant. I think you should go."

He took another drink, larger this time. "Think again."

"Whatever possessed you to confront him as you did?"

"Someone had to do it and you, apparently, were not going to."

"You had no right to interfere in my domestic affairs."

"As your fiancé, I have every right."

"That is a *sham,* Charles! Mere subterfuge. I will thank you to remember that."

He turned to her and took her glass to put it beside his on the sideboard, then pulled her into his arms. "Not as much a sham as you might think. In the eyes of the ton, and your servants, we are now bound to each other. I hope I will not be forced to remind you of that too often."

He was impossible! "We must end this. I was foolish to agree to such a plan. You have a talent for finding me in unguarded moments."

"Still not good enough for you, Georgiana? Objectionable? Still lacking in assets? Well, I can think of one thing, at least, in which you do not find me lacking."

"What—"

He covered her mouth with his, catching her unprepared. She brought her hands up between them, ready to pummel him if necessary. But from the moment his tongue touched hers, she was lost. Her mind became hazy and her knees grew weak. Instead of pummeling, she clung. She knew in some distant part of her brain that he was not going to stop with a kiss, but she didn't care. The mere memory of what he'd done in the coach was enough to keep her standing there, uncaring of the world around them—for as long as it took him to do it again. To her shame, she wanted to feel that thrilling pleasure. Wanted to feel cherished, to feel as if she belonged to someone or something greater than only herself.

Could she? Could she allow him such liberties and still be whole when he left again? And he *would* leave. That was what Charles did when he'd gotten what he wanted. But…if he only wanted the conquest, and if she let him have it, he would go away and leave her alone. He would lose interest in his game.

He would be safe from her curse.

Yes, to end the ruse, then. And more importantly, to prevent him from sharing the fate of her husbands, she'd let him have what he wanted. And pray the loss of him would not be so painful to bear this time.

Selfless of her, really. Even noble.

She surrendered to his kiss, entering into the strange seduction with an abandon she hadn't realized she possessed. She had given access to her body to her husbands, just as Aunt Caroline instructed, but she had never felt this pull, this compulsion. Nay, *desire*.

She felt the change in him when he realized that she was no longer resisting. One arm tightened around her and the other wandered down to cup her bottom as he bent slightly to lift her against him.

Where? Oh, dear Lord, *where*? The settee? The deep carpeting before the fireplace? Her breasts tingled in anticipation of his touch. Of his mouth. She was desperate to feel that again. Desperate to experience that final transporting thrill just before he had stopped. Oh, but tonight, he would not stop. She would not let him.

He headed for the door and she realized his intent. For the first time, she had misgivings. The servants…

But he kissed her again, then nibbled her ear. His breath, hot and moist, caused her to shiver. All thought of denial fled as he started up the stairs, his steps muffled by the carpet.

His voice was low and hoarse when he echoed her unspoken question. "Where?"

"Last door on the right," she said with a breathless gasp.

Clara opened the door just as they arrived before it. Her eyes grew as round as saucers and she covered her mouth to stifle either a giggle or a cry of shock.

"Good night, Clara" was all that Charles said, but his voice was dark enough to send her scurrying away.

He kicked the door closed behind him and placed Georgiana gently on the bed, kissing her cheeks, her throat and her lips. She reached up and circled his neck, but he disengaged her arms as he sat back. "Let me enjoy this, Georgiana. I think you owe this much to me for all the sleepless nights you've caused."

The thought perplexed her. "I?"

He nodded as he pulled the satin slippers from her feet and tossed them over his shoulder, then ran his hand up her leg until he found her garter and the bare flesh beyond. He rolled the white stockings down her legs, then slid the garters downward, too, grinning when she gulped.

He was so practiced and skillful—she did not want to think how—that he found the fasteners to her gown quickly and divested her of it. Reaching behind her, he undid the laces of her corset and cast if off to leave her in nothing but her chemise.

He tugged the ribbons securing that last vestige of modesty, and the chemise slipped down to her waist. A moment later, it lay atop the heap of her discarded clothing. She shivered in the cool night air and looked for something to cover her. Charles looked down at her tightened nipples and groaned. "You won't be cold much longer, Georgiana. Bear with me."

She was embarrassed. The other times—with her husbands—the lamps were off and she was under the blankets in her nightgown. Never naked. To be exposed to his view seemed so…naughty. So erotic.

As if he sensed her fears, he leaned over and blew the candle out leaving the soft glow of the firelight—revealing, but somehow kinder. She sighed in relief. She did not want him to find her lacking in any way.

He smiled and she was momentarily reminded of that younger Charles. The one who had wooed her so sweetly, the one she'd given her heart to. But this was a new Charles. Experienced, determined and relentless.

He sat on the edge of the bed and pulled the pins from her hair. "Like silk," he murmured as he tangled his fingers in the curls. Bending slightly, he lifted a strand and held it to his cheek. "You are so completely beautiful that you take my breath away. What is that scent, Georgiana? It reminds me of spring."

"L-lilacs," she said, amazed that he would notice such a thing.

"Lilacs…" He straightened and stepped back from her bed to shrug out of his jacket. His gaze never leaving her, he removed his cravat, waistcoat, shirt, shoes, stockings and trousers in that order. She felt heat sweep up from her toes as he turned to her and undid his drawers and let them drop to the floor.

Good heavens! She'd never seen a man naked before.

Mr. Huffington had worn a nightshirt and joined her beneath the blankets. Arthur had tumbled down the stairs in his nightshirt on his way to the water closet, but Gower had stayed the course—twice. With a little fumbling, he had managed to find the parts that fit together and finish the job rather quickly. The discomfort he'd caused had come and gone as quickly as he.

This, she gathered, was going to be an entirely different experience.

Charles's physique was stirring. She noted an angry red scar high on his left shoulder and knew what had caused that damage—the shot he'd taken when standing beside Adam Booth. But then all she could see was his strongly muscled chest, narrowed waist and hips and…and that he was impossibly large below. Though she hadn't actually *seen* Gower's member, it couldn't possibly have been this large.

He lay down beside her and she turned from her side onto her back, ready for him. She hoped that he would do some of the things he'd done to her in the coach first, though.

His hands, as deft as she'd ever known them, slipped over her form, from her shoulders to her knees. His eyes were closed and his mouth was open in a sigh, as if he were blind and learning what a woman was for the first time.

"I've wanted you for so long. You are everything I thought you'd be, Georgiana."

Had he? But why had he run away after that first fierce kiss? Why had he not gone further then? She opened her mouth to ask the question, but he kissed her, blocking all thought and reason, as consuming as their first ill-fated kiss. She prayed it would not end the same way and moaned when he finally lifted from her lips. Why couldn't that kiss go on forever?

But he turned his attention to the hollow of her throat and she could feel the heat of his breath there. The soft brush of his lips quieted her protest, alerting her that he was not done with her yet.

Her muscles relaxed and she felt as if she were melting. She was ready when he moved lower and took one firmed aureole between his lips and nibbled. An instant tingle began deep inside her. She couldn't describe it, had never felt it before but had come close that night in the coach. She only knew something inside her was tightening, tensing for some unknown event, drawing ever closer with an indescribable compulsion. Whatever it was, she knew she wanted it, needed it. He moved his hand downward, touching her, stroking her in that most tender spot. She heard a whimper and realized that it was hers.

Charles made an answering sound, part groan, part growl. Had she done something to displease him? His knee slipped between her thighs and she raised her own knee to welcome him.

He sighed. "Everything and more…"

She twisted beneath him, reaching up to him. "Please," she said, not knowing what she asked for, but knowing she wanted whatever came next. Yes, and trusting that Charles would know what she wanted, even if she did not. *"Please."*

And for the first time, there was something familiar—the experimental push of his shaft against her softness. But with Charles, she wanted it. Welcomed it. She lifted to him in desperation.

"Ah, Georgie," he groaned, thrusting again, harder this time.

He was thick and long and sure. She bit her lower lip

to keep from crying out, knowing *this* was what she'd been waiting for, as he entered and filled her. But he did not stop there. He drew back and thrust again and again, creating an exquisite friction that rapidly built to a new and even more compelling need. So compelling that she could not catch her breath.

She joined his rhythm until a shattering spasm overtook her. Wave upon wave of pleasure washed through her and she was dying. Dying of sheer pleasure. Charles was with her, panting and whispering her name as he thrust one last time.

"Georgie…Georgie…Georgie…"

That was all she'd ever wanted.

Sometime before dawn, Charles bent over Georgiana to brush her hair back from her face and kiss her cheek. "I really must be going. Servants are one thing, but it would never do to have the neighbors see me leaving at the break of dawn."

Her eyes were heavy-lidded and drowsy, and her flawless skin had the glow of a well-satisfied woman. A fact in which he took immense pride. She managed a smile and touched his cheek. "Once more?"

He laughed. When she'd recovered from their first coupling, she'd wanted more, and he'd been only too happy to accommodate her. Then again. And again. If she'd been insatiable, he'd been a satyr. "You wear me out, Georgie. I'd be pleased to accommodate you, but I will need a bit of time. I fear you've drained me."

"Mmm." She gave a feline stretch and blinked. "Is there anything I can do to persuade you?"

He groaned. All she needed to do was ask! If duty did not call he would be content to lie abed all day satisfying her every desire. She'd been worth the wait. Worth every moment, every day, every year.

He'd known from her responses that she'd been new to such pleasure and he thanked God that her previous husbands had not ruined her for this particular sport. She was so inherently sensual that he could easily teach her every delight she could imagine. And others that she couldn't. Yet.

"I will fetch you for Vauxhall Gardens at eight," he said, straightening the lapels of his jacket.

"Hortense has taken to her bed with a cold, so I told Harriett I'd go with her. Will you meet us there?"

Was that a twinge of annoyance he felt? Had he become so possessive of her in the space of one night that he could not share her with her female friends? Did it really matter whom she arrived with as long as he escorted her home? "Very well. I will meet you there. Shall I speak to Hathaway on my way out?"

She sighed and propped herself up against her pillows, pulling the sheets up to cover her breasts. Pity, that. He'd have enjoyed the view. "I shall give him two weeks' notice."

"I think it would be best if he were gone today. Otherwise the next fortnight is likely to be exceedingly uncomfortable."

"Yes, but I cannot just toss him onto the street after so many years of service. He may have financial obligations."

"You are too considerate," he said. "I doubt the man would do the same for you."

She shrugged and the sheet slipped to reveal one rosy semi-circle. He grew instantly hard again, and wondered if he'd ever get enough of her. Or if, when this affair was over, she would leave him still wanting more.

"Give him two weeks' wages instead," he said, "and

send him on his way. I warrant your household will function well enough without a butler. If not, promote your footman or hire another butler."

"I shall think on it." She sighed, her eyelids drooping again.

He savored the sight of her sunken against the pillows, still flushed from his lovemaking. Though he'd always known he'd have her, and that their coupling had been inevitable, he hadn't suspected it to be so intense. So difficult to leave her. Arrogant ass that he was, he'd thought he could seduce her and then turn his back, just as she had turned hers after their first kiss.

He steeled himself against those thoughts. There'd be time enough for regrets later.

Georgiana found the sly looks cast in her direction difficult to endure. Word had spread throughout the house that she had taken a lover. To her chagrin, she'd been forced to perpetuate the lie and tell Clara that she and Charles Hunter were engaged to be married. She knew she could depend upon Clara to share that bit of information with the other servants.

But the worst came when she'd returned from a quick errand to find Hathaway in her bedroom rifling through her wardrobe. When he heard her, he turned very slowly and faced her with an unreadable expression.

"Is something amiss, Hathaway?"

He blinked. "Everything appears to be in order, madam."

Did he really expect her to believe he'd been checking Clara's work? When he'd never done so before? She saw a sly glint in his dark eyes and she'd suddenly had quite enough. "Wait for me in the library, Hathaway. I shall be down in a moment."

The instant he left the room, Georgiana dropped her reticule and tossed her bonnet on the bed. What had the man been looking for? Because she was certain he'd been hunting for *something*. Was it possible…? Could Hathaway be responsible for all her little missing items? But why? They'd been trinkets of little value for the most part. Surely the man would have aimed higher if he was to take the risk of being caught, wouldn't he?

Aunt Caroline's jewelry was locked away in a safe at the estate in Kent and only she had the key now. She opened the little box where she kept her jewelry—and the key. Still there. Then what had he wanted?

She glanced around, searching for any other trace of Hathaway's invasion, and noted that the stack of books by her bedside had been rearranged. Had he gone so far as to…but no, they were all there, though in a different order. And every trace of Charles's presence there last night had been erased.

I think it would be best if he were gone today. Otherwise the next fortnight is likely to be exceedingly uncomfortable. Charles's words echoed in her mind. He'd been right. She did not want to think of the man in her house any longer.

She patted her hair into place, brushed the wrinkles from her gown, and hurried down the stairs to the library.

As she entered the room, Hathaway looked down his long nose at her—no smirk, just a dark look of disapproval. Of superiority, actually. And, perhaps, just a hint of anger? "Yes, madam?"

"Hathaway, it is my belief that you have been unhappy in this household since Lady Caroline's death. I have been painfully aware of the awkwardness between us. I think, therefore, that it would be best for all if we severed our relationship. I am prepared to offer you half pay for the next month whilst you find other employment."

Hathaway stiffened and managed to look even sterner. "Half pay, madam?"

She nodded. She had not expected gratitude, but she had thought he would see the sense in her plan.

"I served his lordship, then Lady Caroline, and since her death—you. Three-and-twenty years, madam, and you think to pay me off with one month of half pay and push me out the door with nary a 'by your leave'?"

She gritted her teeth. Hathaway had been left generous bequests by both Lord Betman and Lady Caroline. What he'd done with them, she had no idea. But had she been unfair? Ungenerous? She, herself, owed Hathaway very little. Based upon his short service in her employ— less than a year—he'd shown her little but impatience and disrespect. She could not imagine living indefinitely with him in her home and subjected to his behavior. But in the interest of expediency, "Full pay, then."

She straightened her back and strengthened her will as she went to the desk and removed the leather packet that held the cash she'd withdrawn from the bank for household expenses. She removed the required sum and pushed it across the polished surface toward him. "On second thought, I would rather you leave today, Hathaway. If you are unable to find lodgings on such short notice, you may sleep here tonight, but I expect you to have made other arrangements no later than tomorrow." Perhaps he could find employment wherever his lady love worked.

His expression was incredulous. Could he really have thought he could treat her and her guests with such disrespect and yet remain in her employ? "Surely you realize most employers would have dismissed you long ago,

Hathaway. I would think you'd be relieved to depart when you find working for me so odious."

His eyes narrowed and Georgiana suppressed the shiver that went through her. Evidently he read the resolve on her face because he snatched the banknotes from the desk and spun on his heel to leave the library without another word.

Lord Carlington signaled the waiter at White's gentlemen's club to pour Charles a sherry and nodded toward the deep upholstered chair across from his. "Good to see you again, Hunter. Coincidence? Or have you come looking for me?"

"Looking," Charles admitted. Indeed, he'd been one step behind the man all day. It was time for their long-delayed talk.

"Something I can do for you?"

Charles settled back against the cushions. "If you are agreeable, I'd like to ask some questions regarding Georgiana."

"I cannot help you with that, I fear. I've seen her across a room on occasion, but never met her until last night."

"Actually, it was more Lady Caroline and her friend that I wanted to ask about. Georgiana has very few memories of her early years, and I hoped you might be able to help me with that."

Carlington grew contemplative. "I knew a few of Caroline's friends. Was there anyone in particular?"

"Georgiana's mother."

"Ah, Mrs. Carson. No, I did not have that pleasure. I believe I heard that Caro went to finishing school with her, but the woman married before she even had a season."

"That is unusual, is it not?"

Carlington nodded. "Quite. If she was of sufficiently

good birth to be accepted at a finishing school and become Caroline's friend, she was certainly eligible to be presented to society. But if she'd been betrothed beforehand, I suppose there wouldn't be much point in a season. Expensive, I hear."

Charles smiled as he realized that Carlington had no firsthand knowledge of female expenses. "Then you don't know Mrs. Carson's maiden name?" He accepted the sherry from an impassive footman.

Carlington shook his head. "Don't believe it was ever mentioned. I knew a George Carson who was a captain in the Royal Navy. Just assumed he was the husband. George—Georgiana, you see."

There was sense in that, Charles thought.

"But you're engaged to the gel and don't know about her family?"

He shrugged. "I am inquiring now, sir. Apparently, I only know what you do. Lady Caroline was silent on the matter at our one meeting."

Carlington sat forward, a spark of interest in his blue eyes. "You met Caro? When?"

"Georgiana's come-out year. She summoned me to discuss her ward. I was a bit smitten by her even then."

"What was she like?"

"Beautiful even then. Lively and quite popular. I had a great deal of competition."

"Not Georgiana. Caroline. That was…*after,* you see. And Caroline would never receive me after."

"After?"

"Her accident. The one that sent her back to Kent, never to appear in society again."

Charles noted the sudden redness in Carlington's eyes, which spoke of threatening tears. "Did you love her?"

Carlington blinked and leaned back again. "Completely. As I hinted at our last meeting, we were engaged, though it hadn't been announced."

So Wycliffe's information had been accurate. Sympathy should have kept him silent, but he had to know. "What happened, Carlington?"

"Coaching accident. I handed her into her coach one night after a ball, and never saw her again. She wrote me that the coach tipped and either the window or the coach lamp broke and cut her badly. What did she look like, Hunter?"

He sighed. Lying would be kinder, but that would be a disservice to the man. After all these years, he had a right to know. Perhaps it would ease his mind. "She wore a veil, but even so, I could see her scars. They were…extensive. I gather the doctors were unable to repair her to any semblance of her former self. I've seen a portrait of her at her town house, but it bore little likeness to the woman I met."

Carlington nodded as if Charles was confirming his own information. "I hoped to persuade her that her appearance mattered little to me. It was the woman I loved, not the face. I even went to see her in Kent but she would not receive me. She wrote to me afterward, begging me never to call upon her again, and saying she could never impede me with an unpresentable wife. I was pleased when I heard that she adopted her friend's daughter. I would not have wished a life of solitude on her."

A life such as his own had been?

"But back to your problem, lad. Would you like me to inquire about Captain Carson? Perhaps we could find her family that way. Or at least learn something about them."

"Thank you, Carlington. Your help would be most welcome."

"You're not thinking of backing out of the engagement,

are you? Based on the information you gather about her family?"

How could he answer such a question when they weren't actually engaged? But if they were… "Blood matters, sir. It is who you are."

"Pah! That's nonsense, Hunter. If you believe that, you'd best not involve yourself with an orphan."

"But Georgiana is of good blood, else Lady Caroline would not have been her mother's friend or taken her in and raised her as her own. Indeed, left her all her worldly goods."

Carlington gave him a sage smile. "Good blood, bad blood—we all stand naked before our maker, stripped of titles, position, wealth, beauty or consequence. We will be called to answer not for who we were born to or where we came from, but for what we have made of our lives and how we have conducted ourselves."

Charles did not know if he could believe that. Surely the Carlingtons of the world were not on equal footing with the likes of Dick Gibbons.

He finished his sherry and stood. "Thank you for your time, Carlington. Send to me if you learn anything, will you?"

"Of course. Oh, and my invitation to bring your fiancée 'round for a chat stands, no matter what you find about her family. I'd very much like to know her better."

Charles smiled as he took his hat from a footman. More likely Carlington would quiz Georgiana about Lady Caroline. "I will, sir."

Chapter Ten

Charles spotted Georgiana and Harriett in the supper box he had reserved for them. Sanders—Georgiana's tall, lanky footman—stood watchfully by. Charles was gratified to see that she'd had the foresight to bring an escort of some kind. They'd learned nothing in the past few days if not that the threat of danger lurked at every turn.

At his elbow, Sir Harry Richardson, freshly back from Kent with no news whatsoever, spotted them, too. "Ah, you've brought a morsel for me. The lovely Miss Harriett Thayer."

"Tread lightly there."

Richardson shrugged. "I know how to mind my manners. More than I can say for you on some occasions, Hunter."

"Ah, but I am wise enough to restrict my amorous adventures to the demimonde." The words were no more than out of his mouth when he realized that had all changed last night.

As he and Richardson wound their way through the maze of boxes, Miss Harriett waved to friends strolling along a path bordering the area. She said a few words over her shoulder to Georgiana and then hurried toward her friends. Sanders looked as if he did not know which woman to escort. Charles could solve that problem, at least. "See that Miss Thayer does not go astray, will you, Richardson?"

His friend grinned. "Gladly."

Perfect. Now all he had to do was to think of some errand to occupy Sanders so that he could have a moment alone with Georgiana. She'd been docile enough this morning, but he could not guess her mood tonight. She was preoccupied with arranging the table settings and he came up behind her to slip one hand around her, pull her back against his chest and cover her eyes with the other. "Guess who."

The tension in her muscles relaxed with the sound of his voice. "Um, Mr. Farmer?"

What? Could she be serious? "No."

"Sir Harry?"

Ah, she was teasing. That playful sense of humor had been one of the things that had made him fall in love with her. "No. Not Harry."

"Not Lord Wycliffe?" she asked with a note of exaggerated shock.

He laughed. "Mr. Hunter."

"And which Mr. Hunter would that be?"

He grinned and lowered his voice as he uncovered her eyes and turned her about to face him. "The Mr. Hunter whose name you cried out in passion last night. The one whose arms you swore never to leave. The one who brought you to a boil and—"

"Ah no, it couldn't be *him*." The delicate pink of a blush began to creep up her cheeks. "Did he not say I had rendered him completely useless for at least a week? *He* would be home recovering on milk toast and weak tea, poor thing."

He laughed. "I recover quickly."

"I had noticed that."

"I think I like this Georgiana," he said, quickly brushing his lips across hers before they could be seen. "She reminds me of a girl I used to know years ago." But, oddly, and much to his discomfort, he found he was growing to like this woman even better.

"Does she? I hope you dealt more kindly with her than you did with me."

More kindly than he had with her? To the contrary, she had been the one to deal unkindly. "Would you care to explain that, Georgiana?"

Her blush deepened. "No, I would not. It is in the past and I would prefer to leave it there."

A serving girl stepped into the box carrying a large tray of thinly sliced cold meats and cheeses along with a selection of fruit and breads. This was not the time to pursue the matter, but he would revisit the subject soon. Twilight had deepened and he signaled Sanders to lay out the light repast.

"Shall we fetch the others for supper?" He took Georgiana by the arm, leading her onto the walk that Richardson and Harriett Thayer's group had taken, hoping to catch up with them.

"And what did Hathaway have to say this morning, Mrs. Huffington?"

She sighed deeply. "I fear I did most of the talking. I found him going through my things."

Charles felt his hackles rising. He'd been right to distrust the man. "And?"

"I dismissed him."

Such an encounter would be difficult for Georgiana, but she'd found the mettle for it. "Sent him on his way?"

"Well…"

"Ah. Perhaps you'd best tell me the rest of the story."

"He appeared to be surprised. I really do not think he understood how impertinent he'd become. How unmanageable. And when I offered him half pay for a month, he—"

"Half pay?" He raised his eyebrows. She was far too generous to a man who'd been nothing but disrespectful. "I imagine he was only too glad to take it and leave before you changed your mind."

"Well…he felt I was being unfair and called his previous service into account. The whole affair was unpleasant, so I agreed to give him full pay for a month just to have it done with."

She gazed off into the distance, as if remembering the scene, and Charles curbed his impatience. "At least he is gone now, and you will not have to deal with him again."

"Actually…"

Incredulous, he stopped and faced her beneath a pool of light afforded by one of the lamplights. "Say you did not allow him to stay."

"Just for tonight. He seemed so at a loss, and could not believe that I would toss him out without so much as a moment's notice. I made it clear, though, that he would have to be gone by tomorrow whether he had lodgings or not."

Charles was torn between anger and amusement. "Hmm. Let me ponder this problem. You found your ill-mannered butler rifling through your personal belongings with God only knows what purpose in mind. Then, though you have every cause to dismiss him on the spot, you negotiate his severance pay to a level unheard of in London—or anywhere else, I might add—and then allow the man to stay on, giving him access to your home and belongings. And yourself, Georgiana. Yes, I rather think he got the best of you.

"Have your situation and recent occurrences not taught you that you can trust no one? Hathaway could, even now, be robbing you blind. Or lying in wait for your return to retaliate in some unspeakable manner."

He halted at the stricken look on her face. Clearly none of what he'd said had occurred to her. "I shall go home with you and deal with Hathaway. If you are insistent that he be allowed to stay the night, I shall remain, as well. In the morning I shall summon a locksmith to change the locks. Are any of your servants more loyal to him than to you?"

"I…I do not think so. I believe he has always set himself above the other servants. I shall ask Clara if there is any talk below stairs."

"Your kind heart does you credit, Georgiana, but you mustn't allow it to blind you to those who would take advantage."

She tilted her head up to him and he lost his thoughts in the green depths of her eyes. Dear Lord, how could he want her more this instant than he had last night? Than he had all those years ago? He lowered his lips to hers slowly, savoring the anticipation of the moment they'd meet, of the lushness of those soft petals, of the sweetness of her tongue.…

The stillness was broken by a sharp report, followed by a cacophony of raised voices. Instantly alert, he released her and stepped away. "Wait here, Georgiana. Do not go anywhere, and do not leave the light." He sprinted forward, certain some disaster lay ahead.

Georgiana watched as Charles disappeared. Though it had been a small alarm, she prayed that nothing had befallen Harriett.

She sank onto a stone bench on the edge of the lamplight and inhaled deeply. The night was cool and fragrant with the scent of spring flowers. Her life had become almost magical since last night. Whatever old anger Charles had been carrying against her had dissipated last night and she could almost believe the clock had turned back seven years. Could she trust him this time? Was this a second chance for them? She glanced up to find a star, then closed her eyes to make her wish.

A hand clamped over her mouth and another held her shoulder, keeping her immobile. Instinctively, she clawed at the hand, squealing as best she could.

"Hush, girl. I ain't gonna hurt you," a hoarse voice whispered in her ear.

The fetid breath that brushed her cheek made her want to gag. She tried to calm herself and do as she was told. Reason told her that if this man wanted her dead, he could have cut her throat by now.

"Do as I tell you an' don't turn around."

She managed a nod.

"Now, I gots things to tell you, so pay attention, eh?"

The hand eased off her mouth. Calculating that her best chances for escape lay with compliance, she nodded, ready to run the moment he released her shoulder.

"You ain't doin' what you should. Stay away from them blasted Hunters. Charlie most of all. You owes me that much. He ain't fer you. I gots plans fer you, an' he don't fit into 'em. I'd sooner cut you than see you wi' him."

"Who…who are you?" she squeaked.

A meaningful chortle was the only answer. "You'll find out soon enough."

"Georgiana!"

Charles! Her heart started beating again. She was on the verge of calling a warning when the voice behind her stopped her.

"Don't do it, Georgie, gal. You'd be in more trouble th'n me. Keep your trap shut if you knows what's good fer you. And fer Charlie Hunter. We gots a secret, you an' me."

"But—"

The restraining hand left her shoulder and something crackled in the bushes behind her. Torn between tears and hysteria, she shuddered violently just as Charles arrived.

"Georgiana, what's wrong?"

Keep yer trap shut if ye knows what's good fer you. And fer Charlie Hunter.

"Just a…a sudden chill."

He removed his jacket and draped it around her, then took her hand and lifted her to her feet. "Richardson and the others are not far behind. 'Twas just an accidental discharge of fireworks. Nothing to fret about. Come, let's get you back to the supper box."

Georgiana glanced over her shoulder as Charles led her away. Was that horrid man still there? Watching? Or had she imagined it all?

Mistaking her distraction and nervousness from the odd meeting on the stone bench as reluctance to confront Hathaway, Charles had insisted upon dealing with the butler himself when he delivered Georgiana home. Her back against her bedroom door, she waited for the raised voices she knew would be coming.

Charles was slipping quite comfortably into the role of fiancé and future husband. She, however, was having constant misgivings. How would she live with herself if her curse struck him down? And now, more than ever, she feared it would. The incident tonight convinced her of that. Whoever that man was, he had warned her to stay away from Charles. From all the Hunters. What frightened her as much was that he'd known her name. That he had *plans* for her. Another violent shudder washed through her. *Who was he?*

Though she'd been warned to stay silent, she feared she knew the outcome if she didn't. Charles would dig his heels in further and refuse to budge. She had never known a man so persistent. So stubborn. So...so wonderfully protective.

A timid knock at her back startled her. "Madam? I've come to turn your bed down."

She took a deep breath and opened the door enough to admit Clara, who went straight to her bed and began turning down the sheets and fluffing the pillows. "Oh, madam! They say you've given Mr. Hathaway the sack! Is that true?" she asked over her shoulder.

Georgiana went to her dressing table and began pulling the pins from her hair. "Yes, Clara. This afternoon. I had hoped he'd be gone by now. Charles is quite unhappy that he is not."

Clara snorted as she laid out her nightgown. "We gathered as much, missus."

"We?"

"The others. Cook, Sanders and me. The day help stayed out of his way. Mr. Hathaway has been in a dither all day, he has. Not two words said to any of us. Just storming around and going all about the house. He was in the attic, missus. What would he want in the attic?"

What, indeed? "I do not know, Clara. Perhaps he'd put his valise up there."

"Hmm" was Clara's only comment as she came to run the brush through Georgiana's hair.

The sharp thud of the library door closing made her jump just before voices carried upstairs from the foyer.

"You've no right here, Mr. Hunter!" Hathaway's voice echoed throughout the house. "Who are you to—"

"I am Mrs. Huffington's fiancé, lest you forget. Sanders! Bring Hathaway's valise!"

"You think you're going to get away with this, don't you?"

"Think? I am certain of it, Hathaway."

Georgiana stood and glanced at the door. Should she go down? Interfere? Mistaking her intentions, Clara began to unfasten her gown.

The voices grew louder. "You underestimate me, Mr. Hunter. You will be sorry you dealt with me thus—you and that little street urchin who is no better than she ought to be. Why, she thinks she's mistress of the manor now."

Street urchin? Heat flooded Georgiana's cheeks. What must Charles think of her now?

Charles's voice had gone low and deadly. "If you know what's good for you, you'll watch what you say about Mrs. Huffington."

There was an ugly laugh before Hathaway responded. "Even if it's the truth? Do you really want to be her next victim?"

"That is a vile insinuation and I'd advise you to watch your tongue."

"You think things are bad for her now. Just see what happens when I'm finished."

The sound of a scuffle rose to the two women. Clara gasped and covered her mouth. A sharp crack and splintering told the fate of the entry table. The front door rebounded and Clara ran to the window.

"Oh, madam! He's given Mr. Hathaway the boot! Oh!" Clara covered her mouth to muffle a giggle. "And his satchel after him!"

Georgiana joined her maid at the window to watch as Hathaway gained his feet and slapped the dust from his jacket. Thank heavens it was late and only a single street lamp lit the dim scene below.

Hathaway snatched up his bag and faced the door where Charles must have still been standing. "You'll regret this, Hunter. Until the day you die. And that won't be long if you keep company with *her*. I know things. Things that could turn this town upside down."

"If you repeat one thing about Mrs. Huffington, derogatory or otherwise, you'll answer to me. Do you understand, Hathaway?"

But Hathaway had turned his back and Georgiana couldn't make out his reply. As the butler faded into the darkness, the front door slammed and she heard Charles's footsteps take him back to the library. For his coat and hat?

"Oh, madam! That was quite thrilling. What I'd give to have a champion like your Mr. Hunter."

Her Mr. Hunter. Georgiana sighed. How she wished that were true.

In a reckless mood, Charles finished his brandy in a single gulp and poured another. No wonder Georgiana hadn't wanted to deal with that bastard! Who the hell did he think he was, calling Georgiana's birth into question? Damn near refusing to leave? Making threats?

He examined his skinned knuckles and decided he wouldn't need more than a good scrub. He actually regretted not doing more damage. How had Georgiana put up with Hathaway for so long?

The hell of it was that he could not even dismiss Hathaway's threats as idle bluster. He had dealt with enough ne'er-do-wells to recognize them when he saw them. In Georgiana's present circumstances, he had to allow for the possibility that the former butler was somehow involved with her misfortunes.

He sank into the club chair by the fire and stared into the flames, warming the brandy between his palms. The flickering, ever-changing patterns in the fire usually calmed him, but at the moment all he could think of was how everything had changed since he'd started this investigation. He'd wanted to prove the woman who'd scorned him was guilty of murder, and now he desperately wanted to prove her innocent. He'd wanted to know if she'd had his best friend killed, and now he suspected she was not capable of such duplicity. He'd wanted to confirm that he'd lost nothing all those years ago in Lady Caroline's parlor, but he'd only confirmed that he'd never stopped loving her. He'd wanted to nurse his mistrust and anger to prevent another disappointment, but he'd begun to trust her and the old bitterness was fading.

God help him, he wanted their engagement to be real.

He finished his second glass of brandy and headed for the stairs. It was time to straighten a few things out with the infamous Mrs. Huffington. He stepped over the scattered fragments of the foyer table and took the steps two at a time. He knocked but opened the door before she'd had time to answer.

Clara dropped a nightgown trimmed in blue ribbon over Georgiana's head, and both of them turned to stare at him in shock. Manners required an apology, but he did not feel like offering hypocrisies at the moment.

"Thank you, Clara. That will be all," he said.

The maid turned to Georgiana and waited for a nod before complying. At least someone in this house recognized Georgiana was in charge.

"Sorry if I've caught you at a bad time," he said.

She retrieved a sheer wrapper from her bed and pulled

it on over her nightgown, which did nothing to cool his lust. "I was going to send for you."

He raised an eyebrow at that. He did not think he would be so lucky.

"We must call off our engagement."

"Disappointing," he murmured. "Do you mind telling me why?"

"I never should have agreed to such a reckless plan. It is not too late to turn back. All we need do is tell the appropriate people that we'd been a bit precipitate. I doubt the rumor has had much time to spread."

He laughed. "In London? Surely you are not that naive. I would imagine society matrons are already ordering gowns for the wedding and their husbands are making wagers as to whether I will make it to the altar alive."

She winced and he regretted his teasing. "Too late for cold feet, Georgiana," he said. "We are bound to go through with this now. We've set the stage, and I think we should start making more public appearances together. The more people who know, the more likely we will provoke a response from our villain."

"But that is just it!" She came forward and placed her hand on his arm. "I cannot risk your life. I cannot."

"I thought we were agreed that it was the fastest way to get to the bottom of our little mystery."

"Oh! It is not a *little* mystery. Three men are dead! And you could be next. How could I live with that?"

"You care?" He strove to sound blasé, but his future hung on her answer.

"Of course I care. You have been very kind to me. Without your help, I would not have come so far."

"And how far is that?"

"I…I…"

"Precisely. Not nearly far enough. We are on the verge

of discovery, Georgiana. We have taken a path and committed to it. We would be foolish to abandon it now."

She looked desperate, as if she were about to cry. "Charles, there was a man tonight. At Vauxhall, when you went to fetch the others for supper."

A tingle of anticipation prickled the hair on the back of his neck. "A man? Why did you not tell me?"

She answered his last question first. "He warned me not to say anything. I thought he might have a weapon and would hurt you. He mentioned that he would rather 'cut me' than have me with you."

Charles's heart went ice cold. "Who was it, Georgie?"

"I do not know. I never saw his face. He came up behind me and warned me not to turn around. He told me to stay away from you and your brothers. He said you were not for me."

"What the—?" Who would warn her against him? "Has he ever come to you before? Did anything like this, any warnings, happen before your marriages?"

"I've never heard that voice before. I swear it. But when he said your name, I feared for you. Oh, Charles, I do not want you to die."

Then she did care. And for the moment, that was enough. What matter if he died tomorrow as long as he had tonight? He pulled her into his arms and looked into her eyes—those captivating eyes that had haunted his dreams for the last seven years.

Her lips parted on a sigh and her hand came up to stroke the back of his neck as she lifted on her toes to meet him halfway. There was something shy and innocent about that kiss that humbled him. He took her offered lips and nibbled at the corners until she moaned and tightened her arms around him.

"Charlie…kiss me, please," she said on a sigh.

And he did just that, plundering the heated recess of her mouth with all the ardor he'd held back when he'd expected rejection. His desire was wreaking havoc with his body. He didn't want to give it rein. He wanted to make love to her as she deserved. Slowly. Softly. Thoroughly. He'd not given her his best last time, and he would not have her again until he could.

And he could not when he half expected Hathaway to return to fulfill his threats. Or when he had to solve the puzzle of who the strange man in Vauxhall Gardens had been. The bastard would rather cut her? Not while he was alive. Damn it all, he would have to make new plans.

While he was still able, he broke the kiss, unwound her arms from around his neck and stepped back. "I will be in the library. Call if you need me. Good night, Georgiana."

Chapter Eleven

Georgiana read the note from Charles for a third time, her mind bouncing between anger and gratitude. It seemed he had spent the night in her library making plans for her safety. When morning came, she found he'd hired a bodyguard, dressed him in footman's livery and sent him to protect her against Hathaway's possible return or any mischief he might have in mind. The man's name was Finn, the note read, and Charles further instructed her to take him with her to any appointments or outings. And he was standing before her in the foyer this very instant.

She cocked an eyebrow at him. The man looked as if he'd been born to a race of giants. He was quite tall, with a large nose and hands the size of hams. "Finn, is it?"

"Yes, madam," he said in a gravelly voice.

"And where did Mr. Hunter find you?"

"I, uh, have worked for friends of his from time to time, madam."

She was certain she did not want to delve further into that explanation. "Did Mr. Hunter give you instructions?"

"Yes, madam."

"And if I dismiss you?"

A look of near panic crossed Finn's face. "Mr. Hunter hired me, madam. I would not go until *he* gave me leave."

Then there was no use in trying to send him away. She had visions of this man sitting on her front steps all day, frightening neighbors and passersby alike. She would simply have to deal with Charles tonight. As surly as Hathaway had been, she could not imagine that he would return. Charles was just being overly cautious.

"Are you day help, Finn? Or staff?"

"Staff, Mrs. Huffington."

"Very well, Finn. Go to the kitchen and introduce yourself to Cook and Sanders. Ask them to assign you a room. I will be in the attic." At the man's indecisive look, she hastened to explain. "I am going through my late aunt's things. I doubt Hathaway will scale a wall in the middle of the day for all the neighbors to see."

"Mr. Hunter told me to watch for danger from any direction, madam, not just from someone named Hathaway."

Oh! She never should have told Charles about the man at Vauxhall Gardens. Really, he hadn't exactly threatened her. Just mentioned that he had plans for her. Hmm. Well, perhaps that *could* be taken as a bit of a threat. She shrugged. "Very well," she allowed. "We shall discuss this further with Mr. Hunter tonight. Meanwhile, please try to make yourself inconspicuous." Though she doubted that was possible for man his size.

He nodded and stepped out of her way as she walked to the stairway. She had no doubt he would come looking for her sooner rather than later and then laughed to herself as she thought of him at La Meilleure Robe this afternoon. Madame Marie would make short work of him, she was sure.

The attic door was unlocked and the narrow windows at each end had been uncovered to allow light to pour through. Yes, Clara had said that Hathaway had been in the attic yesterday. She frowned as she noted that dust covers had been tossed into a heap. Spare furniture had been left bare. Trunks and boxes were open. Someone had been rummaging through Aunt Caroline's things. Hathaway.

A prickle of fear made her shiver as she looked around more carefully. What could he have been looking for? Hidden treasure or something of value? Something to carry off? Or…or something in particular? More personal?

Georgiana had played up here as a child when she and Aunt Caroline had made short trips to the city to tend business matters. She knew every nook and cranny. Every crate, box, trunk and broken chair. She knew right where Aunt Caroline's childhood toys were stored. Where the gowns now out of fashion had been kept for their trims and fabric. She knew where her old lesson books were, and the sheet music from her pianoforte lessons.

And she knew something was very wrong.

She turned on her heel and hurried down to the library and the desk where Hathaway had seen her place the pouch with money for household expenses. How foolish of her not to secure it in the safe at once! That money had to last her until the confusion over inheritance had been settled. She opened the drawer and unfolded the pouch. After carefully counting the cash, she went weak with relief. There! It was all there. She sank into the chair and opened the bottom drawer where a heavy lockbox was secured. She removed the key from her chatelaine, opened the box and placed the pouch inside. When it was secure, she sat back and pressed her fingertips to her temples, trying to think.

If Hathaway had meant to rob her, he'd known right where to go. But he hadn't. Thus, he'd been looking for something more precise than his valise when he'd gone to the attic. But what?

He'd been employed by Aunt Caroline's father a year before his death, and had stayed on afterward. It was not unreasonable to think that he might have collected quite a few belongings in that space of time. All the servants had their own lockers in the cellar to store their valuables, and Hathaway had been no exception. In fact, he'd had two lockers.

No. Hathaway had not been looking for his own belongings. And that meant that he'd been looking for something quite specific.

She did not know how long she'd sat there, trying to think of anything Hathaway might have wanted, but she started when Clara touched her shoulder.

"Madam? That Finn fellow said you'd gone to the attic, but here you are in the library. I came looking for you to get you ready to go to the dressmaker. Finn says he'll be escorting you today."

"Oh, yes. I just forgot something here. Could you get the key to the attic and lock it for me? I won't have time for it until tomorrow."

"Aye, madam. How long is Mr. Finn going to be with us?"

"Not long, I think." She noted the flash of disappointment that passed over Clara's face. "I do not believe 'footman' is his usual occupation, Clara. He will likely leave when the danger has passed."

"Danger? What danger, madam?"

Georgiana stood and went to the library door. "Mr. Hunter seems to think Hathaway could come back to cause trouble. Finn is here to prevent that from happening."

"He's a bodyguard, madam?" Clara asked in wonder.

"Something of the sort." She gave her maid a wry smile. After the discovery of Hathaway's thorough search in the attic, she was suddenly very glad Finn was here.

Charles paged through the betting book at his club and sighed. Yes, there it was. *Hunter—Huffington Nuptials.* Odds were not favoring his surviving marriage to Georgiana Huffington, née Carson. The long odds were giving him a week. On the short end, someone had bet he wouldn't arrive at the altar. Only three had taken odds for survival—Lord Lockwood, Andrew Hunter and James Hunter. His brothers. He hoped he'd make them rich.

But, of course, the engagement and pending marriage were a farce. No one would win. Well, maybe Georgiana if they found the killer.

"I vow, I do not know which odds to take," Wycliffe spoke over his shoulder.

"The only right wager would be no wager."

Wycliffe grinned. "I'm not so certain of that, Hunter. I've seen the way you look at her. And the way she watches you."

Sir Harry Richardson joined them with a hearty smile. "You look to be in a good mood, considering the odds against you."

Charles gave them both a quelling glance and headed for the parlor. They gathered three chairs in a conversational circle with a low table bearing a coffee service in the middle. He poured himself a cup and prayed it would be strong. He'd gotten very little sleep last night between listening for Hathaway's return and thinking of Georgiana. The only new plan he'd been able to conceive was so shocking that he could scarcely believe he'd thought of it. And yet there was a certain logic to it. Nothing else would answer all their needs.

Actual marriage.

He could move Georgiana's household to his, thus thwarting any plans Hathaway might have and enabling him to better protect her. The killer would be forced to act quickly or forfeit his game. Georgiana would be compelled to stay in London. With him. He would have free and unhindered access to her. It was madness. And yet... he would acquire a special license to marry. Whether he'd use it or not remained to be seen.

"So pensive, Hunter?" Richardson asked as he and Wycliffe sat.

"I have a lot on my mind. None of which has to do with the matter at hand."

"And what is that?"

"Richardson, how quickly can you be to Cornwall and back?"

"Where in Cornwall? St. Ives?"

"Mousehole."

"Why in God's name—"

"That is where Lady Caroline finally located Georgiana after her parents' deaths. I want you to find out anything that might have a bearing on this matter."

Wycliffe narrowed his eyes. "What is it that you suspect?"

"Nothing. Everything. I am becoming more convinced that the answer to this problem lies neither in who Georgiana is, nor whom she married, but in her identity before Lady Caroline took her in. Lord Carlington gave me a possible link to her father—a Captain George Carson of the Royal Navy. Carlington said he'd look into it, but see what you can find out about him or his wife. And why Georgiana was abandoned in Mousehole. Find out, too, who cared for her during that time."

"Mousehole," Richardson repeated. "The end of the earth."

"Well, England, at any rate," Wycliffe contributed. "Appears as if someone wanted her lost."

This echo of Charles's thoughts confirmed his suspicions. It was looking more and more as if Georgiana Carson was not at all what she seemed. "How soon can you report back?" he asked Richardson.

The man glanced at the tall case clock standing in one corner of the parlor and still reading an indecently early hour. "How soon do you need the information?"

"Yesterday."

"I can ride for Brighton within the hour and from there hire a smack to Mousehole. With favorable winds and ready tongues once I get there, three days, perhaps four."

Charles nodded and Richardson got to his feet. "I'm going to need a few days to sleep when I get back."

Wycliffe nodded. "You'll get them." He waited until Richardson disappeared and then turned back to Charles, a serious expression on his face. "And the rest of it?"

Damn. The man always knew when he was holding back. "Only a vague notion that all is not as it should be. But why Lady Caroline should be party to a lie, I cannot imagine."

Wycliffe gave him a sage smile. "Can you not?"

"Nothing I'd care to share at the moment."

"Do you think our assailant in this instance has turned his attention to Georgiana?"

"I do. She has had several close calls recently. One just last night in Vauxhall Gardens. A man encountered her along one of the paths and warned her that he had plans for her. That he'd rather 'cut' her than see her with me. *Cut* her, Wycliffe. I think that is a clear threat."

"Did he say why? Did she even know him?"

Charles shook his head. "He was behind her and warned her not to turn around. She said she did not recognize his voice, but I wonder if she would tell me if she had."

"I cannot believe anyone would wish her harm. She is such a pleasant woman. Who could she have given offense to?"

"I can think of at least half a dozen people who might want Georgiana dead, and most of them would profit by it."

"Half a dozen?" Wycliffe scoffed. "Surely that is an exaggeration."

"Not in the least. A conservative estimate, actually. Between the families of her deceased husbands, the newly found potential heirs to Caroline's fortune and her own murky beginnings, there could be more."

Wycliffe sat back in his chair and looked thoughtful. "Two cousins of Lady Caroline's, a displaced cousin of her second husband, the parents of her first husband." He stopped to look pointedly at Charles. "Not to mention various friends and Adam Booth's parents. Yes. You might have something there."

"I would wager my fortune that she had nothing to do with Booth's death."

"Never really thought she did."

"Then why—"

"To get you to accept the assignment, Hunter. You can be deucedly stubborn when you have your ire up."

"Possibly," he mused. What did he actually know about Georgiana? That she'd been raised by Lady Caroline Betman and married twice. That she made love like an innocent and that she used lilac soap to wash her hair. That she had turned him around with barely a crook of her finger. What still lay hidden to be discovered?

"I heard you hired Finn. What prompted that?"

"Her butler has been behaving suspiciously. She dismissed him and he made threats. He and I...well, he knows he'd be a fool to try anything. But fools are born every day."

Wycliffe leaned forward and lowered his voice, glancing right and left before speaking. "Hunter, hurry up. I've heard from the Under Secretary that pressure is increasing to solve these cases. And there appears to be some new development. Information that could implicate Mrs. Huffington in those murders and lead to her imminent arrest."

"Imminent? How imminent?"

"Within a few days. A week at most."

"Why?"

"The pressure was severe a week ago when I put you on this matter. With nothing to acquit her and new evidence to implicate her...it's becoming a losing proposition, Hunter."

"Damn it, what new evidence?"

"Laudanum."

"What does that mean?"

"That was the word whispered to me this morning in my office. It isn't official. Not yet. But, if you can, find out what Mrs. Huffington knows about laudanum."

Charles nodded. He would be seeing Georgiana tonight. If the word meant anything to her, he'd know it.

As predicted, Finn looked quite peculiar sitting in a small wooden chair in the reception area of La Meilleure Robe. That he felt out of his element was obvious by the way he fidgeted and kept turning his hat around by the brim. Every member of the Wednesday League mentioned it when they arrived.

"Who is that great hulk in the foyer?" Lady Annica,

the last to arrive, asked as she entered the dressing room and took a chair.

"Finn. My bodyguard." Georgiana, standing in her chemise and corset, explained the circumstances for the fourth time before she could be asked again.

"As if you haven't enough trouble," Grace Hawthorne added. "Still, Finn is a good idea. I would certainly think twice before accosting you with him in the way."

Sarah shook her head. "My brothers know the oddest people. I wonder where Charlie found him."

Georgiana was spared a reply by Madame Marie's entrance, a heap of pale violet silk in her arms. She stepped onto the low platform and dropped it over Georgiana's head. "Come, chèri. This will be the last fitting, yes?"

Once the gown was settled around her, Madame knelt and began tugging the hem to pull the folds into place for pinning.

Grace folded her hands in her lap. "Now tell us, Georgiana, have you been able to uncover any information that might be useful?"

"I fear I only have more questions." She hesitated, recalling the warning she'd been given, but surely that information would be safe here. "We went to Vauxhall Gardens last evening, and while I was alone on a path waiting for Charles to return, a man approached me from behind. He instructed me not to turn around, so I did not see his face. He seemed to know me, but I would swear I have never met him. I am positive I would have recognized his voice. He warned me to stay away from Charles specifically and all the Hunter men generally. He said I should do as he said and that he had plans for me. He ran off when we heard Charles returning, but not before he said he would find me again."

Sarah's face had gone quite pale. "Dear heavens! Did you warn Charlie?"

"The moment we were alone. He seems to think this may be progress."

"Progress?" the ladies said as one voice.

"That...that someone has come forward."

The ladies shared a meaningful glance, then turned back to Georgiana. "No wonder he has hired Finn," Sarah said.

Madame Marie stood and turned Georgiana toward the mirror. *"Magnifique, n'est-ce pas?"*

Speechless, she nodded. Yes, it was, though it exposed more of her than Aunt Caroline had ever allowed. But she was a widow now and no one would think twice about her gowns. She noted the smiles of the ladies behind her reflected in the mirror. They approved. Thank heavens she would not be criticized by the ton.

With a few deft moves, Madame Marie had her gown unfastened and over her head. She handed Georgiana a wrapper. "François will join you in a minute. I shall 'ave my girls sew the 'em immediately so that you can take it 'ome with you."

True to her word, her husband was waiting. He entered through a side door and assumed his usual position in one corner, almost at ease with seeing a woman in a dressing gown. "Afternoon, ladies," he greeted them. "We have a bit of news, at last."

"Do tell," Lady Annica said.

"I've just gotten back from Kent." He removed a small notebook from his jacket pocket and flipped the cover back. "I fear the news is not all good. No one remembers your mother, Mrs. Huffington. The villagers only recall when Lady Caroline returned from Cornwall with you in tow. You must have been about two or three at the time. Quite a favorite in the village, by all accounts."

Georgiana recalled her weekly trips to the village and smiled. The only friends she'd had growing up were the butcher, the greengrocer and the baker. Later, she'd gone to the tea shop and dressmaker, but all those friendships had lacked intimacy. They were just acquaintances, really.

"I also took the opportunity to meet your cousins, Walter and Robert Foxworthy. They raise horses as well as crops. Told them I was interested in buying a horse and got them to chatting about families. They mentioned you, but did not expand on the matter. Decent sorts, I thought— Robert more than Walter. There was something crafty in Walter's manner. I thought he was simply trying to bargain the best price for his stock, but there could be more. I do not believe there is anything to worry about, but should you meet him, be careful.

"I asked if they'd been in London recently or if they had any plans to come. Robert says he's never been. Walter does all the traveling, it seems. I could not pursue the subject as diligently as I'd have liked without raising their suspicions, but as near as I can tell, Walter makes monthly trips to town, as well as other destinations as business requires. Hard to determine if he was in the area of your husbands' homes at the appropriate times."

Georgiana let out a long-held breath. "That is more than I expected, Mr. Renquist. Thank you very much."

"I'm not done yet, ladies. Walter Foxworthy will be coming to town soon, and I've asked him to look me up if he'd like to meet my price on the stallion I inspected."

Grace clapped her hands. "Excellent."

"I also caught up with some of the rookery lads upon my return. And this is the news that worries me."

The ladies all sat forward in their chairs and Georgiana drew the wrapper a bit closer around her.

"There are whispers circulating that someone from the rookeries has a very singular interest in you, Mrs. Huffington. Just what that interest is remains a mystery, as yet."

Georgiana frowned. "An interest? Is that all?"

"All? There are some very unpleasant men in the rookeries, Mrs. Huffington. It is not a place you would want your name mentioned, or where you'd want to provoke interest."

The voice from last night rang in her head. *We gots a secret, you an' me.* Was he the one with the singular interest?

It could not be Hathaway. He'd only just been dismissed. Whatever threats he'd made, he hadn't had time to instigate them, let alone to have displayed and "interest." Heavens! How many men wished her ill? She quickly told Mr. Renquist about the incident at Vauxhall and her dismissing of Hathaway.

A worried frown played at the corners of Mr. Renquist's mouth. "The blighter at Vauxhall, Mrs. Huffington. That's the one that worries me most. I shall put my men to uncovering that first. As for Hathaway, we cannot eliminate him. He has had access to your home and all your secrets the whole time. I shall see if I can find out more about him."

"Yes, but I only dismissed him yesterday and Mr. Hunter removed him from my house last night. There has not been time for him to cause a stir in the rookeries."

"If he whispered a prayer in the rookeries last night, it would be common knowledge by dawn, and if it were a juicy bit of gossip, sooner." Renquist shook his head. "It is beyond me how guarded they are with outsiders, yet how ready they are to gossip among themselves. Well, I should have more information in a few days. Perhaps even the name of your…admirer at Vauxhall. I will send you a note when I have something to tell you."

Pray it would be soon. Very soon.

Before that horrid man found her again.

Chapter Twelve

Charles strode from Doctor's Commons, his head down and deep in thought. For the sum of five pounds, he'd just purchased the right to marry Georgiana at any place, any time, for the next three months. Two witnesses and a minister were all he'd need. Those were easy.

Georgiana's consent would be more difficult.

He'd spent most of the day after his meeting with Wycliffe and Richardson at the Archbishop of Canterbury's office, and now the shadows were deepening, the sun obscured by surrounding buildings. He crossed the commons to the stables, still deep in thought. He'd have to hurry if he was to make it home, wash, change for the evening and still fetch Georgiana on time.

When she had mentioned that she was at leisure this evening, he had asked her to join him at his brother Andrew's home for a family dinner party—a very good place to introduce Georgiana to the rest of the family. Perhaps he would test the waters there.

He'd find some logical way to present the idea without mentioning the special license. She would, no doubt, be angry that he'd had the presumption to acquire one without consulting her. But, if they were to do it, it would be best to do it quickly. Surely she would see the sense in that.

He winced when he thought of what she would say. *No* would be the kindest thing. After all, she'd said it before. And rather emphatically, at that. He'd have to coax her, convince her that this was the most logical and expeditious course of action considering that her arrest might be imminent and she could be locked away in Newgate or Fleet Prison. Between his name and marriage he might be able to protect her or gain her better treatment. He'd even lie and tell her he'd consent to a divorce or annulment afterward. Seems he had very few scruples where Georgiana was concerned.

The shadow of a movement from behind drew him from his introspection and he turned just in time to see the flash of a blade slicing downward. Instinctively, he dodged to the side and rolled, coming up on his feet. Both slashes would have been killing blows if the attacker had made contact. A second later and he'd have been dead, a knife in his back.

Still a possibility.

His assailant lunged again and Charles bobbed to the side, then drove into the man's midsection with his right shoulder, knocking him to the ground. Through the gloom, he could see that the man wore a black woolen hood with two ragged eyeholes cut out, much like an executioner's mask. Why the precaution unless Charles would recognize him?

"Gibbons," he snarled. "Finally decide to do your own dirty work?"

The man pulled off his mask and grinned, exposing two rows of rotten teeth. "Think yer clever? How clever will y'be when yer dead?"

Gibbons gained his feet and crouched, swaying from side to side in an invitation for Charles to lunge again.

Instead he fell back a step. "Big words, Dick. Back them up."

Gibbons charged forward with his right leg, slashing the knife in a wide arc. Charles dodged to the side, the knife barely missing his midsection. He seized Gibbons's arm, twisted and pulled, fully intending to break the infernal thing.

Gibbons howled in pain, his numbed fingers dropping the knife. Charles slipped his own knife from his boot and advanced. Kill the bastard, or take him in?

The gloom came alive with groomsmen, stable boys and drivers. "'Ere, now! What's afoot, lads?" the stable master shouted, running up behind Charles.

Gibbons used the moment to spin and retreat toward the maze of narrow lanes and alleys outside the commons, his arm dangling uselessly from the shoulder socket. Dislocated, but not broken, damn it all. As Charles leaped to follow, the stable master seized him by the jacket.

"No trouble 'ere, lad. This be a peaceful place."

Charles jerked free, but the delay had cost him the pursuit. He'd never find Gibbons with such a lead—that scum-dwelling assassin.

One of the stable boys, having recognized Charles, brought his horse. He slipped his knife back in his boot, tossed the lad a coin and mounted. As he turned toward home, the wry humor of the situation dawned on him.

He'd been meaning to provoke an attack. If Gibbons had been following him, this had been a perfect place and time to act. But he'd meant to incite Georgiana's tormentor. Not his. Ah, well. All in a day's work.

Georgiana settled in the carriage, trying to calm her nerves. She'd met most of the Hunters, but she'd never met the eldest, Lord Lockwood, or his wife, Lady Elise. She took courage from the fact that she was wearing her new gown and knew she looked more than presentable and every bit as fashionable as Lady Elise would be.

She'd expected Charles to take a place beside her after he handed her up, but he sat across from her instead, facing backward. They started off with a little jerk and he braced himself with a shoe to the seat beside her. A little smile hovered at the corners of his mouth as he studied her. He was so completely handsome tonight that she feared her heart was in her eyes so she glanced away.

"No more country mouse," he murmured. "You will not be easy to ignore."

"Do you want to ignore me?"

"Not in the least, Georgiana. I thought you knew that. Would you like me to show you what I want from you?"

"No!" The last thing she wanted was to arrive at Charles's brother's house looking disheveled and wrinkled. "I'd much rather you behaved yourself."

"Really?" He licked his lips and smiled again.

Her heartbeat hammered rapidly and heat washed through her. She knew too well the havoc that tongue could cause to her senses. To her free will. And was causing havoc to her now with just his subtle reminder. "Behave yourself, Charles."

"'Twill be a long, boring evening if I do."

"'Twill be a mortifying evening if you do not."

"I am not feeling in the least bit civil." He knocked on the roof above him. "Change of plans, Peter. Belmonde's," he called to his driver.

"Belmonde's?" she queried as the coach turned.

"A place where it will not matter how I behave."

"But—"

"I've decided I want you to myself tonight, Georgiana. My brothers will understand."

She masked her disappointment. She'd been looking

forward to being part of a family, if only for an evening. "Are you ashamed of me, Charles? Or have you decided you do not want to involve your family further in our deceit?"

"Ashamed? Good God, no! Selfish, perhaps. And my family will understand and forgive the deceit—if, indeed, there is one."

"But of course there is a deceit. They think we are engaged."

His eyes darkened and he merely watched her until she could not bear the silence.

"What are you up to?"

"Exploring options, m'dear."

"You are being quite cryptic, Charles. What options?"

"The deeper in we get, the more difficult it will be to extricate ourselves. Might as well go through with it."

"Go through with what?"

"The marriage."

She was stunned to silence. The steady clop of the horses' hooves punctuated the silence, and the dim light in the coach made Charles's expression difficult to read. Was he teasing? Serious? Had he forgotten the fate of her husbands? "I—"

"I know. Shocking, is it not?"

"Stunningly so."

He crossed his arms over his chest. "Imagine how surprised *I* was when it popped into my mind."

"How... Why were you thinking of such a thing?"

He shrugged, then rubbed his right shoulder. "We've been unable to provoke an attack until today. Alas, it was my enemy to show himself, Georgiana, not yours."

"Are you well, Charles? Did he hurt you?"

"Only my pride."

Relief spread instant warmth through her. "Do you think the deaths were coincidental after all?"

"I believe Booth's death was coincidental. As for Allenby and Huffington…that remains to be seen."

Relief and disappointment mingled in a confusing blend. "Then we can dispense with our ruse?"

"To the contrary, it is more important than ever. Events have taken on a life of their own."

"Is there something new?"

"Laudanum, Georgiana."

He was studying her for a reaction, but she could not make sense of his statement. Was she supposed to know what that meant?

"Do you take laudanum?" he pressed.

"I have taken it on rare occasions to help me sleep."

"Do you keep it on hand?"

"Aunt Caroline used to. Her scars would sometimes pain her."

Charles shook his head. "We could have a problem."

Georgiana thought of the vial of laudanum at home in her dressing table drawer. Who had found out about that? And why did they think it could have had anything to do with her husbands' deaths? "How can my aunt's laudanum matter?"

"I intend to find out."

The coach drew up outside an elegant establishment in the neighborhood of St. James. Charles alit and turned to help her down. "I am about to become the envy of all my friends. Did you look in a mirror before coming out, Georgiana?"

She looked down at her gown and patted her hair into place. "Am I disarrayed?"

He laughed and took her arm. "You are perfection."

A gloved footman in a greatcoat opened tall glass doors

for them and stood aside as they entered a wide foyer. Georgiana was nonplussed to hear a string quartet playing quietly and nearly drowned out by the sound of conversation and laughter. A man standing behind a desk smiled and nodded at Charles. "Good to see you, Mr. Hunter. Will your companion be playing this evening?"

"I believe so. Shall we say fifty pounds, Biddle?"

"Of course." The man made a notation in a large ledger and gave Charles a small chit, which he put in the pocket of his dark jacket.

Biddle came around the desk and held his hand out. "Your wrap, madam?"

Charles moved behind her and slid his hands over her shoulders to take her shawl. She blushed when he skimmed his fingers over the exposed flesh in the deep V between her breasts as he parted the shawl to lift it away. She shivered, her body remembering the sweetness of his touch. His sigh fanned her cheek before he handed Biddle the shawl and led her toward a second set of glass doors where another footman awaited.

The moment that second door opened, Georgiana realized they'd come to a gambling club—a "hell" she'd heard them called. But there was nothing hellish about this establishment. It was opulent to the point of being ostentatious. Gilt moldings, intricate wallpaper and plush carpeting lent an almost decadent feeling. A stunning crystal chandelier, at least twice the size of the largest she'd ever seen, hung in the center of an enormous room casting rainbows of light throughout. An open stairway led to a mezzanine where people milled about, watching the play below. The women below appeared to be a bit older than Georgiana, while the women above were younger and more daringly dressed. And their companions seemed somewhat familiar in their handling of them. *Demireps?*

Dozens of tables, perhaps more, stood at intervals throughout the room, and players were gathered around every one of them. Some tables appeared to be for cards, some for dice, and yet another held a wheel. Heavy velvet draperies shielded alcoves set into the walls, and while she watched, a couple entered one and a moment later, the drape closed. Whatever could be the purpose of that?

For Georgiana, who'd only played casual cribbage with her aunt or whist with friends, the scene was fascinating. And quite exciting. She waited while Charles busied himself with a man in a booth, exchanging his chit from Biddle for counters to gamble.

When he returned to her, he took her arm and led her toward the tables. "What game do you prefer, Georgiana?"

"I've only learned whist and cribbage. Oh, and backgammon."

Charles laughed. "None of that here. The games you played were for society. There is nothing social about Belmonde's. Gambling is serious business."

"But everyone seems so polite. I do not hear any quarrelling or see anyone doing anything…*déclassé.*"

"Look higher and closer, my dear."

She did. Above them, a young man Georgiana could have sworn she had danced with last year stood behind a woman dressed in vivid green. One of his arms wrapped around her middle holding her back against him and the other lingered scandalously near to her breasts. Would he fondle the woman for all to see? She looked away, feeling terribly gauche in such worldly company.

Charles leaned near to her ear. "Do you begin to see what I meant about civil company, Georgiana?"

She nodded. A shout of laughter went up at a table

across the room, and a croupier pushed a pile of counters toward a woman dressed in elegant cerulean blue. When the woman turned to speak to the man beside her, Georgiana recognized her as a countess much respected in the ton. She was a widow, the mother of three and a popular hostess. Then she looked at another woman, and another. They were accompanied by men, too, and were also women she'd met at soirees and balls.

Ah, these were mature women who had earned the right to do as they please. Women whose reputations no longer needed guarding. Women capable of weathering a storm of gossip. Was that why Charles had dared bring her here? That, twice widowed and therefore obviously not virgin, she did not need to guard herself as unmarried women do? Or was it that Georgiana Huffington, whispered to be a murderess, could withstand so small a scandal as gambling?

Suddenly, his motives were important to her. "Charles, why did you really bring me here?"

He stopped and turned to her. "Someone tried to kill me today, Georgiana, and it wasn't the person I was trying to provoke. Between my enemies and yours, death is a breath away. I did not feel like sitting at a polite dinner discussing the weather, politics or the latest *on dit* regarding this duke or that marquis. I wanted to do something to bring an end to this. To flaunt our relationship wherever it might do the most good. To be seen and noted. Certainly not at a family dinner party. We must flush our quarry out of hiding as soon as possible. We may not have much time left. *You* may not have much time."

His words chilled her. "Do you think he will now try to kill me?"

"Not unless our culprit is Walter Foxworthy."

"Why?"

"Because your death would solve his problems. If his suit to become your conservator fails, he loses everything. But with you dead, he is the heir to the Betman fortune unless you conceive. Odd coincidence, is it not, that your husbands have died before they could impregnate you?" Charles smiled and cupped her cheek as he leaned closer. "But no, that is not my concern. If Foxworthy wanted you dead, he'd have made an attempt when you were still unprotected in Kent. If he merely wanted to prevent a future heir, well then, his target would be your husband. If there is anything you've forgotten to mention, Georgie, anything you've withheld, now would be a good time to tell me. Now, before the authorities close in."

She ignored his question for one of her own. "What *is* your concern, Charles?"

"That you could be arrested." He led her to a table where men were casting dice. He leaned close again. "That I could be killed. That time will slip away from us, Georgie. We haven't a moment to spare."

His sense of urgency caught her. "Cease, Charles. Take me home at once. Disassociate yourself from me. I won't be the cause of your death."

"You care what happens to me? I thought you disliked me."

"I've never disliked you."

He laughed and dropped his entire stack of counters on the table after exchanging a few words with another man. As the play began again, he turned back to her. "You lie so charmingly, my dear. No need. I've come to terms with it."

"Charles, you are the one who walked away from me. One day you were kissing me senseless and the next—"

A cheer erupted from the table, and the man beside Charles clapped him on the back as the croupier pushed the winnings toward him. "Congratulations, Hunter."

"Blast," he murmured. He scooped up a handful and passed them to her. "Hold these, will you?"

She cupped her hands and stood quietly while the play continued. The man next to Charles smiled and stepped back from the table to talk to her. "I say, Mrs. Huffington, if you are so lucky for Hunter, perhaps I ought to have you accompany me to a table or two."

He knew her name, so he had to know that she hadn't been particularly lucky for other men. She forced a smile. "Lucky? I think I shall do you a favor and *not* accompany you, sir. Whatever luck Mr. Hunter has had, he has made for himself."

"You are too modest."

The play over, Charles turned to them. "Luck is where you find it, Converse, and I do not intend to share mine." He gave Georgiana a look that made her knees go weak. It was then that she began to understand. His voice, his manners, his heated looks, made it clear that he was making a slow, deliberate love to her. She should have been embarrassed, but she recovered when she recalled that this was his intent—to make society believe that they were lovers, and were, indeed, engaged to be married. She returned his look and was rewarded by a flicker of surprise in his eyes.

They stared at each other in silence until Mr. Converse cleared his throat and moved away. A slow grin bloomed on Charles's face. "Well played, Mrs. Huffington."

A footman brought a small basket for the counters, and another footman offered a tray of wine glasses. Charles took a glass for each of them and led Georgiana to one of the alcoves and a tapestry banquette where they could sit. He put the basket and glasses on a small table, and when he sat close enough for her to feel his heat and smell faint traces of his shaving soap, she felt her expectations rising. Would he kiss her? In public? Or would he drop the drapery to give them privacy?

"Now, what is this about me walking away after our kiss?"

She blinked. How could he not know? Before she could stop herself, she blurted the words she'd guarded since their reintroduction. "Do you really not remember that kiss in Lord Russell's garden? I was so completely taken with you that I'd have allowed you any liberties you wanted. But then you cooled. I would look for you across a room or at a ball, and you were not there. Or, if you were, you would merely glance at me and turn away." There! She'd brought it into the open and she only felt relief, not shame.

"Me? *I* would glance away?"

"I was young. I did not know what I'd done. But I came to believe that I'd allowed you too much access to my person. Only cheap things come easily. You must have thought me very cheap, indeed."

"Cheap? You think our *kiss* did not cost me? Oh, Georgiana, if you only knew what it cost me."

"Then why—"

"Hush," he whispered as he leaned closer, crooking his finger and lifting her chin.

She was on the verge of tears by the time his lips met hers. Softly, worshipfully. When he ran his tongue along the seam of her lips, she moaned as everything inside her loosened. She opened to him and he accepted the invitation, making small licks against her tongue, inviting her to test him—test his resolve, his passion, his determination.

A deep moan rumbled in his chest and resonated in hers. She could feel his tension like a tightly drawn bowstring ready to snap. Just the memory of what he'd done to her the last time they'd been so enraptured caused a burning in her middle and a moistness at her core. He began to stroke her back, pressing her closer and closer. He would not let her break the kiss and catch her breath. Instead she was falling deeper and deeper into that dark swirling mist of desire until she did not want to breathe. Only to feel. To experience his passion. To be joined to him, locked together in body and mind.

He slipped one hand around to touch her breast, then push one side of the deep V of her décolletage aside so that he could find one soft aureole and tease it into a tight aching bud. He pinched it tenderly and a streak of pure primal pleasure shot down her middle to that other, more demanding, bud.

She was so lost to his seduction that she forgot everything but Charles's hand. His mouth. The pleasure was so intense that she dropped her head back to offer her throat with a deep surrendering sigh.

His breathing was coming quick and harsh. "Bloody goddamned hell," he groaned. "Can you stand or shall I carry you out?"

Chapter Thirteen

All Charles could think of was getting Georgiana home before they lost control. He'd never been so swept up in a moment. But he would not subject her to this kind of scrutiny and gossip. This was private business.

He helped her stand and made for the door. As he draped her shawl around her shoulders, he instructed Biddle to cash in his counters and hold the money for him. His carriage was waiting only half a block away and he had Georgiana safely inside within moments of their kiss. This time his lust was not going to get the better of him.

Though she offered her lips when they were settled and the coach had pulled into traffic, he did not accept. Instead he held her hand, stroking her palm with his thumb. Rather than cooling their ardor, the drive and tension between them heightened it. Expectation quickened their breathing, heated their glances, and kept them mute. Words could only diminish what they were feeling.

Arriving at Georgiana's doorstep, he lifted her down and shouted to Peter to go home. He would not need a driver again tonight. Sanders, like any good footman, had been waiting for his mistress's return and opened the door before they reached it. Charles carried Georgiana up the steps and through the door, ignoring the footman's look of astonishment and Finn's confusion.

Clara's wide-eyed expression quickly changed to one of concern. "Is she fallen ill, Mr. Hunter, sir?"

"No," he growled, heading for the stairs.

He should put her down. She was capable of walking, but he did not want to release her. Something fiercely possessive had been born in him the moment she had said, *Do you not remember that kiss in Lord Russell's garden? I was so completely taken with you that I'd have allowed you any liberties you wanted. But then you cooled.*

Cooled? *He* had cooled? Dear God, there had to be some misunderstanding. He had lived that kiss every night since in his dreams. He had looked for it in every woman he'd kissed since. He'd come to believe he'd never experience it again.

Until tonight. Until her wordless surrender had taken him so by surprise that he'd nearly disgraced them both. Even now he knew gossip would be raging about their hasty departure. He'd wanted that, to flush their quarry, but now he was ashamed that he'd allowed Georgiana to be the subject of such talk.

Love? Georgiana? Again?

Her bedroom door was open and he kicked it closed behind them. No need to lock it since no one would bother them tonight. Clara would see to it. Though the lamps were not lit, the fire had been fed and little flickers of light scattered throughout the room. He placed her on her feet and she gasped and swayed as if she hadn't breathed since they'd left Belmonde's.

Her shawl fell to the floor and he threw his jacket on top of it, nearly overwhelmed with his need to have her naked. Quickly.

"Charlie, I don't…" Her voice was a whisper.

No regrets. No second thoughts. "Let tomorrow take care of itself, Georgie. I'm not dead yet."

For a moment he was flummoxed as to how to remove her new gown, but then he ceased to care. He'd buy her a new one. He'd buy her forty—every one an exact copy, and every one to meet the same fate. She caught his urgency and let the buttons fly when she pulled his waistcoat open and pushed it off his shoulders. She reached for his cravat as he parted her gown at the V of her neckline. The fragile silk gave way like mere tissue, leaving her corset and chemise to be dealt with. This one laced at the front and he drew the strings from their hiding place between her breasts.

That merest of touches sent a deep shudder through Georgiana and he was gratified. He wanted her shivering, trembling at his touch. God knew his own nerve endings were itching relentlessly, exquisitely sensitive and driving him toward release.

Unlaced at last, the corset dropped away onto the growing pile of clothes. His cravat and shirt fared the same treatment as her gown. But he slowed a moment to watch her pull her chemise over her head, her arms high and her rose-tipped breasts gloriously bare. He gripped her around her waist and lifted her to fit his mouth first to the right and then the left, teasing the crowns into tight little beads as she tangled her fingers through his hair.

"Charlie…Charlie…" she chanted, and each little entreaty spurred him on.

He laid her on the bed, pulled her slippers off and dropped them on the floor, then paused as he reached for her garters. Soft violet stockings that matched her gown were held up at midthigh by white satin garters and were so erotic that he decided to leave them.

He finished undressing himself, his gaze never leaving the sight of Georgiana, supine and stunning against pristine white sheets. Her eyes half closed, she licked her lips and crooked a knee to make a place for him between her legs. She could not have contrived to say anything so eloquent as that—the simple need to have him fill her and to kiss those lips.

But not yet.

"I want more from you than your acceptance this time," he told her. "I want your participation."

"Yes," she purred. "Yes, yes…"

He lay down beside her, wondering how long he could maintain his self-control. Not long, he thought. But long enough to slow her down sufficiently to make it last. To make it memorable. There was a fine edge between release and completion, a matter of intensity, and he would teach her the differences and advantage of each.

Release first.

He knelt between her thighs, savoring the sight of her there, her olivine eyes glowing with unquenched passion. *His.* She smiled when she realized what he was doing— learning her, watching her, worshiping her. And she returned the favor, her eyes traveling down his chest to his shaft. Her eyes widened and he watched as she swallowed hard. His flesh tightened as his cock grew and twitched in response. Her breathing hitched and he eased himself downward until his mouth was level with those beckoning rosy buds. He flicked his thumbnails over them and she gasped. Slowly, he began to nibble at first one, then the other, until she crooked both knees to cradle him.

Reading that sign as readiness, he slipped one hand down to her core. Still nibbling her breasts, he stroked her, gathering her dew until his fingers slid easily into her. She moaned and her hips jerked upward. He could feel her internal quivering, and it only took a moment to bring her to a small orgasm. She twisted beneath him, panting, her chest heaving.

"That, sweet Georgie, was release," he instructed.

"Oh!" She gulped. "Th-thank you."

He chortled. "The pleasure was mine. And now for the rest."

"Rest?"

He knew he'd only bought them a little time before the passion built to unbearable levels again. Though used to self-denial, he was not certain he could deny himself much longer.

He kissed his way downward, seeking her mound and the hidden nub with his lips and tongue while he spread her legs a bit wider to accommodate him there. He trailed his fingers down her inner thighs to the garters and stockings, reveling in the smooth heated silk so like her inner sheath. The comparison caused a wanting, an unrelenting need, that seized him, overpowering both reason and reluctance. He wanted Georgiana, and he would have her. Nothing on this earth would stop him. Ever.

He found her with his tongue and stroked deeply, drawing a surprised gasp from her. She tasted of sex and love, and her scent was an aphrodisiac to him. If he didn't take her soon, he'd die of the pain.

Moments later her hands left his shoulders and gripped the bedposts so tightly her knuckles whitened. She began chanting his name again, this time with a hint of desperation. "Charlie...Charlie...*help me, Charlie...*"

Thank God. He rose above her, wanting to do this right. Wanting to give her the most intense pleasure of her life. She arched to him, her hands abandoning the bedposts for the less solid bulwark of his arms. "Now, Charlie. Please."

Those words were piercingly sweet and utterly satisfying. She did not have to ask twice. He found her as surely as the stars point true north. Her thighs quivered as he entered her. She was heated and tight, her inner muscles gripping him in a snug velvet fist. He lifted and sank again, this time deeper. She fit herself to accommodate him again and again until she was writhing and keening as her inner muscles contracted rhythmically and tears trickled into the dark blond masses of hair beneath her.

And, at last, his control snapped. A kaleidoscope of rapture, pleasure and pain controlled him, overwhelmed him as he drove deeper into her one last time in a shattering finish unlike any he'd ever experienced.

When he was coherent again, when Georgiana's eyes opened in sated wonder, he said, "And that, my love, was completion."

Georgiana propped herself up against a mound of pillows and watched Charles dress. Broad chest, narrow hips and long legs all disappeared beneath proper clothing, but she would never look at him the same, clothed or not. She thought she'd always see him as he'd been last night— strong, confident, skilled and so very handsome. And so very...*knowing*. The dark shadow of his whiskers only added to his utterly masculine charm.

He turned to her as he tied an elaborate knot in his cravat. He smiled and his fingers faltered for a moment. "Damn, Georgiana. Must you look so tempting? I have half a mind to come back to bed."

She glanced at the slice of sun intruding through a gap in the draperies and stretched languorously. She did not want him to leave, anyway. "You may as well stay. Too late to fool the neighbors now."

He laughed. "With any luck, they will think I've paid an early call. But it will not matter soon."

"No? Why? Do you know who has been killing my husbands?"

"Not yet. But we shall be married by this time tomorrow."

She giggled. "What are we going to say? That we acquired a special license?"

"I did. We are now permitted to marry without banns at any time and place of our choosing."

"Quite thorough of you, Charles, and rather expensive. But do you really think anyone will inquire at the Archbishop's office to see if we've told the truth?"

He sighed deeply, as if preparing himself for unpleasant news. A few steps had him at her bedside. He took her hands and brought each one to his lips for a tender kiss. "Georgiana, I have business to be about today. First, I am going to my local parish to arrange to be married tomorrow. Then I hoped to collect you so that we may inform my family and ask them to witness our vows. Afterward I have an appointment to interview a man who might have useful information. Oh, and Lord Carlington has invited us to dine at his home tonight. I hope you do not mind that I accepted for us both."

"Mind?" She could scarcely think, let alone form a protest. "Marriage? Will your minister perform a mock ceremony? Surely that must violate some ecclesiastical ethic, Charles."

"Nothing mock about it, my dear. We will be married. In law and in God's eyes."

"No! I mean…no. I cannot marry. And certainly not you."

"I will not leave you to fend for yourself another day. Even Finn must sleep sometime. After our vows I intend to move your household to mine. My servants are used to keeping a lookout for trouble. And cheer up, my dear. If your luck holds true, you shall not be married for long."

Ice formed somewhere in the region of her heart. How could he even jest about such a thing? "You will be hard-pressed to marry me, Charles Hunter, when I am standing there saying no."

He smiled and caressed her cheek. A tingle of desire spiraled upward to firm her breasts. "Last night you said you wanted me, Georgiana. I took you at your word. You certainly did not act as if you found me unacceptable."

She leaned her head against his chest and held on to his shirtsleeves. "Charles, I am terrified for you. I have wished from the beginning that I had not let you goad me into our ridiculous agreement."

"Nevertheless…"

"No."

"The only one trying to kill me at the moment is that scum-dwelling sewer rat, Dick Gibbons. That will not change whether we marry or not."

He lifted her chin and smiled. "If I can keep you nearer, we will both be safer, Georgiana. I find that I am always trying to keep an eye on you, and that distracts me. Aside from that, there are other forces afoot. My name may offer you a measure of protection—privilege, if you will—should the worst happen."

The worst? Should he die? But his deep violet eyes were so clear and convincing that she could almost believe him. "What forces, Charles?" He blinked and she knew he was searching for words. They must be very dire indeed if he did not want to voice them.

"For one, we've been intimate. You could be with child even now."

Shocked, she glanced down at her stomach, suddenly

foreign territory to her. With child? How she would love to have Charles's baby. Warmth crept through her every fiber at the mere thought.

"I warn you, Georgiana, I will not father a bastard. My child will be mine. Recognized and raised by me. My heir. A Hunter."

Her resolve began to crumble. "And when it's over? When we've discovered the truth? And if I am not with child? By then you'd be stuck with me."

"A burden I am willing to bear," he said with a grin.

Married. She was going to be married. Again. But this time she wanted it with her whole heart. And was terrified of the consequences. But she could see his determination in every line of his body. She sighed and nodded. "Yes."

His grin widened and he hugged her so tightly she was barely able to breath, then shrugged into his waistcoat and jacket. "I shall be back at two o'clock to take you to Lockwood's house."

"Please, Charles, tell them alone. They will have concerns and will want to be free to voice them in a way they would not if I were present." She feared that Sarah, most of all, would feel betrayed by this development. No doubt she would never have agreed to help her if she'd thought her brother would be at risk. "I would not start our marriage with their resentment."

"If you are certain."

"There are things I should take care of, too. I have been putting off dealing with Aunt Caroline's personal bequests and I will need to gather her papers if I am to remove to your home."

He studied her face for a moment and she knew he wanted to protest. In the end, he saw the sense in her request. "If you wish. Then I shall call at seven to take you to Carlington's."

* * *

The wide white door opened and Georgiana handed the
butler her calling card. A moment later he opened the door
wider to admit her and Finn, who had been lurking at her
back all day. "Lady Aston will see you, Mrs. Huffington."

Surprised, she gave Finn a nod to wait for her by the
door before she followed the butler down a wide corridor
to another door on the right. She'd only meant to leave her
card and perhaps make an appointment for a later date.
Calling unannounced was discourteous, Aunt Caroline
had always told her.

A flood of warm afternoon light spilled into the corridor and temporarily blinded Georgiana as she stepped
inside wondering what she might expect.

"Ah, you've come at last, Mrs. Huffington," a well-
modulated voice spoke as a woman came toward her, her
hand extended in welcome. "I have been expecting you
since I learned of dear Caro's death."

Georgiana's vision cleared and she smiled. She'd seen
this handsome woman at various functions in the past,
but they hadn't been introduced and she hadn't realized
that Lady Aston had an acquaintance with her guardian.
She appeared to be of Caroline's age. "I am sorry if I've
kept you waiting," Georgiana murmured as she took the
offered hand and dropped a quick curtsy.

The woman laughed and Georgiana instinctively liked
her. No wonder her aunt had not given up their friendship, even if it had been through correspondence since
her accident.

"No need. I have not been on pins and needles, my
dear." She waved at a grouping of chairs. "I knew you'd
come to me sooner or later. Please sit down. I've asked
Franklin to bring tea."

Georgiana removed her gloves and perched on the edge

of a chair facing Lady Aston's. "I shan't stay long, Lady Aston. If you were expecting me, I presume you know why I've come?"

"I do, indeed. You've brought me something, have you not?"

Georgiana opened her reticule and removed the packet she'd found with Aunt Caroline's will. "Her instructions were emphatic that I should deliver it into your hands only and that only you should open it. I shall step out of the room if you wish, Lady Aston."

She waved airily. "Not necessary, Mrs. Huffington. I believe I know what the letter contains." She slipped a tapered fingernail beneath the seal, opened the packet and dumped the contents onto her lap.

A small brooch studded with tiny sapphires and diamonds flashed shards of light as the sunbeams reached it. Georgiana recognized it as one her aunt had often worn. She must have put it in the packet on their last visit to town. Then a folded piece of parchment emerged. Lady Aston unfolded the page and read, nodding at intervals.

Georgiana knew that she was to stay until the packet had been opened lest there be any questions, and now she wondered what questions Lady Aston might have. The whole thing seemed so mysterious.

After Lady Aston refolded the page and slipped it back into the packet, she lifted the little brooch and turned it in her hand, a melancholy smile hovering at the corners of her mouth. "Caro was given this by her father upon her completion of school. I always admired it so and she promised it would be mine one day. I had completely forgotten until I saw it again. How very like her to keep her promises to the end."

"She was always a woman of her word," Georgiana agreed.

"She was also lively and popular. Of all of us at Mrs. Horn's school, she was most likely to marry well. Then... the tragedy. How very sad for a life so full of promise to end that way."

Georgiana studied the stitching on her gloves to cover the quick tears that stung her eyes.

"Yet she wrote of you so often, Georgiana, if I may call you that?"

"Of course, Lady Aston."

"You were her chief interest in life after her father died and she fetched you home. Her letters were full of the news of your accomplishments and successes. And I can see for myself that she did not lie about how beautiful you are."

She never realized that Aunt Caroline had bragged of her. That knowledge was bittersweet. It would have been nice to know while Caroline was still alive. "Thank you."

The thought suddenly occurred to her that, if Lady Aston had been at school with Lady Caroline, perhaps she had known Georgiana's mother, too. "Did...did you know my mother, Lady Aston?"

"I loved her like a sister. She was my best friend," the woman said, her tone lowering with sadness. "And she remained my best friend until she died six months ago."

"Six..." Georgiana could not comprehend that statement. Her mother had died two-and-twenty years ago. Aunt Caroline had died six months ago. Aunt Caroline...

Lady Aston leaned forward and patted Georgiana's hand. "I see you have caught my meaning."

Georgiana's pulse raced and she felt peculiarly light-headed. "Aunt Caroline was...was..."

"She was. Her father would not allow her to keep you. He removed Caroline from their home before her condition began to show and took you away the moment you were born. It was almost three years before Caroline found you. Once her father died, she brought you home."

"But she was not married."

"It happens that way, sometimes, Georgiana. I did not judge Caroline, and neither must you."

Her mind reeled at this revelation. "I am...a bastard."

"Tch! No one must know that, dear. Caroline took every precaution that you were protected from that stigma. I am the only one Caroline told, and you are the only one *I* will ever tell. That is what was in this letter, you know— not the truth itself, but her request that I finally tell you the truth. The facts themselves are not written anywhere."

Then this was why Aunt Caroline had instructed her to wait until the letter had been read. "She...she could have, *should* have, told me."

"She did not want you to know while she was still alive. She was ashamed and could not have endured your disgust. You see, she did not know she was with child when she had her accident. By the time she recovered sufficiently to realize, well, she was devastated by her appearance and had decided to retire from society. She swore to me that there was never a question of marrying your father."

"My father? Who was my father?"

"I am certain that was another thing Caroline would never have wanted to tell you. She never said, though I have my suspicions."

"Who?"

But Lady Aston merely shook her head. "I cannot say. If I am wrong it would be a grave disservice to the man in question, and a stain upon Caroline's honor."

But all Georgiana could think was that her own mother had never told her the truth. Had never desired that relationship. The closeness that only two people of the same blood could share. Georgiana had mourned the loss of a mother and father who had never existed. Her stomach twisted into a knot at the knowledge that she'd been so thoroughly deceived by the only person she'd ever trusted.

"It is not so very unusual, my dear. Why, it happens all the time, and in the best of families. Often the error is discovered in time to rectify with a quick marriage. Other times, the mother must go away and bear her secret alone. But Caroline was exceedingly careful to construct a history for you that would allow you to enter society and to marry well."

Yes, and it also explained why she'd always felt like a "duty" and why her guardian—her mother—had never been able to love her. Georgiana had been a constant reminder of her mother's shame. Hot tears trickled down her cheeks and she pulled a handkerchief from her reticule to blot them away. She had to get away. Had to think what to do.

She stood and wadded her hankie into the palm of her hand. "I beg your pardon, Lady Aston, but I really must be going. So much to do, you know. I was to marry Charles Hunter tomorrow, and I must find him to stop it."

Lady Aston came to her feet, too. "No, my dear. That would be a very good marriage for you. The Hunters are an excellent family, respected and well thought of."

"A good marriage for me, perhaps. Better than I could expect. But Charles? I think not, Lady Aston. Illegitimate children are rarely accepted in the ton."

"No one will ever know you are illegitimate. You are of excellent stock as Lady Caroline Betman's daughter. I beg you, Georgiana, do not do anything rash. Think of all Caroline sacrificed to keep your secret safe. Mr. Hunter need never know. Promise me you will ponder this before you act."

"I promise," she said. In truth, she'd have promised anything to escape that house and unravel this web of deceit.

Chapter Fourteen

Charles knocked on the door of a small cottage in St. John's Wood. Praying the address was correct and the man was still alive, he breathed a little easier when an elderly man with silvered hair peeked around the panel and smiled. "Something I can do for you?"

"Are you Tom Clark?"

He nodded. "I am. And who might you be?"

"Charles Hunter, of the Home Office. I'd like to talk to you about one of your old cases."

"Call me Tom," the man said, opening the door wider to admit Charles, then led him into a small room inside the tidy cottage and waved at two chairs set before a fire.

"Thank you for seeing me, Tom."

"Not too many people come looking for information about things that happened back then. What case is it?"

"I found your name in a file, Tom," he explained as he settled in the chair. "I gather you were one of the first to arrive at the accident."

"What accident was that, sir?"

"A coaching accident involving a young woman—Lady Caroline Betman."

The man frowned as if he was trying to recall the incident. Then his face cleared and he ran his gnarled fingers through his hair. "That wasn't an accident," he said.

"The report says that the coach overturned as it came around a corner. Speculation had it that the driver was going too fast."

"Aye. That was the story. And the driver was dead, so there weren't no arguing the point."

This piece of news was interesting, but could this man's memory be trusted? "And you think it was not an accident?"

"Stake my life on it, sir. One of the worst cases I ever worked."

Charles sat back in the chair. This was a surprise. He hadn't expected to learn anything so very different from the facts in the file. "Then why do the files say—"

"It's who she was, sir. A lady. A peer's daughter. Nobody wanted a scandal. And I was ordered not to talk. Ever."

"Your secret is safe within these walls, Tom. We are on the same side here. Lady Caroline passed away six months ago, and her father a few years after the accident. No one could be hurt by the truth now."

Tom looked down at his hands, resting in his lap. "Then why is it important?"

"It concerns a case I am working on. I think there may be a connection. At the very least, I need to determine if your case has any bearing or effect on the one I am investigating."

"Don't know how…"

"Neither do I, but there are some circumstances that are the same."

"I hope not. The Betman case was awful. Tragic."

Charles tented his fingers and waited. He sensed that

Tom wanted to talk but was still wrestling with his conscience.

After a moment the man sighed and looked up again. "Me and Frank Grayson were first ones there. Someone put a ramp on the inside corner so that when a coach turned the corner, one side of the wheels would raise and it would tip. It wasn't no accident, sir. It was a robbery. The driver was already dead, but not from the wreck. Somebody slit his throat. Blood everywhere. *Everywhere.*"

"What of Lady Caroline?"

"She'd been pulled from the coach and we found her in a nearby alley. She'd been cut real bad. Couldn't even make out her face."

"Were her injuries from the accident or from the robbers?"

"Robbers, we thought. Not enough broken glass to do that kind of damage. Only thing we wondered was if it happened before or after."

"If what happened before or after the accident?"

"What was done to the young lady."

"What *was* done to the young lady?"

Tom looked at him for a long moment, then looked away. "She was dragged outta the coach and robbed, sir. They'd cut her purse strings and pulled her jewelry off. Left marks on her throat where her necklace had been. Even her clothes were in shreds. Whoever did it musta liked his work. Went beyond the usual. Vicious, it was. We—me and Frank—thought she might have put up a fight for her jewels."

Charles stilled as Dick Gibbons flashed through his mind. He and his brother, Artie, would have been operating at that time, and they were notorious for using a knife as their weapon of preference. But even this went beyond their usual methods.

"The lady was incoherent. Couldn't have talked much if she wanted to. Her mouth was cut from the corner to her jawbone and in other places, too."

"Why didn't they finish the job and kill her? Were they interrupted?"

"Maybe they thought she was already dead. She was the next thing to it. Lost enough blood to be unconscious." Tom began to wring his hands, a nervous gesture Charles could appreciate. The retelling of such a gruesome attack could not have been easy.

"Did you have any leads at all? Any clues pointing to who might have been behind this?"

"Nothing. We got a description of what was stolen and watched jewelry shops for more than a year in case anything showed up. Nothing. It was like it never happened."

"You worked the case that long?"

"Me and Frank did. On our own. The Home Office didn't want any part of it. Told us to leave it alone and keep our mouths shut."

"Why? If this had happened to my daughter, I'd have hounded the authorities until this day—if I hadn't already handled the matter myself."

"That's what me and Frank thought. But we were called in and told to stop askin' questions. His lordship had whisked the girl back to the countryside and wanted the whole thing kept quiet. We were to say it was an accident if anyone asked. And we have. Until today, sir."

Charles took a deep breath and sat forward. "I appreciate the truth, Tom. It may help on the case I'm working now. But tell me, when did you retire?"

"Few years ago. Still do some work on the side to keep body and soul together."

"Have you ever heard of Dick and Artie Gibbons?"

The blood drained from Tom's face. "Aye. Run afoul of 'em once or twice. Artie's dead now, I hear."

"Is there any chance this could be their work?"

"Me and Frank wondered that. They'd been at work for a while by then. We wanted to talk to them about it, but, like I said, we were told to drop it."

Lord Betman had evidently been determined to hush the whole matter up. Charles tried to put himself in Betman's place and shook his head. How could the man just let this pass? Yes, he'd have wanted to protect his daughter from scrutiny and scandal, but he should have wanted the bastards who did that to be caught and punished.

Charles remembered the papers in the ancient file he'd pulled at the office. The scant information it contained was largely useless since the report was fictitious. The file had been cleaned of any trace of truth. "I did not find a description of the stolen goods, Tom. Do you recall the details?"

The man shook his head. "I remember there was a necklace, a ring or two, earbobs and a comb for her hair. But I don't remember what they looked like. Her purse was never found. Don't know how much of the ready she had."

Charles knew the habits of an agent—after all, he was one. "Any chance you might have notes on the case?"

"'Twas a long time ago, sir. Might be able to dig something up. Lots of boxes in the attic."

Charles stood and pulled a banknote from his waistcoat pocket and gave it to Tom. "Thank you for talking to me. You've been a great help. Should you remember anything else or find your notes on the case, please come to me."

Reluctantly, Tom took the banknote, stood and walked with Charles to the door. "I've thought of that poor girl often over the years. Whatever happened to her?"

"As I mentioned before, Lady Caroline died recently. I believe she lived the remainder of her life in virtual seclusion, but she took an orphan in after her father died, so she was not entirely alone."

"Aye. That's good, then." The man nodded to himself as he closed the door.

The circumstances of Caroline Betman's tragedy must have haunted the man all these year to have asked such a question. God's witness, it haunted Charles now. One thing was certain. He could not tell Georgiana. She was too vulnerable now to bear such disturbing details.

He mounted his horse and turned back toward the city.

The packet from Lady Caroline to Lord Carlington secured in her reticule, Georgiana settled herself in Charles's coach and met his gaze as the coach started off for Lord Carlington's house. She could not think what to say considering that she dared not blurt what she was thinking. *How could she marry him under false pretenses?*

"You are looking pensive, Georgiana. Care to share your thoughts?"

She cleared her throat and smoothed the soft coral gown that had arrived from the dressmaker's this afternoon. "I was thinking about tomorrow, Charles."

"Ah, yes. Lockwood has insisted that we say our vows at the family home. Lockwood's home, actually. The minister will attend us there, and my family has promised to be present, as well. Lockwood and Andrew will sign as our witnesses."

She twisted the cord of her reticule, dreading the answer to her next question. "And did they try to persuade you to think better of such a rash decision?"

"Hmm. Well, something was mentioned regarding the hasty nature of our wedding."

"How did you answer?"

He grinned. "I told them I could not wait and that you'd tried to dissuade me but I would not hear of it. They said no more. Sarah, however, mentioned that she'd be looking for a new pastime now that all her brothers would be married. And what was said on your side, Georgiana?"

She sighed, beginning to feel a bit better now that she knew Sarah hadn't been angry. "Clara is beside herself. Between our marriage and Finn's arrival, she has more than enough to interest her. Sanders and the others are taking the news in their stride. I think, given our behavior the past few days, they were expecting something of the sort."

"Did you tell them that my staff would be coming to facilitate your move?"

"Sanders said he would supervise. Unless you have need of furniture and household items, Charles, I think we should leave mine in place and only remove the personal things and the few valuables I have."

"My furniture should be adequate." He paused and frowned. "I say, you have not been to my house, have you?"

She shook her head.

"Remiss of me. I apologize."

"For heaven's sake, Charles! That will be remedied tomorrow. We've only been reacquainted for…what? Little more than a week?"

He laughed. "Bit of a whirlwind, eh?"

"I shudder to think what the ton will say. I shall be accused of heaven knows what. I used to wonder how Aunt Caroline…how she found me husbands so quickly. I think I may have beaten her record."

"She chose your husbands? Did you have nothing to say about them?"

"Whatever I thought did not seem to matter. She was

determined to see me settled, and the one time I had a decided opinion, it came to nothing."

"When was that?"

Oh, no. She would not give him that satisfaction. Not yet. He was too smug as it was. She waved her glove airily. "A few years ago. A young man who turned my head and disappeared."

He frowned. "Were you between husbands at the time?"

"Between marriage and mourning, I have hardly been anything *but* between husbands, Charles."

"Your luck is turning, Mrs. Huffington. You stand to be married now long into your old age."

"Pray that is so," she murmured under her breath. But the looming alternative sobered her buoyant mood.

Charles leaned forward from his position across from her and took her hands in his. "Count on it, Georgiana. Count on me."

And she would have, had she been no wiser today than she'd been yesterday. But today she was not his equal. Today she was illegitimate.

They remained holding hands until the coach arrived at a lovely two-story stone manor house. A liveried footman opened the coach door and Charles, ever the gentleman, sprang down to offer her his hand.

She was surprised to find that the dinner party was intimate indeed—just Charles and herself. They were shown to a gilt-ceilinged dining room, where Lord Carlington waited, a glass in his hand.

"When Hunter did not bring you to tea right away, I thought I could lure you here with dinner," he explained. "There's so much I'd like to ask you, m'dear." He held her chair, on the right side of the head of the long table.

Charles sat across from her and Lord Carlington took

his place at the head. At a nod to a footman, the servants brought the first course, a delicious chicken bisque soup.

"I hope you do not mind discussing your late guardian, my dear."

"Not in the least," she said. "Aunt Caroline was a wonderful woman. I have so many happy memories."

He grinned. "Did she grow fat and content in her later days?"

She returned his smile. "She was trim to the end."

"Did she ever speak of me?"

Georgiana considered how to answer the question without hurting his lordship's pride. "She never mentioned names, Lord Carlington, but occasionally, when she was melancholy, she would speak wistfully of a young man for whom she had a deep love."

"Ah." He sighed. "Was she often melancholy?"

More often than Georgiana wanted to admit. She would not strip her mother of her pride, even in death. "Only on occasion. She kept herself quite busy, you know."

"Did she? What sort of thing occupied her time?"

"Me." She laughed. "I fear I was not always biddable."

"And I fear that is a continuing problem," Charles said, putting his spoon aside. "Georgiana has a very strong will."

"Ah. A strong will serves a girl well. Had Caroline a stronger will…"

She would have liked to hear the end of that sentence, but Charles broke the awkward pause. "'Twas all I could do to persuade her to marry me on the morrow."

Lord Carlington looked surprised. "You are to wed? So soon?"

Georgiana felt the now familiar heat of a blush rising to her cheeks as Charles answered for them both. "Not as suddenly as one might think, Carlington. Georgiana and

I have been long acquainted. Sadly, I had not been able to catch her between husbands till now."

Lord Carlington guffawed. "Well done, Hunter! Keep after your quarry until she is yours, eh?"

"If you want something badly enough, it is the only path."

The next course was served and conversation flowed easily. Lord Carlington seemed interested in the details of Lady Caroline's daily life, and in her illnesses, as well. Sooner than Georgiana expected, a strawberry ice was served and dinner was over.

Lord Carlington held her chair for her and they retired to the library.

"I hope you do not mind joining us for brandy, my dear," he said. "I should have invited some ladies to keep you company."

"I do not mind in the least," she said, taking his arm.

The library, a cavernous room with floor to ceiling bookshelves and fireplaces at both ends, was softly lit and inviting. She could not help thinking that Caroline would have enjoyed being mistress of such a house.

Then the thought struck her. Could Lord Carlington be her father? Had he and Caroline...

Lord Carlington led them to a grouping of chairs near one of the fires and indicated where they should sit before going to a side table to pour brandies for himself and Charles. "Would you like tea or wine, my dear?" he asked her.

Still puzzling the sudden notion that this man might be her father, she needed something stronger than tea. "Wine, if you please, Lord Carlington."

He brought her a glass, then sank into his chair with a contented sigh. "I suppose, by now, that you have guessed that I was a little in love with Lady Caroline."

She glanced at Charles and noted his grin. "I wondered at your uncommon interest."

"I wrote her many times after her accident, you know. She ceased to return my letters after a while, begging me to get on with my life, and without her." He drank deeply and stretched his legs out toward the fire.

"I am sorry, Lord Carlington," Georgiana said.

"No. She was right, of course. Had she not pushed me away, I'd still be waiting for her."

She and Charles exchanged a glance and she surmised they were thinking the same thing—that Lord Carlington had not gotten on with his life. He had never married. And, in his own way, he was still waiting for her.

"Was she...was she badly scarred, my dear?"

"I loved her. To me, she was beautiful. But to the outside world, she would have been...hideous. Only her eyes were unaffected. They were beautiful eyes, I recall."

"The most beautiful ever I saw," he agreed. "I wish she had not hidden from me."

"She hid from everyone, my lord. She wore a veil even around the servants. I think her Abigail and I were the only ones who saw her without it."

"Did she ever speak of me?"

"She spoke of her years growing up, her days at school, and then of her life after the accident, but she did not speak of the short time between. That is why I was so very surprised when I found this with her final instructions." She pulled the little packet from the reticule dangling at her wrist and leaned forward to present it to the earl.

His eyes widened and his hand trembled as he took the packet, staring at the writing as if it were something precious. She realized he wanted to open it more than he wanted to breathe.

Charles stood and went to put his glass on the mantel,

a pensive look on his face. "Would you mind if I showed Georgiana the gardens, Carlington?"

He looked up at Charles with an expression of profound gratitude. "Please do. I believe the roses are budding."

Charles gave him a small bow and took her by the arm to lead her out the French door. "You did not mention you'd brought Carlington a present, Georgiana."

"I did not know if the opportunity would arise for me to give him the letter."

"I am glad you did. What was in it?"

She shrugged. "It was sealed, Charles. I haven't the faintest notion what is in it, but there is something more than a letter. I could feel a small lump."

"A love token, unless I miss my guess."

"Do you think...they might have been lovers?" Georgiana glanced back toward the house.

"Appears to be a tragic love story. If she had not encouraged him, if there had not been something deep between them, he would not still be sighing over her all these years later."

Tears stung her eyes. How impossibly sad. Lord Carlington had remained faithful to Caroline all these years. Had lived with hope that she might someday return to him. While she, who had loved Charles since the first time she'd seen him, had allowed herself to be passed from husband to husband because she'd lost all hope.

Charles stopped and turned to look into her eyes. "You are deeply affected by this, are you not?"

"My...aunt Caroline's life was very lonely. I cannot help wondering what would have happened if she had allowed him to visit. To see her. I am tempted to believe that he would have loved her anyway."

Charles was silent as they began walking again and she knew that he doubted her words.

"She really was horribly scarred, you know," she reminded him. "Perhaps, if Lord Carlington were not a public figure, or hadn't had obligations, Aunt Caroline's appearance would not have mattered."

"But he did, Georgiana. And that made all the difference."

Her own guilty secret rose to taunt her. Perhaps, if she weren't illegitimate, she would not have so many misgivings about marrying Charles. Would her circumstances hold him back? Cause him embarrassment? "Do you think it is so terribly important, Charles? Who we are? Should it make a difference?"

He was silent as they strolled past an arbor where fragrant roses would soon bloom. When he spoke, she knew he had considered his answer. "Perhaps it shouldn't, but it does. Futures rest upon who you are and what you do. Caroline was right to have refused to see him. He could not deny his responsibilities. That could only have brought more pain."

"Yet you have overlooked who I am. An orphan with no connections. A woman who has become scandalous by virtue of her circumstances. Marriage to me could damage your reputation or your prospects. We should call it off before it is too late."

He turned her back toward the house. "It is growing late, Georgiana. I think Carlington has had enough time to read your aunt's letter. We should go back."

His lack of a reply to her offer was telling—an acknowledgment that she was inferior in society's eyes but that he was determined to go through with the marriage at any cost. Would he still if he knew the worst of her past? She took his arm again as they turned. "Do you think it is because of her that he is still unmarried?"

"He had an obligation to provide an heir for his title,

and he did not. Any wellborn woman would have fit his needs, yet he remained single. There must be a reason for that."

"I did not realize that men could languish over lost love as women do."

He gave her a wry smile. "Did you not?"

"I have seen no evidence of it. Most men have wives and mistresses. Which do they love, if either?"

"That would depend upon their reason for marrying, Georgiana."

What would that say about Charles's reason for marrying her? "Do you have a mistress, Charles?"

"Not at the moment."

"Will you have one again?"

He coughed. "We are marrying tomorrow."

"Yes, but—"

The French doors opened and Lord Carlington peered out. "There you are. Wondered what happened to you."

Georgiana noted his reddened eyes and his flushed cheeks. Whatever Caroline had written him had affected him deeply.

Charles saw his state, too, and interceded. "We really must be going, Carlington. Much to do tomorrow, you know."

"Oh, of course. Well, thank you for coming." He led them toward the door. "Lovely visit. And I was quite pleased to read Caroline's letter after all these years. Still the most beautiful script. She had a very fine hand, did she not, Georgiana?"

"Yes. I think she was a bit vain about it."

He laughed. "I recall. I used to peek over her shoulder when she'd write in her little journals. She'd shoo me away and say that her scribblings were not meant for men. Did she keep them up, my dear? Those little diaries?"

"Every day, though I wondered what she could possibly have to say when our lives were so quiet."

Carlington cleared his throat as a footman opened the door for them. "If there is nothing too personal, I'd like to read them. I would be interested in what her days were like. And her nights."

Georgiana blinked back her tears. She had not thought of her aunt's journals since she'd died. In fact, she could not remember her aunt writing in them at all after their last return to Kent. Perhaps there were some in the attic at the town house. She would have to read them first, of course, to make certain there was nothing that would compromise Caroline's dignity.

"I will look for them, Lord Carlington. If I should find one or two fit for male eyes, I will be glad to share them."

He took her hand and squeezed it in gratitude. "I shall look forward to it."

Chapter Fifteen

Once Georgiana had finished bathing, Clara dressed her hair into a Grecian knot from which curls were left to dangle down her back, and made shooing motions with her hands. "Go on with you, now! You will only get in my way. Mind you, do not muss yourself. This is your wedding day. Just sit somewhere and look pretty."

Georgiana slipped a modest gown over her head and left her room, noting the whirlwind of activity everywhere in the house. Charles's servants had arrived and were busily crating the belongings she would take with her. And, in a matter of hours, she would be married again.

Fear was growing in her and she was near panic. The closer the wedding, the closer Charles could be to death. How could she go through with it? How could she marry him without telling him the truth of her birth?

One of Charles's servants passed her in the foyer with a muffled apology and she knew she would have to find someplace quiet to think. She turned and went back upstairs to the attic. The windows were still uncovered and it didn't look as though anything had been disturbed since the last time she'd been up here just before Charles evicted Hathaway.

One of the opened trunks was a small one she thought might contain her aunt's—no, her *mother's,* journals. She had never looked in that trunk, respecting Caroline's privacy, but Hathaway had had no such qualms. She fingered the latch and noted that the lock had been forced. What could he have been looking for?

She sat on the bare floor, lifted the little trunk into her lap and began removing the journals to take stock. Each one bore dates on the inside covers but they were out of order. She found one that began when Caroline was away at school with Lady Aston. By matching the date of the last entry of one journal to the date on the insider cover of another, she put them in order and found that only a few were missing. Perhaps they were back in Kent, perhaps never written. Surely Hathaway had not taken them. What use would he have for such things? She searched for the dates she knew by heart. The year that she was born was missing, but she found the one from three years later when Lady Caroline had brought her home from Cornwall.

Oh, she was full of "duty" and "obligation," but there was no mention made of love. She was reported to have been "an amiable child, not overly fussy or demanding." She had "cheered the servants after the bleakness following father's death." None of them "suspected the truth." Reference was made to Caroline's having been sent away to Devon for her pregnancy, so the servants or neighbors would not suspect. They'd been told she had gone to a private nursing hospital to convalesce from her injuries as a result of the accident.

And never—not once—was there mention of her father. Was he living or dead? Was he a secret affair? Or could he have been Lord Carlington?

Georgiana closed the journal and wondered if the answer was in any of the journals, or if the truth would always elude her. What, dear Lord, could she tell Charles? It was bad enough that she'd been born out of wedlock, but that she did not even know the name of her father was untenable. Unthinkable. Surely telling Charles the truth would be easier if she could name her father.

She closed the journal quickly when she heard a scuffle on the stairs. "Madam? Are you up there?"

"Yes, Clara."

"There's a Mr. Foxworthy at the door, missus. Says he must see you at once. I told him you were not receiving today, but he insisted."

Foxworthy? Good heavens! "Put him in the front parlor, Clara, and tell him I will be down in a moment."

She replaced the journal hastily, closed the lid and carried the trunk in front of her as she descended the narrow attic stairs. Finn was waiting for her, his massive arms crossed over his chest and a frown of disapproval marring his brow. She pushed the trunk into his arms. "Give that to Clara, will you? I'd like it packed with the rest."

Finn held the trunk tightly but ignored her instructions. Instead he followed her down the two flights of stairs and across the foyer to the parlor. She paused outside the door to pat her hair and smooth her skirts, took one deep breath in preparation and opened the door, Finn fast behind her.

A man who appeared slightly older than Lord Carlington turned from his study of the garden outside the window. He was not unpleasant looking, but appeared very stern and uncompromising. "Mrs. Huffington?"

She went forward, her hand extended. "Indeed. And you are Mr. Foxworthy?"

"Mr. Walter Foxworthy," he corrected, ignoring her offered hand.

"I did not know you were in London, sir."

"No reason you should. Our branches of the family

have not been close for a generation or more." He gripped the lapels of his brown jacket and puffed his chest out. "I say 'ours,' Mrs. Huffington, but I am referring to Cousin Caroline. You are not a true Betman."

A truer Betman than he knew, but she did not intend to tell him that. "I'm aware of the distinction, sir," she allowed.

"I have just come from Mr. Goodman. He informs me that you are aware of my suit."

"To become my conservator? Yes."

Mr. Foxworthy glanced at Finn. "I believe this is a private conversation, Mrs. Huffington."

She turned and smiled at Finn. "Will you excuse us, Finn? You may wait outside the door."

"I cannot leave you alone with strangers, Mrs. Huffington."

"Mr. Foxworthy is family."

Finn looked between the two of them and finally nodded. "I will be outside," he allowed, leaving the room with the trunk tucked under one massive arm.

When the door closed with a quiet click of the latch, she breathed out and pretended an ease she did not feel. "May I offer you refreshment, Mr. Foxworthy? A cup of tea or a glass of sherry, perhaps?"

"I do not like your people poking around asking questions of my neighbors."

Ah, Mr. Renquist's questions had alerted the Foxworthys. "Surely you can understand my concern when I heard that a man I've never met has filed to control my fortune and my person on the accusation that I am not of stable mind? I think it only natural to inquire what sort of man that might be."

"You see him before you now."

Yes, she did. She let her gaze sweep him from head

to toes. She did not think she would like being under his control at all. "What will you take, Mr. Foxworthy? How much do you want to drop the proceedings?"

He bared his teeth, but she gathered the gesture was not a smile. "You think you can buy me off? You're just like Caroline and his lordship. Looking down your nose at the Foxworthys. Think you're better than us, do you? Think you can buy your way out of trouble? Not for any amount, Mrs. Huffington. We, my brother and I, are going to do what's right."

Georgiana perched on the edge of a settee, fearing her wobbly knees would give out. She knew she could not afford to show any weakness to this man or he would rip her to shreds. "What is right?"

"Stopping you from squandering the family fortune."

"I've been conservative, sir. I've certainly spent less than Aunt Caroline used to."

"This is not just about your spending, Mrs. Huffington. It is about your rash behavior and your…your unseemly decisions. You are frivolous and unstable."

And the fact that she was not a blood relation, no doubt. "Decisions? What controversial decisions have I made?"

"I learned today that you have got yourself engaged to Mr. Charles Hunter. This barely six months after Lady Caroline's death."

Oh, Charles knew society well. News had traveled quickly. "I am past the prescribed period of mourning for my aunt, Mr. Foxworthy, and well past it for my late husband."

"Have you no shame? Your engagement so soon after your return to London has caused a stir in society. Why, it is as if you care nothing for the good opinion of others. You've gone about buying gowns from the most expensive dressmaker in London. You cavort at pleasure gardens and—"

"Cavort?" The man had made it his business to know her comings and goings, for heaven's sake! She clasped her hands tightly to keep from doing something rash. "Has it also caused a problem with your suit, sir? Is that why you came to see me now? Do you fear that a marriage would put my fortune out of your reach?"

"Little upstart!" he snarled, taking two steps toward her. "You are marrying to spite my suit, are you not? If you go through with this, I could petition to have your marriage to Mr. Hunter set aside as fraudulent."

She stood and moved behind the settee, wanting to keep a distance from this man. "You could, but you'd never prove it. I am offering you money to drop your suit, sir, which is more than you deserve. My only reason for doing so is to preserve the peace and avoid the scandal of a public proceeding and not because I think your suit has merit. My future husband, however, will not care about that. I'd advise you to take my proposal now and go away before he can intercede."

The clock in the foyer chimed three times and Georgiana realized that Charles's coach would be here soon to take her to Lockwood's.

Mr. Foxworthy's hands fisted at his sides as he advanced. "You will pay for your insolence, Mrs. Huffington. I will see to it that you do not forget it once I am in control."

Suddenly marriage seemed like an excellent idea. "You will never be in control, sir. I am marrying Mr. Hunter this afternoon. You should have taken my offer. Now you are too late."

Foxworthy's eyes bulged and his complexion deepened to a hue that Georgiana feared indicated apoplexy. "Why, you little—"

"Finn!"

The door opened before his name had faded from her lips.

"Show Mr. Foxworthy out, please."

In three long strides, Finn had seized Mr. Foxworthy by the back of his jacket and lifted him so that only his toes touched the floor. Foxworthy in one arm, and the little trunk still under the other, he strode to the garden door, gave the man a shove and closed the door. "Didn't think you'd want him on the front stoop, Mrs. Huffington."

She resisted the impulse to give the man a hug. "Thank you, Finn. Now, if you will watch for the coach, I must go change. I am getting married this afternoon, you know."

He gave her a wide grin. "As you say, ma'am."

"Put that little trunk with my other things, please. Must we tell Mr. Hunter about this unfortunate meeting?"

"'Fraid so, Mrs. Huffington."

Charles waited impatiently in the small family chapel in Lockwood's back garden. He hadn't seen Georgiana since last night and, to admit the truth, he was more than a little uncertain if she would go through with the marriage. According to Finn, however, he would have Walter Foxworthy to thank if she did.

Yes, he'd thank him, and right after he'd thrash the man to within an inch of his life. Richardson had warned him that the elder Foxworthy was an unpleasant person, and it was appalling that he would stoop to threaten a woman.

Restless and impatient, he started forward. If Georgiana would not come, he would go fetch her. Lockwood clamped a hand over his shoulder and whispered in his ear.

"Patience, Charlie. They'll be along in a moment. Elise

said she wanted to pin some flowers in Mrs. Huffington's hair."

His brothers, along with Ethan Travis and Devlin Farrell, grinned at him. All of them had been down this path, and they knew his anxiety. At the sound of soft female voices, they turned toward the chapel door. His sisters-in-law entered and came to stand beside their husbands, and then his own sister, Sarah, entered arm-in-arm with his bride.

Georgiana was stunning in a pale blush-colored creation with a sheer white organza overdress. Fresh soft pink roses set off the glints of sunlight in her hair and she carried a posy of the same innocent flowers. As she came forward, he could read the doubt in her luminous green eyes. Her lips parted and she began to say something, but he gave her a slight shake of his head.

Too late for doubts now. He would erase them all tonight. When they were alone. He gave her a reassuring smile and was rewarded with her quick response.

Sarah brought Georgiana to his side and then stepped back beside her husband. He and Georgiana turned toward the minister, and the ceremony began. He held Georgiana's gaze steadily and barely listened to the words. He did not need to. He'd have vowed anything to have this done with and Georgiana his forever. And Georgiana did not need to listen. She'd heard the words often enough.

He was so lost in her that Lockwood had to nudge him when the minister called for his consent. "I will," he murmured.

A moment later Georgiana's faint agreement followed his and they recited the vows after the minister—he in a clear, steady voice, and Georgiana in a soft whisper that seemed to caress him. When the minister asked for the ring, Charles slipped the gold band studded with diamonds and emeralds, which he'd purchased at Rundel and Bridge's this morning, from his little finger and placed it on the minister's prayer book to be passed back to him to slip on Georgiana's finger.

Repeating after the minister, he gave his solemn vow, still surprised that he could mean every word when just a week ago he'd mistrusted *her* every word. "With this ring I thee wed, with my body I thee worship, and with all my worldly goods I thee endow…"

As they knelt for the prayers, Georgiana's shoulder touched his and deep satisfaction spread through him. She was his wife. *His.* For as long as he lived. Even if that was only until tomorrow. The seductive scent of roses wafted up to him, and his next reflection was far from godly. The rest of the ceremony became a blur as he indulged in salacious thoughts that were sure to damn him to Hell.

Then it was done and, though it was not a part of the ceremony, Charles lifted Georgiana's chin and planted a proprietary kiss on her lips. They turned to the family to find broad smiles and teary eyes. Lockwood and Andrew went with them to sign the clerk's book and finish the business.

The sun was setting as they strolled across the lawns to the house. "Welcome to the family, Mrs. Hunter," Lockwood said.

Georgiana looked bewildered for a moment until she realized that she was the Mrs. Hunter to whom Lockwood referred. Then she sighed—a sound that spoke more of melancholy than of contentment. Was she wondering if she would be attending his funeral tomorrow? He squeezed her hand and she looked up at him. He gave her a reassuring wink and was rewarded with a smile that warmed her face. Charles vowed to give her all the reassurance she'd ever need tonight.

* * *

The moment they arrived home, Charles's butler bowed and assumed an apologetic smile. "Lord Wycliffe and Sir Henry Richardson are waiting in the library, sir. They say it is urgent."

"Thank you, Crosley." Charles turned to her with a pained expression. "I may have neglected to mention that this was my wedding day. I apologize, Georgiana. I will see what they want and send them on their way. I shall be with you presently."

Clara, who had been waiting for her arrival, took her arm to lead her up a curved central staircase. Every detail of the house spoke of good taste and elegance. She had not suspected that Charles's home would be so charming.

"We've been unpacking all day, madam. Soon as we have everything set out, you'll be quite at home. Your room is lovely. Why, it's twice the size of your old one. And twice the room for your gowns and such."

Georgiana followed her maid down a passageway to a door at the end. When Clara threw it open with a flourish, she blinked. Hers was a corner room, which would admit light in both the morning and evening. And it was, indeed, large. High ceilings, mahogany wainscoting and restful colors soothed her, and she dropped her reticule and shawl on a side table to explore. Deep Persian carpets padded her footsteps as she went forward. The dressing table was twice the size of hers and the bed was enormous. She noted that the headboard had been carved with intricate intertwined vines that spiraled up the posts to the green velvet canopy, and the mattress looked as soft as a cloud. It was the most beautiful bed she'd ever seen.

Clara went to a side door and threw it open. "And your dressing room adjoins Mr. Hunter's. But look! That other door in between? 'Tis a bathing room." She threw the door in question open and gestured proudly. "Have you ever seen such a thing, missus? A whole private room for bathing just for the mister and missus. And just look at that tub. Why, it's big enough for two people. And there's even a coal stove to keep the room warm and to heat the water."

The high-backed tub stood on four sturdy legs and was longer and wider than any Georgiana had ever seen. But this one wouldn't have to be carried up the stairs and filled from the kitchen below. Clean towels were draped over the side, ready at a moment's notice. She trailed her fingers along the smooth side, longing for a bath even though she'd bathed only a few hours ago. A washstand with a large mirror above stood along one wall and she noted a shaving mug and razor on the surface by the washbowl.

The familiar scent of Charles's soap evoked the memory of his kisses, and the mug and razor were a very personal reminder that now she would have no secrets from him. They would share all the most intimate details of their lives. She swallowed to clear the constriction that tightened her throat. She turned away and went back to her bedroom to find that Clara had draped her best nightgown across the bed. Heavens! Her wedding night.

Clara giggled. "You blush like a schoolgirl again, madam. A certain kind of man can take you that way, I hear. And don't you worry. I warrant our Mr. Hunter will last."

Last? Longer than her previous husbands? A cold so deep it chilled her clear through settled in her stomach. Had she condemned Charles to an early grave? Had she married him because doing so was easier than telling him the truth of her birth? Because she could not even tell him who her father was? Because she had been frightened by Mr. Foxworthy? Because she felt so safe in his arms? As if no one could hurt her now?

Desperate to be alone, she gave her maid the bouquet she still carried. "Find a vase for these, will you, Clara?"

"Aye, madam. Then I'll come back and make you ready to receive your husband." Another giggle and her maid was gone.

She went to a bureau and opened the drawers one at a time to find her belongings, arranged just as they'd always been at her town house and at the estate in Kent. The simple sameness gave her comfort that not everything had changed.

A corner of the little trunk holding her mother's journals peeked from under the foot of her bed. She knelt and opened the lid. The journal she'd been reading when Mr. Foxworthy arrived lay atop the others and she took it, along with another, to her bedside table and put them in the small drawer. Sooner or later, she'd find something she could share with Lord Carlington.

She gazed down at the wedding ring on her finger. The golden circle embedded with emeralds and twinkling diamonds in a pattern of a never-ending vine suited her more than her others. Gower Huffington's ostentatious inky sapphire and Allenby's plain golden band rested at the bottom of her jewelry box and would remain there forever. This was the one she would wear until the day she died. She slipped it off and looked at the inside surface to see if he'd had it engraved. *Always and Only You,* it said in a faint script.

Tears welled up in her eyes. Always and only her— until he learned the truth of her parentage. Until he faced the reality of his ill-advised marriage.

Until he was killed?

Chapter Sixteen

Charles went to the library sideboard and glanced over his shoulder. "Brandy?" A quick drink and he'd send them on their way. He was rather anxious to join Georgiana upstairs.

Richardson closed the library door and turned the lock. "Whiskey, if you have it. I need something strong."

"You, Wycliffe?"

"Make mine a whiskey, too."

Charles turned up three glasses and poured. "I gather you are fresh back from Cornwall and have come to tell me what you've learned, but it could have waited until tomorrow."

"Crosley said you were getting married," Richardson said as he took his glass and went to look out the front window. "Say it isn't so, Hunter. Who will I carouse with?"

"Sorry. 'Tis done. Mrs. Huffington is now Mrs. Hunter."

Richardson looked back at him as if he'd lost his mind. "You're a walking target, Hunter."

"I've been a walking target since Gibbons decided he wanted me dead. Mrs. Huffington has nothing to do with that."

Wycliffe took his glass and sat in a chair in front of the fireplace. He stretched his legs toward the fire and sighed. "We will get to Gibbons next. But let Harry give his report so he can get some much deserved sleep."

"Aye. I'm looking for my bed. Something that does not move when I close my eyes."

Charles gave Richardson a long look. The man did look exhausted. He steered them back to the subject at hand. "Did you learn anything new?"

Richardson looked down at his scuffed boots and sighed. "I did. And a few more questions, too. You're not going to like it, Hunter. Especially now."

"Now?"

"Now that you've married the girl."

Charles took a deep breath followed by a swallow of whiskey. "Out with it, then."

"Mousehole is a closemouthed village. They sure as hell do not trust strangers. Took a bit of convincing to get anyone to talk, but I eventually put the pieces together after visiting the parish pastor, a washerwoman, the foundling home and the local banker in Penzance."

Charles gave in to restless pacing. "You've been busy."

Richardson laughed. "Somewhat of an understatement, that. Everyone remembered Georgiana—they called her Jane then. Her circumstances were quite different from the usual. She was not local, but arrived by private coach at the church attended by a wet nurse and a servant. According to the pastor, she was not a toddler. She was barely more than a few days old. A small parcel was delivered with her, which included a letter, a few items of clothing for the child and twenty pounds to pay for her keep for the coming year—an unheard of amount in those parts."

Quite unheard of, Charles thought. He glanced at Wycliffe and detected a hint of surprise. The suspicion that had been growing in him for the last few days was taking on an ominous form.

"The only woman in the village who had enough milk to spare was a washerwoman. The pastor handed the baby off to her for the next two years. And each year another twenty pounds arrived.

"When Jane was two and a half, the washerwoman took her to a foundling home in St. Ives. They refused her. Said they were full. So she took Jane back to the parson. He admits that he only paid the washerwoman five pounds a year for the child's care and kept the rest for the 'poor.'"

"The poor parson, most likely," Wycliffe muttered.

Richardson snorted in agreement. "This time the parson left Jane with an impoverished family who could benefit from the five pounds. They already had six children, so Jane was just one of a neglected brood. She was bright, the woman says, quiet and withdrawn most of the time, and she learned quickly to stay out of her husband's way."

"No one recalls a story about a captain and his heartbroken wife?" Charles knew the answer, but he needed confirmation.

"Quite bewildered when I asked them about it. Pure fabrication, I'd say. Or the best kept secret in Mousehole."

"How long did she stay with that family?"

"Something less than a year, I gather. The woman said that the following summer, a coach arrived and, after asking around, came to their squalid little cottage and a servant got out and asked for Jane. She said her husband did not want to give the girl up because of the money that came with her. After consulting someone within the coach, Jane was purchased for thirty pounds. She was taken into the coach as she was, and they drove away. The woman says she never saw Jane again."

Wycliffe stood and poured himself another whiskey.

"Is there anything to confirm that this little Jane is Georgiana?"

Richardson squirmed and glanced at Charles for one telling moment, then back at Wycliffe. "There was a coat of arms on the coach, and a woman within who wore a black veil. Both of those things were unprecedented in Mousehole. By description, the child was fair, had dark green eyes and had arrived with more cash than most of them had seen altogether at one time."

Charles knew the logical conclusion. And from their uncomfortable silence, so did Richardson and Wycliffe. "Jane was very likely Georgiana," he said. "And Caroline was most likely her mother."

"Do you think she had second thoughts about giving the child up?"

"The trip to bring her back from Mousehole would have happened after Lord Betman's death. Lady Caroline may not have wanted to give Georgiana up, but her father would have insisted because of the scandal it would cause."

Richardson glanced out the window again. "You do not looked surprised, Hunter."

"Not much. It is not unheard of for a peeress to be caught in an indiscretion and have to 'visit the continent' for a while. Nor is it particularly unusual for her to maintain an interest in that child afterward. When we dined with Lord Carlington, he showed us a miniature of Lady Caroline. Georgiana's hair and eyes are remarkably similar."

"Then Georgiana is a—"

"Don't say it, Richardson. Not if you are my friend."

Harry nodded, all trace of his usual mockery gone.

"Blast it all! None of this helps us at all," Wycliffe concluded. "Georgiana's past, while tragic, cannot have a bearing on what has happened to her husbands. Considering her circumstances, her marriages were...quite good."

Above her? And her marriage to him would be considered the same. "I've learned that Lady Caroline arranged those marriages. I have been trying to think what her criteria were. What did Arthur Allenby and Gower Huffington have in common?"

Richardson scratched his head. "Allenby was young, and Huffington was mature. Both had quite comfortable fortunes. Both had little family. Neither were titled. But there is nothing so remarkable in those things."

"Both had country estates and neither was often in town," Wycliffe added.

"Seems as if Lady Caroline wanted Georgiana settled comfortably in the countryside."

"And she achieved that. Twice. But why should that matter to her? She'd done all she could to hide Georgiana's past. We've only discovered it because we were looking for something else and found this instead." Charles thought of Georgiana waiting for him upstairs and wondered how much of the truth she knew.

He swallowed the remainder of his whiskey and poured more. A change of subject was in order.

"About Gibbons?" he asked.

Richardson turned from his position near the window. "Wycliffe filled me in while we were waiting for you. I am asleep on my feet, gentlemen. I'm going home. I'll catch up with you tomorrow."

Charles opened the library door for him and nodded to a discreetly waiting Crosley to see him out. Turning back to Wycliffe, he said, "Hope it's better news than Richardson's."

"Gibbons has been seen loitering around the Crown

and Bear. I find that odd considering he knows you frequent the place and your brother-in-law owns it."

"Odd? Not if he's looking to kill me. Good Lord. I've searched seven months with nary a glimpse of him, and now that my attention is elsewhere, he's everywhere I turn."

"Gibbons must be desperate," Wycliffe said.

Charles stopped his pacing to look down into the fire. "No more so than I."

"What would you say if Gibbons offered a truce, Hunter? Would you agree?"

He shook his head. "He killed Adam Booth and shot me. Those are hard things to ignore. Aside from that, I have no faith he'd keep a truce. Gibbons never honored an agreement in his life."

"And if he asked for a meeting? Would you want to know what he had to say?"

What could Gibbons possibly have to say to him? Now, that was tempting. "Perhaps. Let's go. We can fetch Devlin along the way."

Wycliffe stood and clapped Charles on the back. "Not tonight, Hunter. It's your wedding night. Go upstairs. Make love to your wife. Forget your pride. It will not keep you warm."

"I don't know if I can do that," he admitted.

"Then you are a bigger fool than I'd ever thought possible."

Georgiana's hair spread across her pillow and her lashes lay in dark spikes against her pale cheeks, almost as if they'd been formed by tears. *Regrets, sweet Georgiana?* Her lips—those soft petals that beckoned him—were slightly parted. He longed to kiss her awake but he merely stood there, studying the woman he had married. In the flicker of dim candlelight she looked almost ethereal.

In the face of better judgment, of past rejections, of vague suspicions, he'd married her. Knowing she was keeping secrets from him, he'd married her. He could not distinguish what he was feeling—the odd misgivings. Was it anger? Or something darker?

She'd fallen asleep waiting for him, and he could not regret it. He'd have welcomed any delay in talking to her because he did not know what to say. Would she be shocked to learn that her 'aunt' Caroline had been her mother? Or had she known and kept it from him?

Tomorrow. They'd sort it out tomorrow.

A black leather-bound journal lay facedown against her chest, her hand curled over it. She must have fallen asleep reading. Carefully, he slipped the slender volume from under her hand and smiled at her soft sigh.

He glanced at the writing, wondering if it were hers, and wondering if he would learn more about her from these pages than he had in the past week of conversations and confessions. But the date of the entry was from years before, and the handwriting was not Georgiana's.

June 7, 1816

Thank heaven the unpleasantness is past. I have spoken with Mr. Hunter, and I believe I have successfully misdirected him by telling him Georgiana is embarrassed by his attentions. My conscience troubles me little over the lie, though I was distressed to see the depth of his attachment. Had I known how close they were growing, I would have ended it sooner. After Georgiana's encouragement, he had every right to expect a different outcome.

As for Georgiana, I have warned her against fast behavior and told her that Mr. Hunter has lost interest in her. She is crushed, but it is for the best. I simply cannot have her marry into such a family as the Hunters. Despite their country seat, they are city dwellers. Some London busybody would snoop into Georgiana's past to everyone's ruin. 'Twill be better by far to have her settled in the country with no one to ask questions. Mr. Allenby seems a good prospect, as he is so smitten that he will believe she is exactly what she appears to be. His parents will not object, owing to the size of her dowry.

If only she would not cry into her pillow every night....

So, after all these years, he finally knew what had happened that long-ago spring. Lady Caroline had betrayed them both. No wonder, then, that Georgiana had been so cool and distant when they'd been reintroduced. No wonder she'd been confused by his thinly veiled anger. She must have thought him quite a bounder. Lady Caroline had driven a wedge between them that would have lasted a lifetime had Wycliffe not coerced him into investigating her husbands' deaths.

He flipped the pages to the end and read how Georgiana had begged Caroline to recant her engagement to Allenby, and how Caroline had remained firm, nearly pushing her down the aisle. Enlightening, to say the least. Georgiana had not loved Allenby. All the easier for her to kill him?

He shivered. Where had that thought come from? They were married now. And he knew now that she had never deceived him. The time for doubts was past.

He closed the volume, wondering, how much more might he learn from Caroline's other journals? And where were they? After tonight, he would most especially like to read the account of Caroline's "accident" and Georgiana's birth. Though he was fairly certain he knew it, would the name of her father be mentioned?

He glanced at Georgiana again. His earlier suspicion

had likely been right. Her spiked lashes were due to tears. He could not imagine the pain of learning that the person she'd trusted most in the world had betrayed her. Had forced her into two marriages she hadn't wanted.

He opened her bed-table drawer to put the book away, vowing to discuss the matter with Georgiana tomorrow. As he slipped the book into the drawer, his fingers brushed a thick vial. He pulled it out and read the label in the guttering candlelight.

Laudanum. A vague suspicion began to nag at him. Wycliffe had warned him to look for it, and here it was.

Damn. This was not how he'd thought he'd spend his wedding night.

Georgiana woke and stretched. She sat up in bed and looked around, disoriented. The last she could remember was waiting for Charles. And she'd been reading her... Caroline's journal. Good heavens! It was gone!

She threw her covers back and dropped to her knees to look under the bed. Had it fallen from her hand?

"It is in the drawer, Georgiana."

Her pulse pounded and she sat back on her heels, searching the shadows. Something stirred in the chair in the far corner. A dark figure unfolded and rose like a specter. She could only see his form, but it was enough to reveal that it was Charles. Relief washed through her.

"Oh! You frightened me half to death. What were you doing in the corner?"

"Waiting for you to wake."

She glanced toward the draperies to see a thin line of daylight where they met. "Have you been there all night?"

"Yes." He came toward her.

Something was wrong. Some change in his manner. Not the slightest bit of warmth in his voice. Her pulse, which had begun to steady, skipped a beat or two. "Why did you not wake me?"

"You looked as if you needed the sleep."

"I tried to wait up for you, but after all the excitement, I think I was more exhausted than I realized." She accepted his offered hand and got to her feet.

"I've been thinking, Georgiana. I have decided to hold off making the formal announcement that we've married. Nor shall I post notices in any of the newspapers."

Perversely, though that had been her thought last night, she now took offense to it. "Hold off? But I thought that was the whole point of marrying—to alert the villain that I had married again. To draw him out."

He gave a negligent shrug. "Or draw her out. Did you ever think our culprit might be a woman, Georgiana?"

"I…I never considered that. Why would a woman want my husbands dead?"

"Jealousy? Dislike?" His voice had been offhand, but it lowered a moment later. "To do you a favor and extricate you from unpleasant or unwanted marriages?"

She had never seen Charles in such a strange mood, almost as if he were trying to tell her something but did not want to give it voice. "Why?"

He released her hand and stepped back, then snatched her wrapper from the foot of her bed and tossed it to her. "Put your wrapper on, Georgiana. I cannot think with you standing there half naked."

Embarrassed, she looked down at her sheer lawn nightgown. It did reveal rather more of her than was modest. She slipped her arms into the sleeves and secured the tie. "Sorry," she murmured.

He went to stand in front of the banked fire. "Have my servants made you comfortable?"

"They…they've been most hospitable. Clara and Sanders are settling in well. Clara is taken with your bath-room. She says the tub is the largest she's ever seen."

One corner of Charles's mouth quirked in the sem-blance of a smile. "There is another in the servant's wing, though the tub is not as large."

"She will be delighted, I am sure." She looked around and tried to hide her nervousness and the questions that rose to her mind. Was it odd that Charles had not come to bed with her but had preferred to spend the night in a chair?

She turned to see if there was a bell-pull by her bed. "Do you want tea, Charles?"

He was silent so long she turned to look at him. He rested one elbow on the mantel and was watching her with what she could only describe as detached curiosity. "I've told the servants to stay away unless I call them."

Things were not going well at all. Perhaps it would be best to be blunt. "Why do you not tell me what is wrong, Charles? What do you want of me?"

"Answers, Georgiana."

A feeling of dread settled in her heart. For all his con-trol, she now understood that Charles was quite angry. His earlier comment, that perhaps the killer, if there was one, was a woman, suddenly became clear. "Do you think... Can you be suggesting that *I* killed my husbands?"

"The possibility crossed my mind."

"Before or after our marriage? Because if you sus-pected me before, Charles, you'd have been insanely reck-less to have gone through with it."

"So I've been told."

"By whom?"

"Never mind that, Georgiana. Just answer the ques-tion. Was it you?"

She gripped the bedpost to brace herself and sat on

the side of the bed before her knees could give out. He thought she was a killer! He thought her capable of the most heinous crime possible. He had seduced her, slept with her and now married her, and he could believe such a thing of her?

Tears stung in her eyes. That he could even ask....

"Would you believe my answer? Or would you require proof?"

"Proof, if you have it."

"I do not. How could I have proof of something I have not done?"

"Then you are saying you are innocent?"

Something snapped in her mind and her anger bubbled up from deep inside. "That you can even ask such a question disgusts me. Why did you marry me, if you think me guilty of such a crime?"

He spread his arms wide in a bewildered gesture. "I think I may not have had all the facts when I made that decision."

She glanced toward her dressing table. He'd said the little journal she'd been reading was in the drawer. Placed there by Charles. Had he read it? She had thought he'd be pleased to learn she had not jilted him her first season. Instead he had become a suspicious tyrant.

"You are thinking I read your aunt's journal." His voice was deep and steady, and she realized this was a part of him she'd never seen before. "You are wondering how much I know, are you not?"

She met his stare and did not flinch. "Did you?"

"You answer my question first, Georgiana. Did you rid yourself of your husbands?"

A deep well of pain churned inside her. He'd never believed in her. He deserved to believe whatever he pleased. "Will you be able to sleep knowing I am in the next room?

Wondering if you will be my next victim? Waiting for my footsteps?"

"Damn it, Georgiana! Give me an answer."

"Not until you are rational." The servants would not come unless he rang? Well and good. She went to the outer door and shouted at the top of her lungs. "Clara! Tea, if you please!"

By the time she turned, he was gone.

Chapter Seventeen

"Thank you for coming, Hunter. I am painfully aware that I have torn you away from your charming new wife, but I thought you should hear this."

Charles expressed no opinion about precisely how charming Georgiana had been when shrieking for her morning tea. He merely nodded and sat across the desk from Wycliffe.

Wycliffe leaned forward, resting his forearms on his desk. "Walter Foxworthy is being held for questioning regarding Allenby's and Huffington's deaths."

This was surprising news. Maybe he wouldn't have to thrash Foxworthy after all.

"I do not know how long we can hold him. The motive and possible opportunity are the only things that ring true. There is no actual proof. Alas, the Secretary was forced to act."

"How was he forced?"

"Allenby's father and Huffington's nephew are insisting that something be done. Of course, they think your wife is the guilty party, but they cannot prove it any more than we can prove it is Foxworthy. Still, he is the only one with a clear motive—control and use of the Betman fortune and Georgiana. But we will need more proof if we are to get a conviction. The good news is that this development has bought us another day to uncover the truth."

Charles met Wycliffe's gaze and knew that there was more. "And the bad news?"

"A Mr. Hathaway has come to the Home Office and made an official report. He claims that Georgiana killed her husbands with laudanum. Perhaps—" he paused to clear his throat "—even killed her guardian."

The bottle of laudanum in Charles's waistcoat pocket felt like a lead weight. Laudanum and a loveless marriage had provided work for more than one gravedigger. The irony that he'd made the same accusations this morning was not lost on him. Anger tore through him like a winter wind. "Lady Caroline? Why, that's absurd."

"I know. But Hathaway's claim is that she put laudanum in Allenby's wedding cup, and that more than mere revelry accounted for his drunken behavior, and that his tumble down the stairs was a result of having been drugged with laudanum."

"And Huffington?"

"That she put it in his toddy before he left for his daily walk about his property, and by the time the laudanum overtook him, he was too far away to make his way back."

Charles could guess the rest. "And that she simply gave her aunt an overdose of her usual amount for sleep and no one suspected the truth since Lady Caroline was prone to taking it?"

Wycliffe nodded. "Hathaway contends that, although Lady Caroline was in a decline, the end came too quickly. Furthermore, he saw the vial in Georgiana's bed-table drawer."

Charles took a deep breath, hating what he was about

to do. "Search for it, Wycliffe. I grant free access to Georgiana's home and mine."

"You must be quite certain to make such a sweeping statement."

Damn the man! He met Wycliffe's stare and did not flinch.

"Charles, if something is found to implicate Georgiana, you know I will have to do my duty."

"Hathaway is a bitter former employee. He would say or do anything to spite me or her. He and I had words on more than one occasion, and it was necessary for me to expel him from Georgiana's house. He made a threat when he was leaving. I was expecting some sort of retaliation, but this goes beyond reason. Surely you see that?"

"Nevertheless. We had been on the verge of arresting Foxworthy when Hathaway's report came in. Foxworthy's arrest is my ploy to buy you time, Charles. And there is not much of it. Act quickly, because the moment we release Foxworthy, we will have to arrest your wife."

"You will find nothing to implicate Georgiana."

Wycliffe stood and turned to look out his window. "You are certain, Hunter?"

"Positive."

"Foxworthy is likely to be released by the end of the day. Tomorrow morning at the latest. Attention will return to Georgiana."

"I understand."

"Now what will you do?"

Charles sighed. "I have no idea where to go from here," he said. Though Lord Carlington might be a good place to start.

Georgiana watched out her window until she saw Charles leave. She had no wish to encounter him again until she could control her temper. The man could be so maddeningly infuriating!

Was he going to acquire an annulment? Was that why he hadn't consummated their marriage last night? That thought sent her mind spinning. She understood why it would be for the best, but her heart tore in two at the thought of losing him again.

She'd tried to read a few of Aunt Caroline's—she could not yet think of her as her *mother*—diaries, but her attention kept wondering at the sameness of Caroline's days and the loneliness of her nights. When she mentioned Georgiana, it was with the objectivity of an observer, never the fondness of a mother. Georgiana had been daily evidence of Caroline's shame, and yet she had done her duty and accepted responsibility for her.

She put three journals aside for Lord Carlington, hoping he would not be bored to distraction. She'd chosen one volume where Caroline had mentioned that 'Owen' would laugh at something that had happened in the village. She thought he might like to know that Caroline had still thought of him.

In an attempt to escape her ennui, Georgiana donned a bonnet and went down to the back garden to cut some flowers for the foyer and dinner table. She found a pair of pruning shears and a basket in the garden shed adjoining the stable and took the path most likely to lead her to flowers. The grounds were not extensive and she arrived by simply turning a corner around a hedge.

Though it was too early in the year for blooming roses, there were lavish lilac bushes and soft pink and lavender anemone. The sun warmed her skin and she sighed happily. At that moment she could almost believe everything would come aright. She sank to her knees and began taking cuttings of the anemone, hoping there would be enough for a small bouquet for the foyer table.

Her anger at Charles faded as she worked the rich soil and took careful cuttings so she would not deplete the garden. She thought of various ways to mend the rift between them when he came home.

The lilac bushes rustled and she smiled. Perhaps it was a hummingbird looking for nectar, or a robin seeking worms in the soft dirt.

"Aye, yer right pretty, ye are."

Georgiana squeaked and toppled backward onto her bottom. Before she could scramble to her feet, a man emerged from the bushes. He was rough looking and dirty. The gardener? How long had he been lurking there?

"Who are you?" She gripped the shears in her fist like a weapon.

"Why, I'm yer pa."

She recognized that voice. She'd heard it in Vauxhall Gardens. She'd almost forgotten him and his "plans" for her. "No, you are not."

"Aye, yer my gal, right enough. I've been watchin' you yer whole life, Georgie gal. Ever since you was brought back to Kent. Finest thing I ever done. Think it was me, but coulda been Artie. An' everything we done after was fer you."

Watching her? And who was Artie? She could not take this in. Could not comprehend what he was saying. But there was something familiar about him, something vaguely disquieting. Yes! He'd been across the street the night of Lord Carlington's ball, waiting for her and Charles to come out. And she thought she might have seen him before that. In her village in Kent. Hadn't he once given her a rock candy when she'd gone to market with the cook? All she could remember was that he smelled bad and his teeth were yellowed and broken when he smiled. She had thrown the candy into the bushes on her way back to the manor.

Another brief memory flashed in her mind, and then another, until she wondered how he could have been so present in her life and she not recognize him. The disquieting feelings of being watched, being followed, had been true! He'd been a specter weaving in and out of her entire life. Dear God! Could this horrid man she'd dismissed as a demented villager actually be her father? But Aunt Caroline would never—

"I do not believe you."

He grabbed her upper arm and squeezed. "Don't you be gettin' saucy with me, missy! A gal's bound to do what her pa says. I'da come sooner but that blasted giant Hunter hired is always in the way."

She shuddered with revulsion. "Let me go!"

"Not yet, Georgie gal. I got plans fer you. But I gotta get rid of Hunter first. *Hunter,* fer Christ's sake! I oughta whip you fer marryin' him like you done. I warrant he's ridin' you hard but you ain't a tart. You was raised better. That fancy ma of yers saw to that."

She felt sick to her stomach. Surely she would wake from this nightmare any moment. This horrid man would be gone and his hideous claims would go with him.

"A gal's bound to do what her pa says. Now that yer ma's gone, I'm yer boss. D'you understand?"

"Y-yes." She'd say anything to make him release her.

"That's better."

He eased his grip and she stepped back, drawing a deep breath of clean air. "What do you want?"

He smirked, certain he'd won their contest of wills. "Yer comin' with me. Once I put Hunter outta the way, you'll marry who I say. No more of them country squires an' the like. Yer fit fer a duke." He laughed and slapped his thighs with enjoyment. "T' think. My whelps is gonna be swells. Aye, the Gibbonses is risin' in the world."

She took another step backward. Put Hunter out of the way? The man was quite mad. Caroline would never have allowed a man like that to touch her. But, somehow, he had become obsessed with Georgiana in the village and built a fantasy around being her father. And now that Caroline was dead, he thought he had the right to control her.

She still held the pruning shears in her hand. She tightened her grip and drew her arm back to lend force to her blow.

"Mrs. Hunter!"

Finn's voice was blessedly near! "Here, Finn!"

The man snarled at her and glanced over his shoulder, backing into the lilac bushes the way he'd appeared. "Looks like I'm gonna have to teach you not to cross yer pa. You ain't too big to whip. Use the cane on you, I will."

And then he was gone. She sank to her knees, fighting the tears that were crowding forward and trying to still her trembling.

"Need help with the basket, Mrs. Hunter?" Finn asked as he came around the bend in the path.

"Yes, please." She took a moment to get to her feet, waiting until she was certain her knees would not fail her and trying not to meet Finn's discerning eyes, then busied herself by smoothing her skirts and collecting her emotions.

She did not want to tell Finn about the encounter with that horrid man. She did not want to tell anyone what he'd wanted with her. A pack of lies, certainly, but…but she did not want to give them voice. Or was it her own nameless fears that kept her silent? That he could be behind the attacks on Charles. That she, through the obsession of this demented man, could actually be responsible for the deaths of her husbands? That he would keep his promise and come back for her?

Charles stood at the window in Lord Carlington's study. How could he tell the man what he suspected? It was bound to be a deep shock, perhaps welcome, perhaps not, but a shock nonetheless.

The door opened and Carlington entered. "Ah! Hunter. I was just going to send for you, lad. Finally heard from my man in the Royal Navy."

Ah, yes. He'd been going to inquire regarding Georgiana's supposed father and mother. He'd almost forgotten the offer.

"Sherry? Whiskey? Name your poison, lad. Not too early, eh?"

Charles glanced at the ormolu mantel clock. Five o'clock. "Sherry, I think." He did not want to arrive home drunk. He still had a few matters to settle with Georgiana. And she would need to hear this news, too.

Carlington poured two glasses and brought one to Charles. "To old friends in the navy," he toasted.

Charles drank and waited for Carlington to take a seat in a chair by the window. "Like to watch the world go by now and then," he explained, gesturing to the window and chuckling. "See some of the damnedest things when no one knows you're watching. Sit, Hunter. Don't want to drink looking up at you."

Charles sat in the chair next to him and glimpsed out the window. A very good view, indeed.

"Yes, well, to the point, eh? The Captain George Carson I was recalling could not have been little Georgiana's father. Seems he and his wife both went down on his ship.

No children. I asked my friend to look into any other Carsons who might fit the bill. No luck. Not yet, anyway."

Charles hadn't expected news. He was now certain Carlington could inquire into every Carson ever in the navy and never find Georgiana's father. "I suspect you will not get the answer we want."

"No? Why not?"

"Because I do not believe Georgiana's father was in the Royal Navy. Nor was he ever a captain."

"Well, who was he, then?"

After an uncertain pause, Charles delivered his theory. "You, I believe."

Carlington sat forward in his chair, coughing and sputtering. "I say! That's a bit of a surprise, Hunter."

"Were you and Lady Caroline not in love?"

"Quite. I'd have done anything for her."

"And?"

Carlington raised his eyebrows. "You want the details, do you? Very well. We had pledged ourselves to each other. We were going to marry. We were, perhaps, a week or two from a formal announcement. And, had everything gone well, we'd have been married by the end of the season."

"What happened?"

"Her accident. I never saw her afterward. But I've told you all that. It still does not explain why you think I am Georgiana's father."

Charles took a deep breath. "Because Lady Caroline was her mother."

He thought Carlington might challenge him, or call him a liar. Instead, the older man just sank back into his chair and sighed. "Ah. I wondered. She looks like Caroline, you know. Same eyes. Same honey hair. Perhaps even a bit more beautiful."

"I'd like to know what you intend to do about this, Carlington."

"Do? Why...nothing."

"You will not claim her?"

"She is not mine."

"But you said you and Caroline were—"

"We were in love, Hunter. Not that it is any of your business, but we were never...intimate."

Charles could not hide his shock. "Then who...?"

Carlington nodded. "Who, indeed?"

"Was there anyone else she might have been interested in? Or who might have been interested in her?"

"Certainly no one I knew about. But are you certain Georgiana is Caroline's? Could you be mistaken about that?"

"I do not think so, sir. The resemblance... Did Lady Caroline have female cousins or other relations? Could Lord Betman have fathered a by-blow?"

Carlington snorted. "Not bloody likely. A stuffy old man if ever there was one. Stickler for propriety. Caroline was afraid of him. That's why we never risked... well, you know."

Charles did know. He had his own regrets about not protecting Georgiana from the consequences of an unwanted pregnancy.

"But you are married to Georgiana now, are you not? You will not cast her off, will you?"

"Why would I do that?"

"All that nonsense you spouted about birth and blood, and it being who you are."

"I do not consider that nonsense."

Carlington's brow lowered in a stern manner. "I warned you not to involve yourself with an orphan if that mattered to you."

"And if she is Lady Caroline's daughter—"

"Then, although she is of good *blood,* she is illegitimate. Will you punish her for something she could not help?"

The conversation was taking a turn he hadn't bargained for. He finished his sherry in a gulp and stood. "Who and what Georgiana is remains to be seen. Thank you and good day, Carlington."

Finn met Charles at the front door and barely gave him time to hand his greatcoat to Crosley before voicing his concern. "Quiet day, sir, but I think there's something wrong with the missus."

"Why?"

"I found her cryin' in the garden, sir."

A quick stab of guilt shot to his heart. He'd been churlish and suspicious this morning. Trusting did not come easy for him, but to accuse Georgiana of murder was a bit much, even for him. His only excuse was that he'd still been reeling from Richardson's report and learning that his new wife was Lady Caroline's love child. And then he'd found the laudanum in her drawer.

Laudanum! Damn. He'd meant to drop the vial in the Thames upon leaving Wycliffe's office, but he'd forgotten after his errand at Rundel and Bridge's. He'd apologize to Georgiana at once and then remedy that omission. "Where is she, Finn?"

"In her room, sir. Clara informed the staff that she wishes to be left alone. I believe she has a 'crushing headache.'"

More than likely she was trying to avoid him. "Thank you, Finn. I shall look in on her and be down in a moment."

He climbed the stairs, thinking how different his house

was in just twenty-four hours. Before, there had only been himself, Crosley and the cook. Now his staff had more than doubled. Though he was not used to so many people, he did not mind. The bustle reminded him of the house he'd grown up in with three rowdy brothers and one dainty sister. They'd been a boisterous lot and there'd never been a moment's peace. Now his house felt more like a home.

He knocked on Georgiana's door and waited. When there was no answer, he tried the latch. Locked. That was going a bit too far. His anger returning, he turned, entered his own room, crossed through his dressing room and opened the door on Georgiana's side. The room was dim and she'd been reclining on a chaise with her eyes closed. She sat upright when he burst in.

"Charles! I...I didn't know you were home."

"And still would not if I were a respecter of locked doors, madam."

She gave him a timid smile that made him ashamed. "Well, you have found your way in, and since it was never my intent to close you out, we can both be pleased."

"If you did not mean to bar me, then who?"

One hand went up and pressed her temple as if it throbbed. "Clara, mostly. She means well, but I cannot think with her constant hovering and coddling. She can be quite distracting."

He did not know about Clara being distracting, but he could well believe it about Georgiana. Was, in fact, dealing with that distraction at this very moment.

She stood and held out her hand. "Charles—"

He took the hand and drew her against him. He wanted her with a banked desire he'd never before experienced. She'd been his wife nearly a full twenty-four hours, and he still had not bedded her.

"We need to talk, Georgiana. I have questions, and

things I must tell you, but at the moment I can only think how beautiful you are." And how he was growing hard just watching her.

She must have read his mind. A pretty blush rose to her cheeks and she looked at the fading light outside the window. "Dinner will be ready soon. I think we've already given the servants enough to talk about."

She was right, of course, but unfortunately he did not care in the least. He led her to her dressing table and held the little boudoir chair for her. When she was seated, he took the small box from his waistcoat pocket and placed it on the table in front of her. She looked at his reflection in the mirror, the question in her eyes.

"My apology," he explained.

She lifted the lid and her eyes, those remarkable olive-green eyes, widened. She traced the circle of twinkling diamonds surrounding the deep emerald pendant with her index finger. "You are...eloquent, Charles."

"It is a match for your wedding ring."

She nodded and lifted it by the chain to examine the jewels more closely.

"Allow me," he whispered, bending over her shoulder to take the necklace from her. He unfastened the clasp, lowered the pendant to its rightful place, and fastened it again.

She held his gaze in the mirror as he settled the object against her chest. Her mouth curled up in a subtle smile and, starting at the back of her neck, he slipped his fingers downward to smooth the links of the chain against her skin. When he reached the pendant resting in the valley between her lush breasts, he left his hands there, and was rewarded by the thump of her heart against his palm. "There," he said. "Perfect."

Her eyelashes fluttered and her lips parted in a faint

sigh. He watched in rapt fascination as the peaks of her breasts made little dots against the fabric of her gown and her color deepened. Ah, she was aroused. This foreplay was causing havoc. Would he last through dinner?

She scarcely breathed and he waited for an indication of what she wanted. Her head fell back against him and she brought her hands up to cover his, still at that voluptuous curvature. "Thank you." She sighed.

"No need."

She turned her head to look up at him and her cheek brushed his erection. Even through the fabric of his breeches, the sensation was electric. His control, already drawn tight as a frayed bowstring, snapped.

Chapter Eighteen

Georgiana wanted to regret her shameless ploy or blush at the brazenness of it, but she couldn't. She wanted Charles. And she wanted him as she'd never wanted him before. Quickly. Before something could happen to stop it. While she could still quiet her conscience enough to deceive him. Now, as the urgency built inside her with a blind nameless need.

The boudoir chair toppled over as she stood and neither of them stopped to right it. She wanted to touch his skin and feel his warmth. Already damp with desire, she pushed his jacket off his shoulders and made a shambles of his cravat.

He groaned. "Allow me."

But she continued to unknot the intricate folds, leaving him to struggle with the fasteners of his pants and kick off his boots. Between them, he was quickly exposed and free to turn his attention to her.

There would be mending to do tomorrow by the number of little rips she heard in their urgency, but she could not regret it. Once her gown was upon the floor and her stockings and garters tossed across the room, Charles seized her and fell back upon her bed, ignoring the rest.

"God help me, I cannot wait," he moaned.

Her breasts swelled above her chemise and were pushed higher by her corset. She reached for the laces and Charles shook his head. "Now, damn it." He lifted the hem of her chemise and pulled her on top of him.

Oh, the perceptive man! He had sensed what she wanted. She straddled him and sank onto his erect shaft, dropping her head back at the sheer deliciousness of the sensation. She ground against him, finding the depth of his penetration to be wildly erotic. She'd have been content to remain there longer, grinding against him, but he finally gasped and gripped her hips, lifting her and letting her sink again, teaching her his rhythm.

As she took to his guidance, he released her hips to skim his hands upward to her breasts and flick the taut peaks with his thumbnails. With both hands free, he worked a sensual magic on her, intensifying her arousal and sending her spiraling higher. She emitted an involuntary sound, half pain, half pleasure, as the quaking began inside her.

Charles must have felt the first stirrings of her tremors because he thrust hard, his hips rising off the bed to impale her inescapably. "Charles! Oh, Charles. Oh, yes!"

She could feel the power of his release inside her and collapsed on him, her loosened hair tumbling around them.

"Georgie, ah, my sweet, sweet Georgie. Will I ever have enough of you?" Still joined, he rolled with her until he had the superior position. "That just dulled the urgency, Georgie. Now let's get down to business."

He began to move inside her again, growing longer and thicker with alarming speed, her own arousal building apace. Resting his weight on his elbows, he brushed her hair away from her face and grinned.

"You surprise me," he whispered, still moving within her. "And I am not easy to surprise."

She smiled and stretched her arms above her head as she lifted her knees to encase his hips. "You make me feel beautiful, Charlie. And unafraid. And confident that you will not chastise me for my boldness."

His gaze never left hers. "I will never chastise you for that. I will thank God every night for it."

And before she could think better of it, she uttered the words she had guarded so long. "I love you, Charles Hunter. I always have."

"Ah, Georgie." He sighed, and she imagined a hint of sadness in the words.

He quickened his pace and she writhed beneath him, seeking to take all of him and to bind him to her for eternity but knowing it was just for tonight. Tomorrow? Why, tomorrow would likely see an end to all her foolish dreams.

The next morning Charles was barely aware of his surroundings as his coach stopped outside the Home Office and he stepped down. "Do not wait, Peters," he called to his driver. "I will not need you again today."

As the coach pulled away, he was distracted by thoughts—memories, actually—of last night and of Georgiana. She'd been surprisingly eager and deeply sensual. He had not rung for dinner to be brought until sometime near midnight and then they'd fallen back into bed. He'd held her and they'd succumbed to the deep dreamless slumber of utter exhaustion.

And still, his every instinct told him that she was hiding something. Afraid of something. He wanted to reassure her and tell her that everything would come aright, but he very much feared it wouldn't. If Foxworthy was released today, Georgiana would be arrested by tomorrow. And then it would be too late to save her.

The laudanum bottle still weighted his greatcoat pocket. He'd forgotten about it again last night, and he could not throw it away in daylight. He might be seen and remarked upon, or the bottle could be retrieved by some observant boatman. He would have to find a safer way to dispose of it.

From the right corner of his eye, he caught a flurry of motion. Instinct drove him to lunge right and turn. Something caught in the fabric of his jacket and ripped through. The slash of a knife bit into his skin and a searing pain slashed across his left rib cage. When he reached to catch the hand that held the knife, the wound opened wider and the pain nearly doubled him over. If he could not rally, he was a dead man. The sound of shouting and running feet reached him and, even as the man pulled away, a whiff of the sewer revealed his identity.

"Gibbons!"

His admission was a deep snarl. "Blast ye, Hunter! Ye've got more lives than a cat." He crouched, his arms out to his sides as he measured for another attack. "Ye done this to spite me, didn't ye, ye blighter?"

Done what? What the—

"I mighta let ye go, but now yer gonna have t' die."

The wicked looking blade came up again and slashed outward to define an arc across what would have been Charles's belly if he hadn't ducked and slipped under Gibbons's arm to come up behind him. He knew better than to get close enough for the man to make another cut. He already felt the wet flow of blood down his side.

"You came looking for me, Gibbons. I've done nothing to you."

"Ye killed my brother."

"Is this about Artie? Damn, Gibbons! You shot me and killed Booth. I was home having a ball dug out of my shoulder. I couldn't have killed him."

"'Twere one of yer brothers, then. Or Farrell. I'll kill ye all."

"You'll be dead first."

A wild gleam lit Gibbons's eyes. "Yer blood will cover the street, Hunter. Count on it."

"Empty threats, Gibbons."

Gibbons's filthy lip curled, his anger making him incautious.

Charles rallied for another lunge and knocked Gibbons's arm out of the way. But the knife was a part of him and he did not release it.

Gibbons loomed over him, hatred in every line of his body. He was getting ready to slash when he glanced up and scowled, then broke into a run. Charles followed the moment Gibbons turned and made for an alleyway.

Richardson rushed by him. "You're hurt. Stay out of the way!"

Hurt? Charles stopped long enough to feel his side, now stinging like fury, and when he looked up they were gone. A crowd had begun to gather and Wycliffe took his arm to drag him inside the building.

"The bastard will not give up," he muttered.

Once they were in Wycliffe's office, he shrugged out of his jacket and waistcoat to examine the damage. His white shirt was stained with blood along his left side. He pulled the tattered remains from his waistband and bared the flesh. Not deep, but wide. The blood was already beginning to thicken to a sticky consistency.

Wycliffe took the whiskey bottle from his desk drawer and poured some on his handkerchief. "Good God, Hunter. Are you trying to make Georgiana a widow already?"

Charles winced as Wycliffe applied the handkerchief to his side. "I've been trying to kill the sod for months now. He's slippery. Knows every hole and crib in Whitechapel. He's been invisible for the past six months, and now he's coming after me every time my back is turned. He must be desperate to have me dead."

Wycliffe called his clerk and told him to bring a shirt for Charles, then turned back to him. "We are getting closer to finding where he's been holing up. We have it narrowed down to three blocks near Halfpenny Lane."

"You will let me know when you get to within one block?"

"Our usual informants will not talk. They are afraid of Gibbons. They know he'll come after them if he suspects they've betrayed him."

Charles inspected his side again. With the blood cleaned, he could see that the cut should have stitches but would heal without them. Bandages would suffice. He wondered how he would explain this to Georgiana. She'd be certain her "curse" was responsible.

Wycliffe wound gauze strips around him several times and secured the end by tucking it in the folds. His clerk returned with a clean shirt and Wycliffe tossed it to him. "Have Crosley return it to my house, will you?"

Charles laughed. "Does this confirm the rumors that you live here?"

Wycliffe grinned. "I've found it is always convenient to have a fresh change of clothes. I believe I might have a jacket that would fit you, though not a waistcoat."

Charles tucked the shirt into his breeches. "I'll take the jacket and be grateful. What news have you?"

Wycliffe scribbled a few lines on a piece of paper and pushed it across the desk. "That's Hathaway's address. He's rented a room there. The watch hasn't seen him yet. And—" he sighed and shot Charles a worried look "—Foxworthy was released this morning with a warning to stay away from your wife. Charles, it won't be long before she is arrested. Tonight or tomorrow morning, likely."

Charles folded the paper and put it in his waistcoat pocket. "How much time will it buy if I send Georgiana to the hunting lodge in Scotland?"

"They'd be barely a day behind her. Go sit down, Hunter. I'll see if I can hunt up Richardson."

Charles retreated down the corridor to his own office. He sat at his desk and sighed. Not even noon, and he'd almost been killed. He was hoping his day would get better when a sharp knock sounded at his door. "Come," he called.

The door opened a crack, and Tom Clark peeked in. "You got a minute, Hunter?"

"Yes." He stood to welcome the old Bow Street Runner.

The man came in, shut the door behind him and pulled his soft cap off his head. "Got that information for you."

Charles gestured to the chair in front of his desk and they sat. Clark reached inside his jacket and removed several sheets of paper with ragged edges. "These are my notes on the Betman robbery." He unfolded the papers and slid them across the desk to Charles.

There were rough notes written in blurred and faded lead, and a few rough sketches. Clark had recalled the details clearly. Everything he'd told Charles was written on these pages, but the sketches were new. They'd never been entered into the official file. One of them detailed a brooch in the form of a Scottish thistle with the notation "solid gold, amethyst center." A necklace with an elaborately swirled jeweled clasp that fastened in the front bore the inscription "solid gold, amethyst and diamond stones." And earrings had the simple notation "pearls."

"May I keep this, Clark? Or have the clerk make a copy?"

"You can keep it, sir. Put it in the file. They wouldn't let me do that back then, since it wasn't supposed to be a robbery. Weren't interested in the truth after his lordship called them off."

Charles shook his head. "I am still amazed that Lord Betman would rather the villains got away than that justice be done for his daughter."

Clark squirmed in his chair and twisted his cap. "There were reasons, sir."

Charles leaned back and looked at the clock. A bit too early to offer the man a drink, but he needed to put Clark at ease to get the rest of the story, though he was beginning to suspect the truth. "Tea?" he asked.

"Thank you, sir, but no. If there's nothin' else, I'd best be on my way."

Charles was sure Clark knew more, and certain, too, that he wanted to tell it. To unburden himself of the bad taste the case had left in his mouth. "Are you certain there's nothing else, Clark?"

His hesitation was enough of an admission.

"If I don't know it all, I may miss something."

"Don't know how it could help anyone now."

"You can trust my discretion. I will not repeat anything you tell me."

The older man sank into his chair again and let out a massive sigh. "Aye, then. That girl. Lady Caroline. When we found her in that alley, she was tore up real bad. Blood everywhere. Gave a good fight, like I said. But what wasn't in the report was that she was raped. Brutal. They'd ripped her unmentionables off and there was plenty of blood...down there, too. She'd been a virgin, I warrant."

Charles groaned. For the first time, he saw past Lady Caroline's haughtiness to the events that had changed her forever. From the sweet young girl Carlington loved to the bitter woman Charles had met, she had endured the worst that could happen to a woman. And found the strength to survive. "Why did you not put that in the report?"

"Didn't seem right, somehow. She'd been hurt enough. Didn't need me and Frank writin' things down where anyone could read it. There'd be a worse scandal than there already was."

A sick feeling settled in the pit of Charles's stomach. So much to think about. So much to unravel. He stood and reached into his ripped waistcoat pocket to remove a crown and flipped the coin to Clark. "Thank you. I appreciate your candor. If you should remember anything else, you know where to find me."

Georgiana and the other ladies sat around a low table in the back dressing room at La Meilleure Robe while Gina, now her sister-in-law, poured tea. Georgiana realized with a bit of wonder that she was now somehow related to everyone in the room with the exception of Lady Annica and Grace Hawthorne.

"Whatever happened to that woman who stood before us swearing never to marry again?" Lady Annica teased with a broad smile.

"I…I…"

"She hadn't bargained on Charlie," Sarah finished for her. "My brother can be quite persuasive."

Georgiana blushed, thinking of all the things he'd persuaded her to do last night. "More than I'd realized. Though, were I to be honest, I would have to admit that I have always had a *tendresse* for him."

"How sweet," Grace said. "I do so love a story that ends happily."

A polite rap at the rear door of the dressing room drew their attention. *"Entrez!"* Lady Annica called.

Mr. Renquist came in, his little notebook in his hand. "Ladies," he said with a small bow.

"Mr. Renquist, would you like a cup of tea?" Sarah asked.

His lips quirked in a quick smile, but he shook his head. "I've got to catch up with some of the lads and see what else they might have found. But I have had some success on the matters we spoke of last time."

"Did you meet with Mr. Foxworthy?" Georgiana asked.

"Aye, just after your meeting with him, apparently. Did you, indeed, marry Mr. Charles Hunter?"

She nodded. "Mr. Foxworthy was upset when I told him."

"He called you several, um, unkind names, Mrs. Huff—er, Mrs. Hunter. Seems to think you married Hunter just to halt his petition as conservator."

She looked down into her teacup. "Of course not. Though I will admit, that was a happy result."

Mr. Renquist squirmed uneasily and looked away. "And how is Mr. Hunter?"

"Still alive." She gave him a dry smile. Was that little sigh he emitted one of relief?

"Yes, well. I've had news of Foxworthy's arrest."

"Whatever for?"

"The murder of your husbands. I believe it is being said that he had motive for keeping you childless, and that his intent was always to become your conservator in order to wrest the Betman fortune from you, but he could not while Lady Caroline was alive. He did not expect you to become engaged so soon after your guardian's death."

"But that is wonderful!" Gina exclaimed. "Then the mystery is solved. You are safe, Georgiana. Charles will be so pleased!"

"I fear not," Mr. Renquist interrupted. "It is being said that there is no proof. The case against Mr. Foxworthy is thin, at best. There are whispers in the Home Office that he will be released and you will be arrested next, Mrs. Hunter."

She'd been expecting something of the sort. She took a tight rein on her emotions. "Thank you for the warning, Mr. Renquist. I shall put my affairs in order. And Mr. York?"

"He appears to have borrowed heavily in expectation of inheriting the bulk of his uncle's estate. His creditors are nipping at his heels. I think, if you offer him a reasonable sum, he will take it."

"I shall have my solicitor draw up an offer," she said. "I would like these details cleared up before…before I may not be able to attend to business."

"As for your Mr. Hathaway, he has not been seen recently. After a few meetings with several individuals, he has gone missing."

"Who did he meet with, Mr. Renquist?"

"One of my men followed him to your solicitor's office, the Home Office and the Cat's Paw, a disreputable public house just off Petticoat Lane. I can only guess at his business."

"Please do," she invited. She had her own suspicions, but she would like Mr. Renquist to confirm or deny them.

"I suspect he may have gone to your solicitor to ask for hush money—that he would not discuss the intimate details of your home if he were paid to keep his silence. When that did not work, he likely went to the Home Office to offer evidence of some sort against you, and that is why we are hearing whispers of your possible arrest. As for the Cat's Paw? That is anyone's guess. My man did not recognize the person Mr. Hathaway met with, but said the man was of an unwholesome nature."

"Why am I not astonished?" she muttered, more to herself than to the others.

Mr. Renquist looked ready to comment and then took a deep breath before continuing his report. "In regard to the man who accosted you in Vauxhall Gardens, Mrs. Hunter, I believe you have become the object of some very unsavory attention. I suspect that he and the man from the rookeries could be the same. If so, you are in grave danger."

"Does this man have a name, sir?"

"Gibbons. Richard Gibbons. Known as Dick."

Of course. Had there ever been a doubt? She braced herself for the next question. "Can you tell me what his business is with me? Or anything else about him?"

"I cannot imagine, Mrs. Hunter, unless it has something to do with your husband."

All the possibilities whirled in her mind until she could barely think. But she needed to know if there could be a single ounce of truth in the things he'd said to her. "I… Please tell me what you know about him."

"He is the lowest of all possible levels, Mrs. Hunter. His deeds would shock you to the core. I do not wish to speak of them in mixed company. Suffice it to say that he might be seeking to use you to hurt Mr. Hunter. He has tried countless times to kill him, and perhaps he has settled on hurting you instead."

He did not need to speak those deeds aloud. Her memory of the night in the coach was clear enough. Charles had had no such qualms about voicing them. *The vilest of the vile… They robbed, raped, pillaged and murdered*

*their way through London. They were known for their filth
and utter lack of morals. If it's birthed a Gibbons, you'd
do the world a favor to exterminate it before it can spread.*

"I see Mr. Finn is still with you, and I urge you to
go nowhere without him. Be careful, Mrs. Hunter. Very
careful."

She wanted to thank him, but her throat had closed and
her mouth had gone dry. She expended her entire energy
in gaining control of her emotions.

"Excellent advice, Mr. Renquist," Sarah said for her.
"The more people you are with, Georgiana, the less likely
he is to approach."

But he already had done so. The horrid claims he'd
made and what he wanted of her. She felt physically ill.

"I will keep inquiring, Mrs. Hunter," Mr. Renquist
vowed as he put his notebook back in his coat pocket.
"We shall get this sorted out as quickly as may be."

The door closed behind him and Georgiana let out a
sigh. "If there is time enough…"

The dressing room fell silent and none of the ladies
would meet her gaze. They knew how dire her circumstances were, and they did not want her to see their fear
for her. Long moments passed while Georgiana tried to
find the words to tell them what she suspected, but nothing would come. Not even the confession that she was
Lady Caroline's natural daughter.

Lady Annica was the first to speak. "Well, we needn't
worry overmuch. We have never given up a case, nor
have we ever been unsuccessful in the past. We are not
about to fail with you, Georgiana. We have another day.
Perhaps two."

Some cynical part of Georgiana's mind noted that an
unbroken record was bound to be broken sooner or later.

Chapter Nineteen

Georgiana had pushed the unwelcome thoughts of her origins out of her head until she arrived home and closed the library door behind her. Alone, unwatched, she could finally surrender to her deepest fears. She gripped the back of a chair and held on for dear life as pain so intense she could not credit it shot through her. She doubled over with it and clung to a side table to keep from crumbling to the floor.

It couldn't be true. It *couldn't!* Please, God, it couldn't.

If it's birthed a Gibbons, you'd do the world a favor to exterminate it before it can spread.

How could Charles ever forgive such a thing? How could he ever look at her and not think of who she was? Gibbons blood flowed through her veins—would flow through his children's veins! How could he ever accept that? How could she? But it had to be true. All the pieces fit, including that horrid man's interest in her. He'd told her the truth in the garden, and yet she'd hoped he was lying or deluded. Hoped that Lord Carlington had sired her.

It was a full five minutes before she could stand erect again. On shaky knees, she went to the sideboard where the decanters were all lined up in a civilized row. Her hands trembled as she removed one stopper after another, trying to find the most potent brew. She settled on a rich amber whiskey and poured a full glass, ignoring the way the lip of the decanter rattled against the crystal rim.

The first swallow burned its way down her throat and threatened to come up again. She closed her eyes and breathed deeply, steadying her nerves as well as her stomach. The second swallow was easier and spread a calming warmth outward. Another deep breath. Another swallow.

Why, I'm yer pa.

Despite the fading of day, she did not stop to light a lamp on her way to the fireplace. There, she sank to the hearth, glass in one hand and decanter in the other, needing the heat of the fire to bring feeling back to her numbed limbs and needing the courage of the liquor to face the truth. Dear God! What was she going to do? What *could* she do?

I've been watchin' you yer whole life, Georgie gal. Ever since you was brought back to Kent. Finest thing I ever done. Think it was me, but coulda been Artie. An' everything we done after was fer you.

When the contents of her glass were gone, she poured more and drew her knees up to rest her forehead on them, then circled them with her arms. She rocked as if she could comfort herself, but there was no comfort in who and what she was. A Gibbons. Her husband's enemy.

A gal's bound to do what her pa says. Now that yer ma's gone, I'm yer boss. D'you understand?

After a time—she did not know how long—she wiped her tears away with the back of her hand. She had survived the deaths of everyone she'd ever loved, and she would find a way to survive the loss of Charles for the second time. But how could she face him? Confess her heritage? Watch his dawning horror, loathing and disgust? Oh, Lord. Anything but that. The gallows first!

What a wretched coward she was! She could not tell him. Now or ever. She would have to find another way to give him his freedom.

Informed by Clara that Georgiana had arrived home and gone to the library with instructions that she not be disturbed, Charles knocked at the door. When there was no answer, he turned the latch. The room was in shadows but he could see Georgiana by the fireplace. She was sitting on the hearth, hugging her knees—the very picture of contemplation. He stepped in and closed the door behind him. He did not want the servants overhearing the conversation they were going to have.

"Georgiana?"

She shuddered and turned to look at him. Her face was streaked with tears and her eyes were reddened.

A sudden and unfamiliar mix of anger and concern struck him in the chest. "Good Lord! What has happened? Did someone hurt you?"

She gulped, and he realized it was a sob. Whoever—whatever—had hurt her would pay for that.

He knelt beside her and recognized the whiskey in the bottom of her glass. And in the decanter beside it. What had sent her to the bottle? Whatever it was, it had torn her apart. He'd never seen her so distraught. He took the glass from her hand and put it on the hearth next to the decanter.

"Georgie, tell me what happened."

She sniffed and he handed her his handkerchief. "I cannot talk about it, Charles. 'Tis still so…so fresh."

"Then have another glass of whiskey, m'dear, because we are not leaving this room until I have the whole of it."

Taking him at his word, she reached for the whiskey.

He smiled and took it from her and set it back on the hearth. If he was any judge, she had yet to feel the full effects of what she'd already consumed. Even without more, she'd be drunker in ten minutes than she was now. "Just tell me, Georgiana. Whatever it is cannot be all that bad."

She laughed and the sound bordered on hysteria. "You would think not, wouldn't you? But I cannot imagine worse."

"Say it, Georgiana. Whatever it is, we will sort it out."

"It cannot be undone, Charles. It is far too late for that."

"I warn you. I will not rest until I know."

She sighed and rested her forehead on her knees. When she spoke at last, her voice was so soft he barely heard her. "I am not what you think I am."

Ah, so she knew. The question was, when had she learned the truth. "I do know what you are."

"You couldn't. Caroline Betman was…was my mother, and—"

"I know."

She looked up at him and blinked. "How?"

"I sent an investigator to Cornwall. I had Carlington make inquiries in the Royal Navy. There were no Carsons who had a baby girl. But you were born nine months after Lady Caroline's departure from London. And she came back for you once her father was gone."

"I see."

"And you look a bit like her, Georgiana." But he had to know the rest. Had she deceived him? "When did you find out?"

"The day I went to see Lady Aston. My…mother set the facts out quite plainly to her, with instructions to tell me only after she was gone."

"That was the day before we married, was it not?"

She nodded and looked down at her knees again.

The first stirring of anger twitched in his stomach. "Did you not think this was a fact I should know concerning the woman I was about to marry?"

She frowned as if she was trying to remember something. "I did not have time. When Sarah and I arrived at the chapel, you were all waiting. I started to say something...but you shook your head."

Charles remembered that incident. He'd been impatient to have the nuptials said. He'd thought she was having doubts and was going to beg off and hadn't wanted to give her the chance. "You should have insisted," he said, knowing that was unfair.

"I wish I had. Oh, if only I had."

Tears brimmed in her eyes again and he was afraid she'd begin crying at any moment. He took a tight rein on his rising anger. "That is your only excuse? That people were waiting and I shook my head?"

She looked up at him again and he was surprised at the depth of despair in her eyes. "And...and that I thought I'd be safe with you. You made me feel...less alone."

He'd hoped to hear those words again—that she loved him and always had. He could forgive her anything for the sake of that. "But if you knew then, Georgiana, why are you crying only now?"

"Shame, Charles, for what I've brought to your door. I am suspected of murder and will be arrested soon. Hathaway went to the Home Office and accused me. And, somehow, I've... I am connected to the man who is trying to kill you. Oh!" Fresh tears rolled down her cheeks, ravaging her face with grief or guilt, he couldn't tell which.

A cold feeling settled in his heart. He had been shunning the thought from the moment it had entered his mind this morning. Between Gibbons's mysterious accusations and Clark's revelations, he'd been fighting the suspicion.

He'd denied it in his mind, refused to believe it, sought for other answers.

And still, he had to ask. "Connected how, Georgiana?"

"No, Charles. No…"

"Tell me."

"I cannot say the words."

Then he would say them for her. "He is your father."

She gagged and he feared for a moment that she would vomit.

And still he could not relent. He stood, needing to put distance between them. Needing to harden himself against her pain. "Admit it."

She gasped for air, clearly fighting her hysteria. "Charles…"

"Damn it, Georgiana!"

"Yes," she moaned. "Yes, he says he is my father."

He took two more steps away from her. "When did you know?"

"I wonder if I always knew. When I think back, I remember his face in my village, or on the street when I came to London. There was always a shadow behind me. A feeling I could not dispel."

Charles could scarcely comprehend her admission. Had she married him knowing who she was? Had she deceived him deliberately? "When did you know?" he asked again.

"He told me yesterday."

After the wedding. Thank God for that much. "You met with him?"

"He waited in the garden."

He recalled Finn's remark that he'd found her crying in the garden. And then he'd gone upstairs and made love to her. He'd lain with her, touching her, knowing her, *loving* her in ways too intimate to speak of. And all the while, she'd known she was Gibbons's daughter.

"He means to kill you, Charles. 'Put you out of the way,' he said."

Nothing new there, at least. There was only one last question he had to ask.

"Were you his accomplice, Georgiana? Were you helping him?"

She looked up from her knees, her eyes wide with horror, and then reached for the whiskey without saying a word. The crystal stopper shattered on the stone hearth as she knocked it off and lifted the decanter to her lips without bothering to fill a glass.

God, how he wished he could join her. Sit with her before the fire, drinking until the memories fell away, until it no longer mattered that she was a Gibbons by birth, but he doubted there was enough liquor in the world to accomplish that. All he knew for certain was that he'd go mad if he stayed in this room a moment more. That he'd surely say or do something he would regret tomorrow.

He turned and walked away, closing the door softly behind him.

It was late afternoon before Charles nodded at Wycliffe's man loitering across the street and looked at the folded paper again, confirming the address Wycliffe had given him. The tenement looked respectable enough for all that it was in a declining neighborhood. He opened the door and climbed the stairs to the second floor. The unwholesome stench of cabbage and spoiled meat followed him. Halfway down the passageway he found the number he was looking for. He knocked and waited a moment.

A door opened across the way and a man peeked out. "Real popular man, that Hathaway. Keep tellin' folks he ain't in."

The door closed again and Charles turned back to

Hathaway's room. He tried the lock with no luck. Odd, how no one had seen Hathaway for several days. If Wycliffe's men hadn't found him, no one could.

He was halfway down the stairs when he realized the odor was stronger upstairs. He spun around and went back, removing a pick from his pocket. The lock was easily forced and Charles stepped through with a glance over his shoulder to be certain he hadn't been seen.

The smell was overwhelming now and recognizable. Decaying flesh. He threw the only window open and breathed deeply before turning back to the inside.

In a darkened corner, he saw the crumpled form. Hathaway by the length and breadth of him and by his fastidiously polished shoes. No wonder no one had seen him. Charles held a handkerchief over his nose and mouth as he inspected the bloated body. He'd been dead for several days judging by the number of flies, the state of the body and the fact that death rigor had come and gone. Probably killed after his visit to the Home Office.

A knife had made a single slice across his throat. Dried blood had stiffened the man's dark coat. A knife. Altogether too many coincidences. Dick Gibbons, then. But why? For Georgiana's sake? In retaliation for reporting her to the Home Office? Just because he felt like it? Or had they been in collusion and argued?

He searched Hathaway and found only a crumpled scrap of paper in one corner of his waistcoat pocket. No coins, no banknotes, nothing of value whatsoever. Gibbons, if it had been Gibbons, had taken everything. He smoothed the wad of paper and read an address in Whitechapel. An address within the area Wycliffe's men had narrowed to Gibbons's crib.

He quickly searched the rest of the room, but found nothing useful. It appeared that Gibbons had come to see Hathaway, killed him for some as yet unknown reason, had taken anything of value, and left him to rot. He must have missed the little slip of paper with directions to his room.

A grim smile found its way to his lips. No time to waste if he was to catch Gibbons this time.

He closed Hathaway's door behind him and hurried back down the stairs and across the street. He handed the man the paper he'd taken from Hathaway's pocket and turned toward Whitechapel. "Hathaway is dead. Give that to Wycliffe at once. Tell him to meet me there."

Charles knew it had been too much to hope for to find Dick Gibbons at home. He kept his disappointment in check and decided that this could be his only opportunity to search for any proof of the Gibbons brothers' complicity in a myriad of crimes. He stepped inside.

Whether it was the oppressive atmosphere of the room or something more, a warning tingle spiraled up his spine. Something felt wrong. Something that nagged at the back of his mind. He would wait for Wycliffe, but there was no time to waste. A candle stub waited on a shelf just inside the door and he found the tinderbox to light it.

The single room in the back stables of a squalid public house gave testament to the Gibbons tolerance for filth. Despite the lock he'd had to pick to gain entrance, there looked to be nothing worth stealing. As he stood in the open doorway, Charles wished he had a shovel. Still, knowing that Gibbons could come back at any minute, he decided not to wait for Wycliffe's arrival.

The room was small and airless. No windows offered light or ventilation. Cobwebs and rat droppings were everywhere. He'd have likened it to a fortress, but there was no watchtower. Not even a peephole. A searching glance around the room gave him no clue where he might start his hunt.

He moved the torn blankets covering a single pallet and found only more blankets. He lifted the lot with the toe of his boot to find that there was no bed beneath, just a pile of discarded blankets too worn to be mended. He'd have felt sorry for anyone else, but he knew full well that the Gibbons brothers had extorted fortunes and charged exorbitant rates for their services, be they assassinations or pickpocketing. Where that money had gone was a subject of endless speculation by the Home Office.

A pile of objects in one corner offered a place to start his search. Old playbills and torn posters had been smoothed and stacked, but for what purpose? Charles could not imagine. Buttons of the sort that might have been lost on the cobbles filled an old glass jar. Scraps of ribbon, empty bobbins and brushes missing half their bristles were in a single pile, as if kicked aside.

He continued around the perimeter, reasoning that not even Dick Gibbons would leave anything incriminating or that could be of value in the open center of a room. He touched as little as possible, moving things aside with his boot.

A few moments later, Wycliffe appeared in the doorway, his tall frame nearly blocking any light. "What a bloody mess," he said. "Shall I call in help?"

Charles shook his head. "I am beginning to wonder if we will find anything here."

Wycliffe tilted his head toward a tin plate of stale bread and overripe fruit. "Looks like supper. Think he's coming back?"

"Not if he sees us here."

"A search of this place will take us hours. Richardson

is outside, keeping watch. He will stay and send word when Gibbons returns."

A sensible plan. Charles nodded and slid his boot under another rag pile. The scrape of his sole against a wooden plank invited closer inspection. He knelt and moved the rags, Wycliffe peering over his shoulder. The board was level with the dirt floor, as if it had been set in a hole. He removed the pick from his pocket and pried one edge up. Yes, there was a hole beneath.

He flipped the board over and peered into the hole. A metal box with a hinged lid appeared. Rather than open the lid, he lifted the entire box out and placed it on the floor. Wycliffe knelt beside him and flipped the lid back.

The glitter of gold flashed in the candlelight. So this was the Gibbons treasure trove. There were not many pieces, but why had they kept these when they were wont to sell everything they stole within a day of two of the theft? Were these fresh acquisitions? Had Dick not had time to dispose of them?

Wycliffe pulled out a chain, from which a dainty oval amethyst dangled, and held it to the light. This was no tawdry imitation, but the living model of Clark's sketch of Lady Caroline's stolen necklace. There, too, was the Scottish thistle brooch and pearl earrings. If he had needed confirmation that the Gibbons brothers had been the thieves who robbed Lady Caroline's coach, he had it now. There were other items, too. A tiny ring meant for a child, a dainty garnet necklace, an opal ring and a bracelet of wrought gold. And, most damning of all, a locket with a miniature portrait of a younger Georgiana.

"These were Lady Caroline's," he said, pointing to the first items. "The jewels she wore the night she was robbed."

Another warning chill invaded Charles's vitals as he

stood. After all the time he'd spent chasing Gibbons, this was too easy. Too convenient. How had Gibbons missed the paper with his address when he'd stolen everything else of value from Hathaway's room? Unless *he'd* left it there? He stepped outside and glanced around. Was it a trap?

Wycliffe gave him a questioning look, as if he'd felt it, too—this nameless suspicion.

No. Not a trap. A diversion. A red herring meant to keep them occupied. The hair on the back of Charles's neck stood on end, and a deep dread filled him. "Georgiana," he whispered.

Chapter Twenty

Knowing she could never get drunk enough to drown the facts of her birth or even dull the memory of Charles's face when she admitted the truth, Georgiana gave up the attempt. Darkness had fallen by the time she left the library and went up to her room. She found a valise in her dressing room and put it on her bed.

She only needed to pack a few things. She could send for the rest later. The journey home would not take that long. Charles could handle the details of the annulment. There shouldn't be too much of a scandal since they'd never even formally announced their engagement. Heaven knew he had grounds enough. Fraud. He hadn't known who she really was. Though she hadn't known she was a Gibbons at the time of the nuptials, she had known she was illegitimate—Lady Caroline's illegitimate daughter.

And, should the authorities wish to arrest her for her husbands' deaths, they would know where to find her. Even that eventuality did not seem to matter now. Odd, how only days ago her life had been quiet and ordinary, and now everything was turned upside down.

Had she dealt so much with death that it had lost its power to horrify her? Was she simply numb from the revelations of the past few days? Or had something died inside her with the look on Charles's face when he realized who she was? Some spark of humanity that she would never be able to reclaim? No, she would never be the same. Even now the pain of losing him again was almost more than she could bear.

She opened her bureau drawer and removed a nightgown and robe, as well as some stockings and handkerchiefs. A breeze wafted from the open window and brushed a stray curl across her cheek. She shivered and tucked the curl behind her ear.

"Oh, there's a good girl. You knowed I was comin' fer you, eh?"

Georgiana jumped, her heart pounding wildly. Dick Gibbons stepped from behind the draperies and grinned. Her hand came up to cover her heart and she was so frightened that she could not speak.

"Madam? You want dinner?"

She spun to look at the locked door in horror, then back to Gibbons, who had drawn a knife and was scowling. She knew with cold certainty that he would kill Clara if she entered the room. And that he was completely unhinged.

"No, Clara. I am not hungry. I do not wish to be disturbed the rest of the night, please."

"You need help undressing, madam?"

"I can manage. Good night, Clara."

Gibbons nodded approval.

If only she could think of a way to summon Finn! When the maid's footsteps faded down the corridor, Gibbons gestured with the wicked-looking blade, light flashing from the razor-sharp edge. "Quick thinkin', Georgie gal. I knew you was smart."

She noted the faint sound of a door opening and closing somewhere below. Finn? Charles? She had to keep Gibbons talking. Distracted from the sounds of the house. "Where are you...where are we going?" she asked as she placed her little stack of clothes in the valise, knowing her only chance of survival lay in indulging him.

"Why, it don't matter. Maybe back to that big house in Kent. Maybe not. First we gets you away and then I can kill Hunter."

She noted the gleam of madness in his eyes and suddenly it was all clear. "You killed Allenby, didn't you?"

Gibbons merely gave her that inane grin.

"And Mr. Huffington?"

"Not with my own hands, but they wasn't good enough fer you, Georgie."

She sank to the bed, feeling light-headed with shock. "And...and Adam Booth?"

"I was aimin' fer Hunter that night, but Booth stepped in his way. Artie took the second shot and hit Hunter. Shoulda killed him, though."

"Artie?" If she could keep him talking, perhaps Finn would come to check on her.

"My brother. Yer other pa."

He'd made some sort of reference to that before. "I don't understand. My other father?"

"Aye. We don't know what one of us sired you. We both had her that night. Yer ma was the only fancy lady we ever got at. Cut 'er up good, we did, so she couldn't be with anyone else. We kept watch on 'er and found out she was breedin'. We followed 'er to Devon where the nuns took care of 'er. If you'da been a boy, we'da stole you away. But you was only a girl, so we didn't bother. The old lord took you away when you was born, though, and we thought he mighta drowned you or left you in a ditch. Then *she* fetched you home."

Her stomach cramped and she feared she was going

to be sick. She could not even imagine Caroline's agony. Nor could she comprehend that she would never know which monster sired her.

But she could not think about that now. She had to stall, to keep him talking until she could think of some way out of this mess. "I remember seeing you in the village."

"Aye. We come to keep an eye on you every now an' then. When we saw how pretty you was, that's when we started makin' plans."

"What sort of plans?"

He chuckled to himself. "Yer pretty enough to catch a lord. Maybe a duke. We was gonna have you rise in your station, gal. Make the Gibbons clan high-flyin' dandies. Have Gibbons blood minglin' with royalty."

Good heavens! He was really quite mad. So mad that he could not see the flaws in his plan. No peer would ever marry without being certain of his wife's lineage. Preserving the integrity of the title was too important. Caroline had understood that, and had been careful to marry her to country squires where such a secret could be kept. She'd even thought Charles too dangerously close to the peerage. Dare she tell Mr. Gibbons that? Would he dispose of her, too, if he thought she was of no use?

"Do you still think that is possible?"

"Why not? By the time yer mournin' is done fer Hunter, we'll come back to town and hunt you up a proper lord. You'll marry who I tells you to this time."

"What if none of them want me?"

"Clever gal like you? You'll know how to bring 'em to heel. Why, I warrant you've learned a few tricks from Hunter."

Nausea churned in her stomach at the thought of doing any of those things with anyone but Charles. "And if I can't…bring them to heel?"

He scowled at her and brandished his knife. "You damn well better, chit. Everything we done since that day we saw you, we done fer you. You owe us and yer no use to me if you don't do as I tell you. Now get packin'."

She could not stall him much longer. She went back to the bureau and chose a chemise. "I cannot imagine how you were able to keep track of me all these years. I saw you in the village occasionally, but have you not spent most of your time in London?"

"'Twere easy once we hired yer ma's fancy man."

Fancy man? "Do you mean Hathaway?"

"Aye. He sent word now an' then. Took that little likeness of you from yer ma and sent it to us so's we could see how pretty you was. He were the one took care of Allenby an' Huffington."

No wonder Hathaway hated her. He'd known who she really was. *That little street urchin who is no better than she ought to be....*

"He'd bring us some of yer gewgaws so we'd know you was good. Charged us a pretty penny, too."

So that was the answer to the mystery of all her little missing items, and why she'd found Hathaway snooping in her room on occasion. Oh, she'd been so naive!

"What if Hathaway tells someone? Tries to blackmail you?"

Gibbons snorted. "Hathaway ain't tellin' anyone anything."

Her heart stilled and she swallowed her horror. She did not have to ask to know that Hathaway was dead.

She studied the man for a long moment, trying to find anything familiar, anything redeeming or endearing in him, and failing. Even his supposed fondness for her was merely another means to achieve riches or glory for himself. She was a tool to be used, not a cherished daughter.

As she tucked her chemise into the valise, she thought she saw a movement in the dressing room. Finn? How long had he been there? Oh pray he did not bumble in. Pray he realized the situation before he, too, was killed. Was there some way to warn him?

"I need a dress." She held Gibbons's gaze. "I will fetch one from the dressing room."

"I'll pick it fer you," he said, starting for the door.

"Never mind. If we are going home to Kent, I have enough there."

He frowned at her, glancing between her and the dressing room. "You tryin' to get away, Georgie gal? Gonna go in there and lock me out?"

"No. I… You did not tell me for certain where we'd be going."

He grunted. "One dress is enough fer any gal. C'n only wear one at a time, anyways."

She closed her valise, buckled the straps and lifted it from the bed. "We had better be going." She wondered how he intended to get her out of the house. Surely not the same way he'd come in. She looked toward the window.

He cackled when he realized what she was thinking. "We're gonna walk outa here, proud as you please. Yer the woman of the house. Won't anyone stop you. Not even that man Hunter hired, if you tell him to stand back."

She glanced at his knife again and nodded, resigned to doing anything he asked to keep him from killing anyone else because of her. "I will need my cloak."

Charles, straining to interrupt Gibbons and Georgiana for the past five minutes, shot Wycliffe a warning glance. They'd heard Gibbons confess to everything. Georgiana had led the conversation almost as if she'd known they were listening.

And he'd heard the hopelessness and despair in her voice and knew she believed he'd deserted her. Abandoned her to whatever darkness was awaiting her. In his shock, he'd walked away without giving her any reassurances or a single word of understanding.

What a fool he'd been. What an utter ass. He loved her, and that was all he'd ever need to know about her.

But Gibbons was not going to take his wife anywhere. Wycliffe nodded and released his hold on Charles's arm.

He slipped the small pistol from his boot and edged forward. As he cleared the dressing room door, he came face-to-face with his old enemy.

Gibbons blinked and brought his knife up even as he seized Georgiana's arm. "Stay where you are, Hunter." He began to back toward the door.

Georgiana's eyes met his and he was struck by her fear—not for herself, but for him. He could feel Wycliffe at his back. Gibbons did not miss with a knife. If he threw it at him, Charles would die, but Wycliffe would save Georgiana. Slowly, he raised his pistol and took careful aim.

Gibbons realized the decision he'd made and jerked Georgiana's arm to bring her in front of him. He tightened his arm around her waist, using her as a shield, and held the tip of his blade to her throat. "I'll kill her before I let you have her, Hunter, so you better let us go," he snarled. "You ain't good enough fer her."

Charles kept steady aim. "I daresay you are right, Gibbons. But she stays with me."

The tip of Gibbons's blade made a depression in the soft flesh at the hollow at the base of Georgiana's throat. The bastard would actually do it! And Charles could see in her eyes that she knew it, too. And did not care.

She closed her eyes and swung her arm out from her

side. For the first time, he noted that she held a small valise, and that she intended to use it against Gibbons. The
jolt would ruin his aim if he threw the knife at Charles,
but would surely drive the blade into her throat if he held
it steady. Ah, sweet Jesus, she meant to sacrifice herself
for him.

But Gibbons was a head taller than Georgiana. In that
split second before she could complete her swing, Charles
steadied his pistol and squeezed the trigger.

The shot reverberated in the small room and a pungent
cloud of sulfur and vaporized blood rose in the air. Gibbons fell backward, dragging Georgiana with him. Once
they hit the floor, neither of them moved.

The outer door splintered and dropped flat on the floor
as Finn trampled over it like an enraged bull, Clara behind him waving an iron pan.

Charles stepped forward and kicked the knife away
from Gibbons's limp hand. He needn't have bothered.
A pool of blood was forming beneath him, and a ragged
black hole in the center of his forehead gave evidence that
he would never wield a knife again.

He lifted Georgiana in his arms and carried her to the
bed, relieved that her only sign of injury was a small bead
of blood at the base of her throat. At the very point where,
when he kissed her there, she would sigh and tighten her
arms around him.

He wiped the single bead of blood away with the pad
of his thumb, only vaguely aware of Finn hoisting Gibbons over his shoulder and taking him away.

Wycliffe gave orders to remove the Persian carpet and
any traces of the incident. He ushered Clara, craning her
neck in curiosity, from the room. When they were alone,
he lowered his mouth to that vulnerable spot and brushed
his lips across it.

Georgiana's eyelids fluttered even as she curled her arms around his neck. "Oh, Charlie. Oh, thank God."

"Thank *you*," he corrected.

"I nearly got you killed."

"No, Georgiana. You gave me back my life."

Epilogue

Georgiana kneeled on the deep grass bordering the flower beds and began digging weeds. So much had changed in just one week, and she had found a sense of peace, though she still did not know her future. Something would need to be settled soon. She could not go on living here, loving Charles and knowing it could all be over the next second.

She had met with the ladies of the Wednesday League and Mr. Renquist to explain the events of that night, though she hadn't found the heart to tell them the whole truth. She'd said only that Mr. Gibbons was a man who'd become obsessed with her when he'd seen her in her village many years ago, and that his delusions had set her husbands' deaths in motion. They'd all been relieved it was over at last. When she was finished, Mr. Renquist had smiled and nodded at her and she wondered if he knew more than he was saying. If so, she knew her secret was safe with him.

Shockingly, she'd learned that Richard Gibbons and his brother, Arthur, had amassed a sizeable fortune. Somewhere in the range of one hundred thousand pounds, their solicitor informed her. She was their sole heiress, and she wanted none of it. Since there was no way of knowing from whom they had stolen, extorted or blackmailed it, the ladies had helped her establish a philanthropic fund for the purpose of housing and educating foundlings.

Finn's services had not been required and he had been dismissed, and yet she would find him lurking around the kitchen, loitering in the garden and sighing as he watched Clara go about her duties. She feared she would be losing a maid when she returned to Kent.

But, most comforting of all, she had finally come to terms with her mother. Instead of wondering why her "aunt" had been unable to love her, she marveled that her mother had loved her enough to lift her from the poverty she'd been left in, take her home and show her kindness and consideration every single day, protect her from the disturbing truth, provide for her future and leave her all her worldly goods. She'd been a good woman who'd tried her best to do what she believed was right. She'd only wanted to find Georgiana a safe harbor and an honorable life. That was love enough for her.

Charles had been busy every day and long into the night, working with Lord Wycliffe to unravel the full extent of Mr. Gibbons's—she would never be able to think of that man as her father—crimes. And in the still hours before dawn, he came to her, wordlessly making a passionate, almost desperate, love to her, as if he was trying to tell her something for which he couldn't find words. Was he simply telling her that he still craved her body? Was it an attempt to sate his desire before she was gone? Or was it a lingering and bittersweet goodbye?

The sun dipped behind the house and Georgiana removed her bonnet as she worked the soil. The simple work was rewarding and soothed her nerves. Her hand spade hit something solid and she dug carefully around it. A rock?

She turned and looked up as a shadow fell across her shoulder. Charles. Her peaceful feeling abandoned her and her pulse sped. Was he finally free to deal with her?

He sat on the grass beside her, an uncertain expression on his face. She looked into his eyes and wondered if this was the last time she would feel as if she were drowning in the violet-blue depths or lose her train of thought when he smiled.

She left the trowel stuck in the dirt and sat back, ready to hear him out. Annulment? Divorce? Denouncement? Quiet retirement to Kent and banishment for life so that he would not have to see her every day? Whatever he had decided, she braced herself to agree and accept it with good grace. She would remain as much a lady as her mother had been.

He inclined his head toward the trowel. "Did you find it?"

"What?"

He pushed the trowel deeper and scooped the object out of the earth. When the dirt fell away, she saw the laudanum vial. She gave him a puzzled look.

"I had to get rid of it. Wycliffe warned he would send men to search the house. Because of Hathaway's lies, that is all they would have needed to arrest you, Georgiana."

"I wondered what had become of it." She smiled, touched by all that Charles had risked for her sake. "You wouldn't have let them arrest me?"

"Over my dead body."

She laughed. "That was a distinct possibility, Charles."

"Aye. If Gibbons had had his way."

She bowed her head and removed her gardening gloves. "I have tried to think what to say to you. How to explain—"

"It has taken us a while, Georgiana, but we now have

the loose ends tied up. Wycliffe and I have gone to the families and explained that you are completely innocent and that the murderer has been caught and dealt with. We told them only that he was a madman who had become obsessed with you and did not feel anyone was good enough for you."

"Cold comfort, I would imagine. They still must hold me a little responsible."

He shrugged. "They must deal with that however they can. That is the official story and is what will appear in the files. The case is closed."

She nodded as she busied herself wiping the dirt from the laudanum vial.

"I want you to know that the only one aside from me and Wycliffe who will ever know the truth is Lord Carlington. I thought he deserved to know what Lady Caroline…your mother…had gone through and what had formed her reason for never seeing him again."

"I hope that brought him comfort."

"It did. Though he said he was not entirely certain he was not your father."

She looked up and met his gaze. "How very kind of him, though we both know that is not the case."

"Nevertheless, he swears he will claim you as his should Lady Caroline's secret ever come out—though we've been quite careful that it will not."

"But the facts of my parentage remain."

He nodded somberly. "They do indeed. And the facts are these—that you are the daughter of a peeress. She alone formed you and nurtured you. You are well educated and intelligent. You risked your life to save mine though I wouldn't have been able to live without you. And I have loved only you since the first day I saw you."

"But you said—"

"Do not remind me what I said. I was…I *am* a complete idiot and my foolish prejudices nearly cost me the one thing I hold dearest." He took her hand and lifted it to his lips. "When I saw you standing there with Gibbons holding a knife to your throat, I realized, with clarity uncommon to me, that you were all I cared about. That I could not breathe without you. He was right, Georgiana. You are too good for me. But I would be honored if you would consent to remain my wife, to bear my name and my children as well as my occasional idiocies."

Tears stung her eyes. She could not speak for the lump in her throat, so she nodded instead. He threw his arms around her and they fell back on the soft fragrant grass. As he looked down at her, she only had one last apology to make.

"I am so sorry to have turned your life upside down, Charles. And I regret the scandal, gossip and danger I have brought you."

"No apologies necessary, my love. I am counting on our daring liason to keep me from growing bored. Have I not told you that I have a deep passion for loving dangerously?"

* * * * *